Praise for *Sinking Suspicions*

IR

"A riveting beginning, a fascinating background, and an engrossing story m̥ *Sinking Suspicions* another excellent book in Sara Sue Hoklotubbe's superior series."

—CAROLYN HART, author of *Ghost Wanted*

"Sara Sue Hoklotubbe's *Sinking Suspicions* will weave its way into the tapestry of your literary life with characters that will charm you, frighten you, and, best of all, surprise you—one heck of a good read."

—CRAIG JOHNSON, *New York Times* Best-Selling author of the Walt Longmire Mysteries and the basis of A&E's hit drama *Longmire*

"Action, romance, and even bit of World War II history combine to make *Sinking Suspicions* a memorable story that leaves readers satisfied—and with a grin on our faces. Sara Sue Hoklotubbe returns to the world of spunky Sadie Walela, a can-do Cherokee crime solver with a heart as big as the plains of her native Oklahoma."

—ANNE HILLERMAN, author of *New York Times* Best-Selling *Spider Woman's Daughter*

"In *Sinking Suspicions,* Sara Sue Hoklotubbe's third Sadie Walela mystery, her likable and resourceful heroine takes a solitary trip to Hawaii. On her way to the islands, Sadie learns that a Cherokee neighbor has gone missing and that her partner Lance is doing his best to find him. Sadie's island journey, full of light and enchantment, is described beautifully by Hoklotubbe. Meanwhile, back in Oklahoma, Lance's crime solving is full of darkness. Hoklotubbe deftly explores the darkness and the light in this fascinating mystery."

—JUDITH VAN GIESON, author of the Neil Hamel and Claire Reynier mystery series

"Another intriguing mystery from a gifted storyteller. With a sure hand, Sara Sue Hoklotubbe ratchets up the suspense while exploring the myths, passions, and fears of modern-day Cherokees. If you haven't yet caught up with this author, *Sinking Suspicions* is a fine place to make her acquaintance."

—MARGARET COEL, author of the Wind River mystery series

"There are only a handful of Native American writers in genre literature, and even fewer who feature Native main characters. This is a solid mystery with excellent Native themes and characters."

—LEE FRANCIS IV, National Director of Wordcraft Circle of Native Writers and Storytellers

SINKING SUSPICIONS

SINKING SUSPICIONS

SARA SUE HOKLOTUBBE

THE UNIVERSITY OF
ARIZONA PRESS

TUCSON

The University of Arizona Press
www.uapress.arizona.edu

Printed in the United States of America
19 18 17 16 15 14   6 5 4 3 2 1

Cover design by Leigh McDonald

This is a work of fiction. Names, characters, and incidents are products of the author's imagination and are not to be construed as real. Any resemblance to actual events or persons, living or dead, is entirely coincidental.

Library of Congress Cataloging-in-Publication Data
Hoklotubbe, Sara Sue, 1952–
  Sinking suspicions / Sara Sue Hoklotubbe.
    pages cm.
  ISBN 978-0-8165-3107-3 (pbk. : alk. paper)
  1. Women detectives—Fiction. 2. Theft—Fiction. 3. Murder—Investigation—Fiction.
I. Title.
  PS3608.O4828S27 2014
  813'.6—dc23
                              2013047274

♾ This paper meets the requirements of ANSI/NISO Z39.48-1992 (Permanence of Paper).

For The Indian,
my husband, best friend, and warrior,
with love

Acknowledgments

I am grateful to Judy Soriano, retired English teacher extraordinaire, for her ruthless red pen; Pam Daoust, whose writing counsel and friendship are unparalleled; Major Nick Elias of the Oklahoma City Police Department, who kindly answered my law enforcement questions and freely shared his insight; Shirley Van Lear, who shared her nursing experiences and allowed them to seep into my manuscript; and Weynema Smith, Cherokee elder and friend, who graciously helped me with the Cherokee language. Any error in the language is solely mine. I am indebted to the people of Maui, too numerous to name, who shared their stories with me about life in the islands during the war. Mahalo. I am thankful for the advice of a veterans' trauma counselor and social worker, who shall remain nameless at his request, for helping me understand how post-traumatic stress disorder (PTSD) affects our combat warriors and how to make it real in my story. I extend my appreciation to Kristen Buckles, acquiring editor, and the entire staff at the University of Arizona Press for their support. A big "mahalo" goes to Susan Campbell, my copyeditor, who has an amazing gift for understanding me and my work. And finally, words cannot express how thankful I am to my husband Eddie for his endless love and support. *Wado.*

SINKING SUSPICIONS

Prologue

Buck Skinner pulled an envelope out of his mailbox, wondered how many days it had been there, then spit on the ground as he slammed the box shut. He hated the U.S. government.

Looking past the house toward a tree-lined meadow streaked with early morning sunshine, he stuffed the envelope into the front pocket of his bib overalls and began mumbling to himself in Cherokee as he marched up the rock walkway and into the old, one-story farmhouse. His first impulse was to simply rip the letter in half and drop it in the trash; let it mingle with the rest of the smelly rubbish. Instead, he took it out of his pocket and dropped it on top of three more envelopes lying on the kitchen table with the same return address—the Internal Revenue Service, Washington, DC.

He had told the woman on the phone three times that he did not lie on his tax return. He had never worked at a meatpacking plant in Texas, nor had he ever worked in a chicken plant in Sycamore Springs, Oklahoma. He did not have thousands of dollars stashed under his mattress or buried in the backyard in an attempt to commit tax fraud.

During the last phone call, the same insolent woman had threatened him. Either cooperate or get an attorney, she had said. He would not win in a standoff with the IRS.

He was tired of arguing.

Buck picked up the letter again, pulled a pocketknife out of his pocket, and slid the blade under the flap of the envelope. The letter was brief and to the point. The IRS had the necessary court order to attach a lien to his property. If he didn't come up with $30,000 in thirty days, they would seize his ranch for unpaid back taxes and penalties. He could protest the seizure by filing a form . . .

Buck refolded the letter, stuffed it back into the envelope, and let it fall onto the kitchen table. He walked out to his back porch and sat down to think. How had he come to this unhappy station in life? Why would someone want to destroy his peace of mind? And what was he going to do about it?

After World War II ended, Buck never wanted to intentionally harm anyone again. Killing had scarred his soul. The U.S. Marines had taught him the skills to hurt other humans, or to kill, to be more precise, and those abilities still lay embedded inside him. He fought the desire to reawaken them, but lately, this situation with the IRS had caused troubling thoughts to resurface. The man at the Cherokee Nation Veterans Office in Tahlequah had told him it was a sign of post-traumatic stress disorder, called it PTSD. But Buck thought it was too late to seek counseling for something that had happened some sixty years ago on the other side of the world. Buck wanted to be left alone, that's all, and he and his horses would be just fine.

A few minutes later, his anger flared. If they weren't going to leave him alone, he'd have to take care of it himself. He wasn't going to let the government or anyone else take his ranch away from him due to some ridiculous misunderstanding or bureaucratic paperwork mix-up. At the age of seventy-eight, he had absolutely no intention of sitting idly by while some thieving lowlife tried to steal his social security number, ruin his name, and take his ranch. He would kill or die first, and at this moment he didn't particularly care in which order.

Buck returned to the kitchen table and cursed. He reached for the wall phone and then changed his mind when he saw the red message light still blinking, just as it had for the past two days. The call would be from his niece in California, who thought it was her responsibility to hound him on a daily basis about where he'd been and what he'd last eaten. He couldn't decide if she meant well, was just plain nosy, or had less than honorable intentions, but the conversations were always the same, and he wasn't in the mood for another one today.

What day was it, anyway? He ran his gnarled finger across the feed-store calendar tacked on the wall next to the phone. Saturday, August 6, 2004, it read. How had he managed to live so long?

Hearing the crunch of tires on gravel, he watched from the kitchen window as a red car with Texas plates slowed, then rolled to a stop in front of his house. "Lost *unegvs*," he muttered to himself, referring to the white folks in the vehicle. "And they've been lost ever since they landed on this continent."

Buck didn't hate all white people, but he had spent most of his life fantasizing about what it would be like had the Spanish never tromped up through Mexico, or the English never sailed in from the east, to invade Indian country. The white settlers had arrived with an attitude of superiority, believing they had the authority to kill or remove the "heathens" they encountered and steal the land for themselves. They had made life miserable for all Indian people, and the elitist attitudes had persisted throughout history—white people always looking down their noses at their Indian neighbors. Now the descendants of those same pushy settlers had begun to search every historical document and cemetery they could find for some unknown relative who might have had a drop of Indian blood to which they could lay claim. Buck snorted. If they knew what it was truly like to endure daily discrimination, he thought, even in a so-called Indian community, they wouldn't be so eager to be Indian.

He opened the front door and leaned against the doorjamb. He was right. They were looking for the Eucha Indian cemetery, in search of some long-lost relative's grave. He gave them directions in Cherokee and returned to his house, letting the screen door slam shut behind him.

From the cabinet next to the refrigerator, Buck retrieved a plastic bread sack full of venison jerky. He pulled out four strips, wrapped them in a paper towel, and stuffed them in the front pocket of his bib overalls. He would never be hungry, he thought, as long as he had a good supply of jerky on hand.

Returning to the phone, he punched in a number he'd written on a notepad a few days earlier. After a minute, he grunted and hung up. He placed a well-worn straw hat on his head, marched out the back door, and climbed into his truck. Someone was going to be very sorry they had messed with an old Cherokee warrior named Buck Skinner.

Chapter 1

The plane lurched in the air and the knot in Sadie's stomach tightened.

"The pilot has turned on the 'fasten seat belt' sign while we experience some air turbulence," the flight attendant announced. "Please take your seats. We will be making our descent shortly."

Sadie felt the plane vibrate and realized she hated flying. She could never quite convince herself that it was normal for something as heavy as an airplane to safely soar thousands of feet above the earth. Or, in this case, above water—lots of water.

She glimpsed her reflection in the TV screen on the back of the seat in front of her and wondered who the person with the long black hair and blue eyes was staring back at her. She pushed her hair behind her shoulders and shifted in her seat. At the age of thirty-seven, she couldn't help but think her life lacked direction. This trip would change all that.

Excitement began to stir through her body as she marveled to herself how easily everything had fallen into place. She had bumped into Jan Goss in the grocery store parking lot three weeks ago. Jan had been booking organized travel tours for the area for close to twenty years. Sadie had never traveled much, but she had heard a couple of people at the bank where she used to work rave about the Hawaiian vacations Jan had set up for them.

Jan told Sadie she needed to find someone who could run the well-established travel business for her. She had two new grandbabies, and she intended to take over their upbringing rather than allow her alcoholic son to ruin their lives the way her ex-husband had ruined her own children's.

Jan's job offer sounded very attractive to Sadie now that she'd sold the American Café in Liberty, Oklahoma. Sadie had loved fulfilling her dream of owning a restaurant; it had been a wonderful experience. However, she believed that, in the end, everything had worked out right. She felt good about the day a few months earlier when she'd handed the keys of the café to the rightful heir.

Sadie had considered returning to the banking business, but she couldn't quite erase from her mind the violent and deadly robbery she'd lived through a few years ago. The image of her coworker slumped on the floor in a pool of blood simply wouldn't go away.

The bank's personnel director had given her an open-ended invitation to return to work—after all, she'd spent twelve years working there—but Sadie thought that career had provided enough trauma to last a lifetime. A recent phone call from one of her former bank coworkers detailed a bomb threat that had come in a letter to the old branch where Sadie used to work in Sycamore Springs. The conversation had sent a cold chill down her spine.

It was a sign, Sadie thought. Putting together vacation packages for happy travelers sounded a lot more appealing than dealing with bank robbers and bomb threats.

A week later, Sadie sat down with Jan in her office to discuss the agreement. She would earn a commission on every trip she booked, and that included the travel club at the bank that had already scheduled seven tours in advance. If Sadie still liked the job after six months, it was hers to keep. Jan would send Sadie, free of charge, to Maui to meet with Mr. Yamaguchi, the owner of Playin' in Paradise Travel, the parent company of Jan's travel agency, to finalize the contract. Before Sadie knew it, she was on her way to becoming a travel agent extraordinaire.

She wished Lance had come with her on this trip, but he wouldn't have any part of it. He reminded her that he couldn't leave the town of Liberty in the hands of two green officers while their police chief went gallivanting halfway around the world with his girlfriend. In addition, he argued that, in his opinion, the trip wasn't exactly necessary for her to learn how to book vacations on the computer for other people.

They had argued. You're suffocating me, she had told him. His response consisted of hands on hips, a long sigh, and an even longer stare into space before simply walking away.

Undeterred, she continued with her plans to go alone. She would only be gone five days—one day to get there, one day to meet with Mr. Yamaguchi, two days for sightseeing, and one day to fly home.

She thought about her wolf-dog Sonny and her stallion Joe. They would be fine on their own until she returned home. They both had access to fresh springwater in the creek, Joe had plenty of grass to munch in the pasture, and she had left a hunk of venison for Sonny. She wasn't sure how much wolf blood flowed through Sonny's veins, but she thought she was better off not knowing what he ate when he disappeared on his own from time to time.

She dismissed her animals from her mind and thought about Lance again. Twelve hours earlier, he'd kissed her good-bye at the entrance to the Tulsa airport. She hated waving at him as he drove off—without so much as a backward glance—but she dismissed her disappointment with a shrug and rolled her bag into the terminal to make her way through the crowd of people. From Tulsa to Dallas, and then on to Los Angeles—she embarked on her first flight over the Pacific packed like a sardine into the coach section of a plane on its way to the state of Hawai'i.

She tried to read during the flight, but instead fell into a restless sleep, dreaming about her grandfather, Andy Walela. He had served in the U.S. Army during World War II and had been stationed in the Pacific for four years. He disliked talking about the war, but he loved to tell stories about the people of Hawai'i and how friendly they had been to the soldiers. He called it the "spirit of aloha," and although she knew a lot would have changed in the past sixty years, she looked forward to relaxing in what she imagined was a casual atmosphere.

If she had time, she wanted to search for information about World War II history on Maui. Even though she thought Andy had been stationed on O'ahu, she might be able to find out if his unit had ever done any training on Maui. Visiting a place where her grandfather may have been stationed during the war fueled an exciting thought: She might gain some insight into his past. He had been a single man during the war, and since he had always spoken with so much affection about the islands, the romantic part of Sadie wondered if he might have left a lost love behind.

The plane broke through the clouds and Sadie could finally see land. The woman sitting next to her pointed out the left window.

"That's Haleakalā," she said, emphasizing the final syllable. "If you're going to be here very long, you should drive to the top for sunrise. It's an experience you'll never forget, seeing the sun come up above the clouds." The woman then gestured out the window to their right. "Those are the West Maui Mountains. My family lives in Lahaina on the other side of those mountains."

Sadie smiled and nodded, continuing to gaze out the window. As the plane circled and began its descent into the Kahului Airport, she could see odd-shaped rectangles of sugarcane fields sprawled on the valley floor below. Houses sat clustered closely together high up in the crevices of the West Maui Mountains. Sadie, so used to wide open spaces, wondered if these people had any privacy at all.

As the plane moved closer to the ground, Sadie craned her neck toward the window, trying to see the airport. After barely clearing a highway, the plane suddenly dropped onto the runway. The pilot slammed on the brakes, and the knot in Sadie's stomach cinched her chest to her throat as the small airport flashed by on her left. The plane came to a jolting stop that made Sadie glad she hadn't loosened her seat belt. The pilot maneuvered a U-turn and taxied the aircraft back toward the terminal.

Sadie let out a long breath and looked at the woman seated next to her. "Good grief," she said. "That was quite a landing."

The woman smiled and said, "Welcome to Maui."

"I don't know why we had to stop so suddenly."

The woman unlatched her seat belt. "Because if we hadn't," she chuckled, "we'd be swimming in the ocean right now."

As the plane emptied, Sadie pulled her carry-on bag out of the overhead bin and made her way off the plane, through the Jetway, and into the airport. Hawaiian music filled the air, instantly infusing her tired muscles with energy. As she rode the open-air escalator down to the baggage claim, the warm trade winds blew her hair across her face, and she smelled an unfamiliar fragrance of flowers. This really is paradise, she thought.

She stood with the other passengers and patiently waited for the luggage to arrive inside the terminal. The carousel jolted to life and she stood nearby, waiting for her bag to fall onto the conveyor belt. Finally, it did, wedging itself into the parade of identical black bags moving around the huge oval. She grinned and shook her head when she recognized the piece of silver duct tape Lance had insisted on attaching to the handle. He had been certain no other Maui-bound traveler would apply the sticky fix-all tape to their bags and she would be able to spot her bag instantly. He had been right on both counts, for which she was grateful.

After securing her bag, she retrieved her cell phone from her purse and turned it on. To her amazement, the signal indicator climbed to full strength. A few seconds later, the phone beeped, indicating that she had two messages. They were both from Lance.

She smiled while she listened to his message. She could see him push his cowboy hat off his brown, chiseled face while he spoke, his penetrating, coffee-colored eyes searching the horizon for some bad guy to take off after. His voice reflected his personality, strong and confident, yet gentle and calm. Don't worry about anything, he'd said. He would check on the house daily and make sure her dog and horse were okay. He missed her already. Would she please be careful and come home soon. She saved the message so she could listen to his voice again later and waited for the second message to play.

Lance's voice had changed to an official business tone. She switched the phone to her other ear so she could hear better. Her neighbor Buck Skinner was missing, and since she knew that part of the country better than anyone he could think of, and if she got this message in time, could she call and tell him where to look?

Surely he couldn't be serious. She followed the other passengers outside, found a place to sit, and parked her bags on the sidewalk next to her. Perched on the edge of a concrete planter, she dialed the familiar number. While waiting for the connection, she calculated the five-hour time difference. It would be about 8:30 p.m. in Oklahoma. Lance's voice mail answered after the first ring. That meant either he had turned off his phone or he was somewhere void of cell phone service, which was most of the Eucha area—and that's where he would be if he was still searching for Buck. She left a message and promised to call back as soon as she settled in to her vacation rental, a condo in a place called Ma'alaea.

She looked up and saw a beautiful middle-aged woman, a flower securing her long black hair behind her left ear. The woman held a purple and white lei in one hand and a sign with Sadie's name on it in the other. Sadie gathered her things and walked toward the woman.

"Hello," she said. "I'm Sadie Walela."

"Aloha," the woman said. "My name is Pua Keola. Mr. Yamaguchi sent me." She smiled and placed the lei around Sadie's neck. "Welcome to Maui."

"Thank you," Sadie said, holding the flowers to her face, inhaling the delicate fragrance. "These flowers smell wonderful."

"It's the white tuberoses. They are heavenly, aren't they?"

"They are." Sadie nodded and adjusted the strap of her purse so it wouldn't interfere with the lei.

"I came to offer you a ride," Pua said.

"Oh my. How nice. But I've made arrangements for a rental car if I can figure out where to find it."

"No problem. I'll help you."

As the two women strolled down the sidewalk toward the car-rental windows, Sadie drank in the sunshine, the nearness of the emerald green mountains, and the tall palm trees bending ever so slightly in the pleasant August breeze. When she arrived at the car-rental counter, Pua conversed with the attendant while Sadie fished in her purse and presented her confirmation number. Soon, she waved at Pua as a shuttle whisked her down the street to pick up her car. The personal attention surprised Sadie, and she wondered if everyone who arrived on Maui was treated like royalty. It was nice. She liked it.

The car-rental attendant gave her a map of the island and politely pointed out the route she should take to Ma'alaea. It looked pretty straightforward on the map. She hoped it would remain so when she got on the road.

She placed her bags in the backseat and maneuvered the economy car onto the highway, following the flow of traffic away from the airport. She drove past throngs of tourists with luggage piled high in convertibles, SUVs, and vans. Just think, she thought to herself, I bet all these people have travel agents back home.

As she drove, she found it hard to read road signs and dodge moving vehicles at the same time. Suddenly, she felt very alone. Why had she come all the way to this magnificent place by herself?

Sitting in traffic at a very long red light, her thoughts turned to Lance. He had told her more than once that she was the most stubborn Cherokee woman he'd ever met. They were both strong-willed people. Maybe that was the attraction. She knew he loved her independence, and his strong personality made her feel safe, but she wasn't sure two headstrong people could ever settle down together and be happy. She loved him, but the conflict was ever present.

Maybe it was the age difference. Having just turned fifty, Lance was thirteen years older than she was. He'd been falling in love in Vietnam when she was throwing rocks at boys in elementary school. Was that the problem? A generation gap? Did their tastes, values, and outlook on life differ that much? She didn't think so. Besides that, she believed that love, their love, could conquer all obstacles, including a few extra years.

Her thoughts moved to her neighbor, Buck. Like Lance, Buck was a strong Cherokee man. She had known him since she was a kid and always believed he could do anything. His age had nothing to do with it. He would be strong and resilient until he took his dying breath. That's just the kind of man he was. Thinking he could be lost somewhere was absurd. Then a wave of fear engulfed her. Even a strong man like Buck could get into trouble in triple-digit heat and humidity if something unforeseen had happened. She quickly convinced herself he was all right.

As the traffic light turned green, she surged ahead once again. The attendant's instructions were clear: Go straight at Costco, straight through the light at the big church, left at the T intersection, exit left when she got to the Ocean Center, turn onto Hauʻoli Street, and look for her condo building on the right—the building with all the plumeria trees in front, he had said. When she told him she had no idea what a plumeria tree looked like, he laughed and told her to look for a row of trees covered in white and pink blossoms.

The trees turned out to be unmistakable. She turned into the Maʻalaea Banyans's parking lot and found a place to park.

Inside the open-air lobby, Sadie picked up her key from the young woman at the front desk. Like Pua, the woman exuded such welcoming kindness that Sadie felt sure this must be what her grandfather had been trying to describe as the "aloha spirit." Sadie slung her carry-on over her shoulder and pulled her other bag into the elevator. When she found her room, she let herself in, dropped her purse on top of her bag, and gasped. She walked straight to the patio door, slid it open, and stepped out onto the balcony. The view took her breath away.

She stood and stared at the palm trees swaying slightly in the breeze, the ocean sparkling in the sunlight, and the grandeur of the dormant volcano—the woman on the plane had called it Haleakalā—its flanks sliding into the water and curving around the bay. The colorful shrubbery looked familiar, but completely unlike anything that grew in her garden back home. Children laughed and splashed in a nearby pool, and a young couple held hands while they dipped their toes into the surf. A boat filled to capacity with sunburned tourists sailed toward the harbor, and several surfers bobbed in the water, waiting for a wave to ride to shore.

"Oh, Lance, where are you?" she whispered.

Chapter 2

Lance stood next to his truck and searched the simmering horizon for some kind of a sign that Sadie's neighbor Buck Skinner was still alive. If he was, he wasn't moving. Not that Lance could see, anyway.

On the northern slope, a small herd of white-tailed deer entered the pasture. One by one, they bounced over the fence and congregated. From his position, Lance could distinguish four does and two fawns. They gathered near a bare spot in the tall grass and began to eat. Lance shook his head and chuckled when he realized Buck must be providing corn for the deer. Only someone with too much time on his hands would indulge in such a pastime in northeastern Oklahoma, where natural food for animals was plentiful, thought Lance.

A large buck bounded over the fence and cautiously approached the herd. One of the does faced the intruder and stomped her front hooves on the ground. The male obliged and retreated to the edge of the fence, as if waiting for the females to finish eating before approaching again.

Suddenly, the entire herd scattered in two directions and disappeared before Lance could see what had startled them. He retrieved his binoculars from the front seat of his truck and searched the area. He could see nothing unusual, but that was more movement than he'd seen since he and the others had started this search.

Lance wished Sadie was there. She would know exactly where to look. In his mind he could see her jump on her paint stallion and ride off in a gallop with her wolf-dog Sonny running out front as point. Her property joined Buck's, and she probably knew every hill and valley as well as she knew her backyard vegetable garden. But she wasn't there. Not even close.

He had dropped her off at the Tulsa airport earlier that morning for a flight that would take her thousands of miles away, across the Pacific on an unnecessary trip he was still unhappy about. He couldn't imagine why she wanted to be a travel agent, but he wasn't surprised. Right after college, she'd started out in the banking business. After she quit banking, she'd decided to go into business for herself and ended up buying and selling a restaurant in less than a year. Here she was, once again, searching for a new direction in life. She danced to her own drum, and he supposed that was why he was so crazy about her.

They had both been hurt, suffering in their own way. He had never been able to completely silence the crashing sounds of artillery that took his lover's life in Vietnam. It would have been so much easier if he could have died with her. But he didn't. Instead, the smells, the sounds, the feelings of utter helplessness from that awful night frequently came to him in the dead of the night. He hoped someday the memories would subside.

He knew Sadie had her own nightmares. He had met her right after she'd survived a deadly bank robbery where her coworker had been killed. It wasn't long after that he learned of the mental and physical abuse she'd endured from her jailbird ex-husband, a drug dealer who had died a violent death not far from her property. Then she'd been deceived by a man she thought loved her, a man whose whole existence was nothing more than a lie, including his love for her.

All this had made Sadie as leery of men as he was of women. Even so, they both waltzed around their anxiety and misgivings, trying to build a trusting relationship.

Everyone has baggage, he thought, but he didn't want a little unfortunate history to ruin their future together. He wanted to be the man who could convince her to overcome her fear. If she could do it, then he could, too.

Sometimes he thought she just wanted to assert her independence, push him away. He had felt the strain between them when he kissed her good-bye.

He wanted to marry her, something he was sure she knew, even though he had never actually uttered the words. And now that he thought about it, that's probably why she had fled like a hummingbird, zipping away after stealing nectar from a blood-red flower. He was the flower.

He thought about saddling Sadie's horse and using him to search for Buck, but decided against it. Joe was a gentle giant around Sadie, but the stallion had a tendency to turn his head and flatten his ears every time Lance came near. Lance figured the big guy might not take kindly to an impromptu ride by anyone other than Sadie.

Sheriff Percy O'Leary and numerous volunteers had been searching for hours on foot and on horseback but had found no sign of Buck. The sheriff had assigned volunteers to the wooded ridges that lined both sides of the valley between Buck's home and the abandoned house where Buck's truck had been found. Lance thought O'Leary's theory about Buck's whereabouts seemed unlikely, so he decided to search the upper pasture alone, where he could spend some time trying to sort out his thoughts. All he had to do was put himself in Buck's shoes for a little while, he thought, and then maybe he could figure out what the old man had been thinking when he disappeared. He ran what he knew through his mind.

They were looking for Buck because a hysterical woman had called from California and reported that she hadn't been able to reach her Uncle Buck on the phone. Once O'Leary had ascertained that Buck was indeed missing, he moved unusually fast to get the word out, simply because of the brutal August heat. If some calamity had befallen the old man, time was not on their side.

Lance had volunteered to help because of his proximity to the search. Even though Sadie had assured him that her wolf-dog Sonny and her stallion Joe would be fine on their own, he had driven from the airport back to Eucha instead of home to Liberty to make sure everything at Sadie's place was okay. It was, except that her elderly neighbor wasn't where his niece thought he should be.

Before heading out onto acres and acres of densely wooded land, Lance and the sheriff had searched Buck's house. The door was unlocked, which wasn't unusual for the area. Nothing appeared to be out of place, and there was no sign of foul play. However, a stack of envelopes on the kitchen table, all from the IRS, caught Lance's eye. He couldn't imagine Buck having trouble with the IRS, and the letters seemed irrelevant to finding Buck, so he moved on.

The sheriff asked about Sadie, echoing Lance's own thoughts that she would know more about her neighbor than anyone else around. The only information Lance could offer was that she wouldn't be home for a few days, and that he had already left her a message. Finding nothing of any interest, the two lawmen had left the house and joined the other volunteers in their search of the property. So far, their efforts had been fruitless.

Lance leaned against his truck and continued to think. Buck appeared to be an independent old man, who could be anywhere from fishing in Lake Eucha to looking for horses in a neighboring state. Lance doubted that Buck thought he had to answer to anyone, including a relative who lived fifteen hundred miles away. Buck could've simply gone on an out-of-town trip and not bothered to mention it to anyone. The only problem with that assumption was that Buck's old truck had been found that morning on the property. If he'd gone fishing, how did he get there and who did he go with?

Lance got into his vehicle and drove across the pasture, rolling to a stop next to Buck's worn-out Chevy truck. It sat near a springhouse in front of a dilapidated farmhouse that appeared to have been uninhabited for decades. Lance got out and glanced into the truck. He could see nothing unusual. But why exactly would Buck leave his truck there? Maybe it wouldn't start. The keys were missing, so there was no way to know whether the truck was operable without getting a mechanic to come out and test it. Then again, maybe Buck thought the old truck deserved a nice final resting place, and that spot was as good as any.

Lance walked over to the springhouse and went in, taking pleasure in the coolness of the rock building. He squatted by the stream that flowed through the structure, scooped some fresh water with his hand, and splashed it on his face. It felt good. He lifted another handful to his face, sipped, and relished the iciness of the water. After a few minutes, he returned to the sunshine and slowly turned in all four directions, trying to imagine the path Buck would have taken if he had chosen to walk home from there.

Lance decided the worn trail in front of the house that ran east back toward Buck's house seemed the most logical. He would retrace it, spreading out in both directions. With the heat index inching higher, closing in on triple digits, there was no time to waste. Buck could be dehydrated and disoriented.

Lance chose his steps carefully, ever mindful of the plentiful copperheads and rattlesnakes that could so easily blend in with the surrounding landscape. Steamy air rose around him and sweat slid down his face. When he reached a rundown fence, he walked up and down the row looking for evidence in the tall grass that Buck might have crossed. He found no trace of Buck and, thankfully, no sign of snakes.

Lance returned to his truck and threw his binoculars on the front seat, then drove slowly across the pasture, hoping that if the old man had fallen he would see him before he ran over him. As he neared the spot where the deer had been feeding earlier, he stopped and killed the engine. He leaned out the window and yelled Buck's name.

Nothing.

The grasshoppers sang around him and a crow called from a nearby tree. The staccato bursts of a woodpecker echoed in the valley below. He called out Buck's name again and listened.

Still nothing.

The day wore on, until the relentless Oklahoma sun finally started its descent in the sky. Lance had searched acres of pasture, bottomland, ridges, and valleys. He was hot, hungry, and dog-tired. He flicked a brown, spotted deer tick off his arm and out the window of his truck. If the other volunteers came up empty-handed as well, then the sheriff would most likely call off the search. After all, Buck could be anywhere.

Lance nosed his truck back toward the makeshift command center at Buck's house to regroup and try to call Sadie again. Maybe she would answer this time.

His path took him through the pasture back by the old farmhouse where Buck's truck still sat. When he reached the springhouse, a thought occurred to him. Had anyone even bothered to look in the abandoned house?

It could be dangerous. The roof had already begun to cave in over the front door and there was a possibility the floor could be equally rotten. Sadie's presence was never far from his mind, and he could hear her cautioning him to not go in alone in case something happened. He knew her concern for his safety reflected her love for him, but he brushed away the echo of her voice. He parked his truck and walked toward the house.

With flashlight in hand, Lance carefully pushed the side door of the house open and called out Buck's name. A bird flew from an unseen perch and escaped through a broken window. Startled, he instinctively ducked. After a few moments, he calmly entered and shone his flashlight around a small empty room that appeared to have been a kitchen in years past.

He continued through a doorway to his left and into a larger room with a very old potbellied stove standing at attention in the center of the room. As Lance moved past the stove, the floorboards creaked and sagged beneath his feet. He froze, calculating his next step. The flooring appeared to be more stable near the wall, so he took that path to the end of the room, where he found another empty room that must have been a bedroom. Next to that doorway, he found a narrow stairway.

Lance looked up to the top of the stairs at a closed door with a glass doorknob. He called out Buck's name again. Silence. He let out a deep breath and began to climb, testing each step before placing his full weight on it. Surprisingly, the stairs felt remarkably strong compared to the flooring in the rest of the house.

He pushed open the door at the top of the stairs and watched the heavy dust float into the air, reflecting in the last slender rays of sunshine filtering through a western window.

"Buck?" he said, even though he knew he was alone in this sad, empty place.

He directed the beam of his flashlight around the small room. A tall, narrow, tarnished mirror leaned against one wall. Three metal clothes hangers lay strewn on the floor. At the other end of the room an old trunk sat in a corner, the kind of chest one would expect to contain a treasure. Careful of his footing, Lance approached the trunk and paused before opening it.

In the early evening distance, a hoot owl began to call into the night. Lance tensed and then cursed. "Not now," he said. How many times had he heard his Cherokee uncle say that an owl was an omen of death? Go away, he thought, I don't have time for you right now.

Fighting the urge to forget everything he was doing and run, Lance returned his attention to the trunk. He took his pocketknife out of his pocket, pried open the rusty latch, and forced open the lid. He had indeed found a treasure.

One by one, Lance pulled out an array of World War II memorabilia, in surprisingly good condition considering its age and whereabouts. Yellowed newspaper articles lay on top of an old military uniform. He pulled the uniform out and carefully inspected the shoulder patch—a gold "4" on a scarlet background—the insignia of the 4th Marine Division. The stripes on the sleeves indicated the rank of corporal. Having been a Marine, and knowing the history of the corps, Lance knew that whoever had worn this uniform had been a part of the famous Fighting 4th, the division that had taken on the Japanese in their own backyard and won. The 4th Marines were legendary.

Underneath the uniform lay a knife in a leather sheaf, a handful of unspent rounds wrapped inside a black silk kimono, a stack of old letters tied together with a string, and a small wooden box. Lance lifted the lid of the box to reveal an assortment of colorful medals and ribbons. He whistled softly through his teeth as he gingerly picked up a Purple Heart Medal, turned it over in his hand, and then respectfully returned it to the stack of other medals. A name badge read "Skinner."

Lance wondered about the trunk and why it would be in the abandoned house, and then he instinctively knew the answer. It held painful memories that Buck probably wanted to forget, yet the old man had never taken the steps to destroy the contents. Instead, he'd left it to eventually rot with the rest of the decaying structure.

The owl made its presence known again, and the muscles tightened in Lance's back. He removed the letters and the box of medals, and closed the trunk lid on the rest of the gear. He quickly retreated to his truck, put the treasure he'd found on the seat beside him, and drove out of the eerily quiet and dark valley.

Chapter 3

Sadie leaned on the balcony railing and stared at the ocean as its waves rolled into the shoreline in front of the building. The view stole her breath away. In the distance she could see the other side of Maʻalaea Bay, which, according to the woman she'd first met at the registration desk, was a place called Wailea. Sadie liked the way it sounded so similar to her own last name—Walela—and hoped to learn the Hawaiian meaning before she went home.

She returned to her carry-on and pulled out the guidebook she had studied on the plane. She stared at the map and then at the landscape. "Molokini," she read aloud. "A favorite snorkeling spot shaped like a horseshoe." To the right of Molokini she could see another island name, Kahoʻolawe. Maybe Pua could teach her how to pronounce it.

The lady on the plane had told her all about it, that the island had been used for bombing practice by the U.S. military during World War II. Sadly, she had explained, it was now completely uninhabitable because of the unexploded ordnance still there. Of course, that was the land that the government wanted to give back to the Native Hawaiians. Sadie thought Hawaiian history must be a lot like Indian history—the white man took what he wanted and, after he ruined it, gave what was left to the Natives.

The gentle surf calmed her as the water repeatedly rose and fell against the rocks in front of the building. The excitement of the trip began to fade as she relaxed in a patio chair, taking in the fragrance of an unfamiliar yet heavenly floral scent that mingled with the sea air.

Her mind returned to Lance, and she recalculated the time difference. It would be almost 10:00 p.m. in Oklahoma. She went back inside, retrieved her cell phone from her purse, and dialed his number again. He answered on the second ring.

"Oh, Lance, I got your message. How is Buck?"

"Lost."

Sadie's heart dropped. "Buck is not lost," she argued. "He's spent his whole life in those hills. He might be hurt somewhere and can't get home, but he is not lost."

Lance let out a long sigh. "I know. But we can't find him, so as far as I'm concerned that means he's lost."

"Oh."

"We've been searching all day, but the problem is we don't really know where to look. We found his truck down at the old springhouse, but the keys weren't in it. So, for all we know, it could have been there for days or weeks."

"Why exactly are you looking for him then? You know he takes off from time to time. I'm sure there's nothing to worry about."

"His niece in California called the sheriff's office and said she had been trying to call her uncle and couldn't get an answer. I guess O'Leary didn't want to take any chances. You know how blazing hot it is." Lance let out a heavy sigh. "Anyway, a group of folks was out looking for him when I got back to your place to check on the animals, so I stopped to see what was going on, and that's how I got involved."

Sadie fought off a vision of Buck, his wiry body sprawled on the ground with a twisted ankle or a broken leg, his straw hat just beyond his reach with the sun beating down on his military-style haircut, speaking quietly in Cherokee to a rattlesnake coiled nearby, trying to convince it to move along.

"He could have caught a ride and gone somewhere," she finally said. "You know he loves to go to those all-night gospel singings down around Stilwell and Tahlequah."

"You wouldn't happen to know who he might've gone off with on this little adventure, would you?"

"No, not really." Sadie tried to lighten the conversation. "Maybe he has a new girlfriend, or something."

"I doubt that."

So did she. "Just kidding," she said.

"I suppose anything's possible. We don't have a lot to go on right now. I helped O'Leary search his house. Nothing unusual there. The only thing that keeps bothering me is the letters I saw from the IRS on the kitchen table."

"The IRS?"

"Yeah, it said 'Notice of Lien' on the outside of the envelope, but I can't imagine Buck having trouble with the IRS. Can you? The only income he probably has is his social security. He seems to be a man who lives well within his means, and if I was a betting man, I'd bet his ranch is paid for, free and clear."

"Oh my gosh, Lance. A few months ago Buck told me someone had used his social security number and messed up his taxes. I didn't know it was that serious." After a few moments Sadie forced a chuckle in an attempt to hide her concern. "He was threatening to run down whoever it was and make them pay with their hide. If anyone could do that, Buck could. You think that's where he is? Looking for whoever stole his identity? You know that's what it is—identity theft. I bet I saw it a hundred times when I was working at the bank."

"I think I'll see if I can get another look at those letters." A long pause meant Lance was thinking on the other end of the line. "I don't know," he continued, "but I'm going to have to get some help from the Cherokee marshals if I'm going to keep looking for him."

"So does that mean you're going back out?"

"O'Leary is calling off the search tomorrow if something doesn't turn up by then. I think I'll call and have him meet me back at Buck's house. There's got to be something there that explains Buck's disappearance."

"Lance, why don't you take Joe and Sonny with you?"

"We had some men out on horseback today. Besides, your horse and your dog don't respond very well to me when you're not around. They act like I'm an alien."

Sadie rolled her eyes and bit her lip.

"I tried to see if your Uncle Eli or Aunt Mary had any ideas, but I couldn't find them, either." Lance sounded exasperated. "Maybe they're all lost somewhere together."

"Oh, I forgot to tell you. Uncle Eli sold a colt to someone out in the Texas Panhandle and he and Aunt Mary went to deliver it. They're going to take their time and stop in Oklahoma City on the way back to visit some friends and do some shopping, so they won't be back for at least a week. Maybe I'd better come home after the meeting tomorrow."

"No, Sadie. There isn't anything you can do. Go ahead and enjoy your trip and I'll see you in a few days."

"I'm not sure I can enjoy anything now. I feel like I should be there looking for Buck. I know I could find him." Sadie moaned. "Besides, I feel awful about coming here without you. Oh, Lance, it is so beautiful. I wish you were here."

"Oh, come on, Sadie. You can't be in control of everything. If he's out there, we'll find him. If he's not, he'll turn up in a few days—one way or the other. I was in law enforcement for a long time before I met you."

His words hurt. Her brain churned with things she'd like to say, things she would most likely be sorry for later. "You know, Lance—" she started, and then swallowed hard.

"We'll handle this," he broke in. "Relax and have a good time. It'll all be here when you get back."

"Fine." Sadie hung up, dropped the phone on the couch, and returned to the endless sound of the surf. She rocked back and forth on the patio glider and thought. Lance could be so serious when he was working, and she didn't like it when he was short with her. Exhaustion began to creep into her arms and legs and work its way into the rest of her body. She went back inside the condo and collapsed on the bed. She whispered a prayer for her good friend Buck Skinner and fell sound asleep to the rising and falling of the ocean.

Chapter 4

Lance checked the time—5:00 a.m.—while he sat in his truck in front of Buck Skinner's house and sipped coffee, waiting for Sheriff O'Leary to arrive. Lance wanted a closer look at the letters from the IRS he'd seen the day before. However, he didn't want to enter Buck's house without the sheriff present in case there were any questions later. Lance spent a lot of time in Eucha due to the fact that he couldn't stay away from Sadie for any length of time, but that didn't put Buck's house or this investigation in his jurisdiction as a lawman.

Lance didn't really have a connection to Buck other than he was Sadie's neighbor and Lance knew Sadie thought the world of him. Lance knew Buck was Cherokee, grew a huge vegetable garden that he generously shared, loved wild horses and homemade chocolate brownies, and that was about it. Buck seemed friendly enough, but always kept to himself, an apt description of a lot of Indians in Delaware County.

Lance had a sixth sense when it came to people. He didn't know if it came from his years in law enforcement or was simply a trait he had inherited from his ancestors, but he didn't think O'Leary, a white man with political ambitions, would spend much more time looking for an old Cherokee man. That uneasy feeling had caused Lance to make arrangements with the Cherokee marshals to cover for him while he took a few days off from his job as the police chief of Liberty, Oklahoma. If he was going to find Buck Skinner and run down who had stolen the old man's identity, he was going to have to do it on his own time. O'Leary had already told him he had other people in Delaware County to worry about and he couldn't keep spending county money looking for someone he wasn't even sure was missing.

Lance also thought that sorting out Buck's problems would help keep his mind off Sadie while she was out of town. He could hear her asking him why he hadn't worked harder at finding her friend, and he knew she'd never forgive him if something really bad had happened to Buck and he had failed to find him.

O'Leary drove up next to Lance's truck and rolled down his window.

"This'd better be good, Smith. I haven't even had breakfast, yet. Hell, it ain't even daylight."

Lance got out of his vehicle and waited for the sheriff to do the same.

"Just wanted to get another look at those letters we saw on Buck's table. If he's not out here on the property somewhere, maybe he went looking for whoever is causing him all those problems with the IRS."

"You've got to be kidding me." O'Leary shook his head and cursed. "You got me out of bed for this? You're on a wild goose chase, Smith."

Lance smiled and followed the sheriff to the door.

O'Leary rapped loudly on the door and then turned to Lance. "He probably came home drunk last night and is inside sleeping it off. That'd be about par for the course."

With a stone face, Lance crossed his arms and waited.

O'Leary pushed the unlocked door open and the two men entered the house. Lance immediately went into the kitchen, flipped the light switch, and found the letters he'd seen the day before. He opened the top letter and studied it, then took a small, spiral-bound notebook out of his shirt pocket and started making notes. When he finished, he turned to the sheriff.

"Mind if we take a walk through the house again?"

"I can't imagine anything has changed from the last time we looked, but go ahead."

The small, one-bedroom house looked like the obvious home of a bachelor—bare and in need of a woman's touch. A tattered map of the Hawaiian Islands and the southern Pacific Rim hung on the bedroom wall, attached with thumbtacks. Lance glanced at the map and noticed it had been marked with an ink pen as if tracing several routes, all beginning and ending on Maui. He continued to the closet, and then checked under the bed and in the bathroom. Back in the kitchen, he noticed the blinking red light on the phone.

"Sheriff, you want to listen to this message on Buck's phone?"

O'Leary rose from the living room chair where he had been waiting for Lance and walked into the kitchen. "Sure, knock yourself out."

Lance pushed the button and began to take notes.

"Uncle Buck, this is Dee Dee, again." The tone of the woman's voice sounded as if she were talking to a child. "You know, I'm getting worried about you because you won't return any of my phone calls. I'm afraid at your age something is going to happen to you . . . and how would I ever know? Are you feeling okay? Eating more than beans and jerky, I hope." The woman chuckled and then her voice took on a more authoritative tenor. "If I need to come out there and take care of you, you know I will. Call me."

Lance shook his head and looked toward O'Leary, who was already walking out the front door. Then a small notepad next to the phone caught his attention, where Buck had scribbled some numbers and words. They made absolutely no sense to Lance.

"Hey, Lance, can you hurry up? My wife's probably got breakfast on the table by now, and I've got a million things to do, including finding some men who are willing to waste their day looking for a needle in a haystack in this heat."

Lance copied the information from the notepad into his spiral-bound notebook and placed it back into his shirt pocket. He nodded his thanks to the sheriff as the two men got in their respective vehicles and drove off in opposite directions.

Lance traveled the short distance to Sadie's house to make sure everything was still locked up tight. In the early morning light, he could see her paint horse Joe grazing in the pasture, but her dog Sonny was nowhere in sight. He rolled down the truck window, whistled, and called his name. Nothing.

He got out of his truck and stood in Sadie's yard, hands on hips, visually searching the nearby pasture, then walked to the barn and looked inside. Empty. In his estimation, Sonny was unpredictable, and that spelled trouble to his way of thinking. The wolf-dog was smart all right, but he thought it unlikely the animal would ever be completely domesticated, no matter what Sadie said. It was quite apparent that the wolf-dog didn't like him, either.

Lance didn't relish the idea of telling Sadie her dog was missing, so he rationalized. Maybe Sonny was kind of like Buck, refusing to answer to anyone right now. Lance pumped fresh water, then retrieved a container of dog food from the barn, and dumped it near the porch where he thought Sonny would eventually show.

Lance's cell phone rang. It was O'Leary calling to tell Lance the search for Buck Skinner had been called off. A neighbor who had heard they were searching for Buck had called and left information about a vehicle they'd seen parked in front of Buck's house the morning he went missing, so the sheriff concluded the old man had simply gone with the driver of the unidentified vehicle. There was no crime in that, O'Leary said, and he was sure Buck would turn up sooner or later. O'Leary's tone annoyed Lance.

He returned to his truck, gathered the stack of letters from the front seat, and entered the screened-in porch of Sadie's farmhouse. A row of empty flowerpots lined the far wall. What's the use in planting flowers in pots, he thought, when you've got an acre of yard space? He scooted the corner pot over with the toe of his boot and uncovered the key Sadie had left for him, picked it up, and unlocked the kitchen door.

The quiet house smelled like Sadie, a combination of vanilla sugar cookies and the subtle fragrance of lilacs that hung in the air after she tossed her long raven hair behind her delicate shoulders. It was as if she had just walked through the room, beckoning him to follow.

He made a pot of coffee and pushed the awareness of Sadie's presence away, allowing his thoughts to return to her neighbor. After pouring a cup of coffee, he sat down at the kitchen table to examine the old envelopes he'd found in the abandoned house. They were letters Buck had sent home during the war, arranged in order by date and tied together with strong twine. Unable to loosen the knot, Lance slid out the top letter and opened it. He sipped coffee as he read.

Dear Mom and Dad,
You wouldn't believe how many boys showed up to fight in
the war. Training has been rough, but not too rough for me.

We've got a baseball team and I've hit the most home runs so far. I don't know where these boys learned to play ball, but our team in Eucha could beat them all. I'm ready to go. I can shoot better than anyone else in my platoon. I told them it was because I'd been shooting since I was a kid. Tell Jake it's okay to use my rifle while I'm gone. One of the men told me his brother died in France a few weeks ago. His parents want him to quit and come home, but they say we can't come home until the war is over.

Love,

Ben

Buck's letter stirred something deep inside Lance. Buck had obviously been very young when he went off to war, and his words reflected the same feelings Lance had had when he joined the Marines and headed to Vietnam—a lot of fear and adrenaline.

Lance returned the letter to the stack and poured another cup of coffee. Something didn't feel right. He couldn't forget about Buck. Maybe a little unofficial snooping wouldn't hurt, he thought, and even though the information he'd gathered at Buck's house was limited, it might be all he needed to find an identity thief. If Buck was indeed out riding around with some unknown person or persons, so be it. Lance could at least help the old guy out with his problems with the government. After what Buck had done for his country, as a fellow Marine, it was the least Lance could do for him.

He picked up the phone and dialed Sadie's cell phone. No answer. He hated being out of communication with her. He hung up and mentally reviewed what he knew so far.

A California woman was in a panic because she couldn't reach her Uncle Buck on the phone. Buck answered to no one and had a tendency to go wherever and whenever he pleased. His old truck was sitting in the middle of his property, but no one seemed to know whether it was running or if it had been there for a day, a week, or a month. Ten men had searched Buck's ranch all day and all night and had found no sign of him. But Lance knew it would take a hundred men a month to cover two hundred acres of heavy woods and dense underbrush, and it would take a lot more than that to find someone like Buck if he didn't want to be found.

What else did he know? The IRS was getting ready to take everything Buck owned. Obviously, someone had been using Buck's social security number illegally and reporting income to the Social Security Administration.

Knowing what little he did about Buck, Lance didn't think Buck would take too kindly to anyone stealing his ranch. The expected response, however, wouldn't be for Buck to disappear. It would be more in tune with greeting visitors on the front porch with a loaded shotgun.

Lance's final conclusion was that Buck might be missing, and on the other hand, he might not. Either way, Lance would follow the money trail and see what he could find.

He picked up the phone and dialed Maggie Whitekiller, the woman who answered the phone for the Liberty Police Department when no one was around. Lance had grown to depend on Maggie for sundry things, one of which was her computer skills. She answered on the first ring.

"Hi, Maggie. Everything under control?"

"Hey, Chief, of course," she said, and then broke into song, "It's a Sunday morning sidewalk." She chuckled and said, "I just heard that song on the radio. Don't you just love Kris Kristofferson?"

Lance shook his head in silence.

"Did Sadie get off okay?" Maggie continued.

"Yes, she's fine. In fact, I'm up here in Delaware County at her house now trying to help locate her missing neighbor, Buck Skinner. Can you look something up for me on the computer?"

"When are you going to get with it, Boss? This is the twenty-first century. Even my grandson can use a computer."

"Come on, Maggie. Don't give me a hard time. You know the City of Liberty can't afford to buy me a computer to carry around in my back pocket."

Maggie laughed. "Okay, what is it?"

Lance pulled the spiral-bound notebook out of his shirt pocket, fed questions to Maggie, and waited. After a few minutes, he began to take notes as she recited information to him. Lance thanked her and made her promise she would call him on his cell phone if anything catastrophic happened. She promised she would, and he hung up.

Next stop would be Sycamore Springs.

Chapter 5

Ga do da jv ya dv hne li ji sa
O ga je li ja gv wi yu hi
O ga li ga li na hna gwu ye hno
Jo gi lv hwi sda ne di yi

When Sadie woke up, it took a minute for her to recall where she was. She had dreamed about someone singing a mournful Cherokee song and the melody still hung in the air around her. She sat up in bed and listened to what sounded like a million chattering birds. They were either arguing over something important or exclaiming the glory of the early morning. She smiled when she remembered the "No Parking—Bird Droppings" sign she had seen the night before under the huge banyan tree in the parking lot. At least it's better than waking up to the sound of an obnoxious alarm clock, she thought.

Sometime during the night she had undressed, left her clothes on the floor, and slid between the clean sheets. She had slept soundly, giving her renewed vigor for her first full day on Maui. She jumped out of bed, fished her swimsuit out of her luggage, and pulled it on.

She stepped out on her third-floor balcony to the same ocean air she had succumbed to the night before. The lawn chairs below had been magically arranged in a straight row across the luscious green lawn. The empty kidney-shaped pool glistened in the predawn hours. No one seemed to be out and about. Must be the time difference, she thought. Once again she made the mental calculation: if it's 5:20 a.m. here, it's 10:20 a.m. in Oklahoma. Her internal clock still ticked in the Oklahoma time zone.

She grabbed her cell phone to dial Lance's number. No signal. Her battery was dead. She groaned and dug in her bag for the phone charger. When she found it, she plugged in the phone, threw it on the couch, and headed for the beach.

She walked a few hundred yards to the end of the street, passing lots of thick, blooming shrubbery, a manicured greenbelt, and several condominium buildings. On the other side of the road lay a huge sugarcane field. She stopped and watched a couple of birds, the likes of which she had never seen before. They looked like redbirds or cardinals, except they had gray bodies and crimson heads. She watched as they picked at seeds on the side of the road and then flitted to a safe distance.

When she got to Haycraft Park, she made her way in the early morning light toward the sound of the surf. When she reached the beach, she stood and stared. The sun had begun to creep over the same mountain she had seen when she landed the day before. The moon hung low on the western horizon. It was the most beautiful morning she had ever seen. She felt exhilarated as she walked.

The beach, listed as Sugar Beach on her map, began at the park and extended as far as she could see around Ma'alaea Bay. For a while, she thought she must be the only living soul out at that time of the morning. But before she knew it, several walkers, joggers, and a couple of fishermen came into view.

She carried her flip-flops and let her toes sink into the fine sand that looked and felt like brown sugar. The gentle surf crawled around her feet as she stopped for a moment and looked across the water. In the distance a tour boat sailed toward the tiny island of Molokini. The magnificence of it all caused her to think about Lance and how thankful she was to have him in her life. If he wasn't so stubborn, they could be walking this beach together, holding hands.

The faint odor of seaweed rose from massive brown and green clumps that lay strewn across the beach. In small natural pools of water, stranded minnow-sized fish waited for the tide to return and wash them back into the ocean.

Sadie had been walking about thirty minutes when she noticed six pyramid-shaped concrete objects sitting in the water near two rows of large lava rocks. The rocks appeared to mark an entrance onto the beach, perhaps into the brackish pond that lay under a boardwalk not far away. She wondered if these indestructible man-made objects were perhaps remnants from the war, placed deliberately to keep small watercraft from landing on the beach. She made a mental note to look for related information if she ever made it to the library to do any local research on the war.

She glanced back at her footprints. They had already begun to fade by the water's continual washing of the sand. In a few more minutes, all proof of her existence on this stretch of beach would disappear, erased by the ocean.

Suddenly, the song from her dream returned—"One Drop of Blood"—a sacred song her ancestors had sung on the dreadful, long walk from Georgia to Indian Territory known as the Trail of Tears. It reminded her of her friend and neighbor Benjamin "Buck" Skinner. She'd heard him singing that song to himself so many times before. Where could he be? Could he just disappear without a trace the way her footprints had? He had probably gone somewhere insignificant, she thought, and when he gets home in a few days everyone will have a big laugh. He was quite a character.

Sadie found a comfortable place to sit on the beach, sink her toes in the sand, and think. She had known Buck for as long as she could remember. He had been a friend to her father, to his father before him, and now to her. His land butted up against the Walela land on the south side of the road. He was a good neighbor, a quiet, steady Cherokee man who kept to himself.

Sadie could remember returning home on more than one summer day to find a brown paper sack stuffed full of tomatoes, cucumbers, squash, or whatever the day's harvest from Buck's garden had been. In return, she would bake his favorite treat, a batch of oatmeal cookies or a pan of double-fudge brownies, wrap the goodies in aluminum foil, and drop them by his house. Buck would carry on over her tasty gifts and make her sit down and have a bite with him while he reminisced.

The stories often centered on the first time Sadie's grandfather balanced her on the bare back of a paint horse. According to Buck, Sadie's mother had thrown a fit. No one knew why she got so upset, because it seemed evident to everyone else that Sadie was a natural-born horse lover. Throughout the years, not even her mother would be able to convince her it was unbecoming for a lady to spend all her time in the barn brushing horses and mucking stalls.

Sadie enjoyed listening to Buck, amazed at his talent for creating those slight embellishments that eventually morphed the delightful tales into his own personal version of her life. Sometimes she actually began to question her own recollections. Only occasionally did he venture into any of his own personal history.

Buck was known in the small community of Eucha as "Buck, the rider of wild horses." As the story went, there wasn't a horse in Delaware County that hadn't bucked, kicked, or rolled over the old man at one time or another unless it had arrived in the county already suitable for riding. He had a multitude of scars and had suffered countless broken bones during his lifetime working with horses, but it had never stopped him from climbing back on long before the throbbing stopped. Those days had long passed, but he still talked about his favorite stallion as if he was a member of the family. Now he settled for the enjoyment of watching wild mustangs roam on his land, and sneaking carrots to Joe when he thought Sadie wasn't watching.

Only once had Buck mentioned a wife and child to Sadie. The baby had come early during a terrible spring rainstorm, the mother home alone while Buck fought swirling flood waters to rescue a new colt. The foal survived; the mother and baby didn't. Buck never forgave himself.

The conversation had been Buck's attempt to comfort Sadie when she had suffered a miscarriage during a brief teenage marriage. They shed a few tears together and the subject never surfaced again.

According to Sadie's father, Buck had endured every bloody battle fought by the 4th Marine Division in the Pacific theater during World War II; that is, until he was badly wounded and had to return to the States. Buck rarely spoke about those lost years at war. Even when Sadie studied history at the university and tried to interview him for a paper, he refused. Instead, he looked off into the distance, grinned as if he knew the world's biggest secret, and then politely walked off.

Sadie felt helpless, but she knew one thing—Buck was a survivor. The crusty old man might be hurt, but he wasn't lost. Maybe he had fallen and hit his head or broke something. She knew if Buck was alive, the old war hero would hang on until someone could find him.

She turned and headed back down the beach to her condo. She had a lunch meeting in a few short hours with Mr. Yamaguchi in his Kihei office. Besides that, Lance might be trying to call.

✣

Hoping no one would notice that she was late for work, Priscilla Blackfox hurriedly swiped her magnetic card at the seldom-used side entrance of the Sisson Farms chicken processing plant in Sycamore Springs, Oklahoma, and pushed on the door. It was stuck. She used her left shoulder and all her strength to push again, only to gain a couple of inches and uncover a dirty sneaker blocking the way. "Open the door," she yelled through the small opening. When no one answered, she pushed with all her might, creating barely enough space to step through.

Once inside, it took a few minutes for her eyes to adjust to the darkness before she discovered the problem. One of her coworkers lay on the floor against the door.

"Get up, Hernandez," she growled. "Go somewhere else and pass out." She nudged him with her foot and then noticed blood on his shirt. "This isn't funny, man. Get up." Suddenly, realizing her friend couldn't hear her, she gasped for air, ran to the door leading into the plant, and screamed as loudly as she could.

Chapter 6

Lance locked up Sadie's house and started to replace the key under the flowerpot, then changed his mind and dropped it into his pocket. The dog food he'd left by the back porch remained untouched. He called out Sonny's name and waited. Still no sign of him. Joe, Sadie's paint horse, stood under a shade tree near the barn, brushing flies away with his tail. Lance climbed into his truck and headed toward Sycamore Springs.

He drove past the Eucha cemetery and followed the road to Highway 20. As he drove, Lance could see the heat radiating from the asphalt. It was going to be another scorcher.

Lance's thoughts turned back to Buck. He hoped the old man really was off on an adventure somewhere and not in trouble. More than that, he prayed Buck wasn't dying a slow death somewhere in this heat. The number he'd copied from the notepad near Buck's phone didn't make any sense until Maggie used her magic on the Internet and came up with the phone number of a chicken processing plant in Sycamore Springs. Lance couldn't imagine what business Buck would have at a processing plant that only sold frozen chickens wholesale to grocery stores. That led Lance to wonder if it had something to do with Buck's predicament with the IRS. Before long, he'd know.

This stretch of highway had become so familiar to Lance he thought he could drive it blindfolded. He hardly noticed the familiar houses along the way, the tree-covered landscape mixed with cleared pastureland dotted with horses and cattle. When he reached the highway, he unconsciously surrendered to the lonely ribbon of curves for the next several miles to the small community of Jay, Oklahoma.

He squirmed in his seat as thoughts of Sadie surfaced. She was never far from his mind. The woman had done something to him, something he simultaneously adored and hated. She had taught him the meaning of love, and the mere thought of living without her made his stomach churn. He'd had that feeling only once before in his life. It had ended very badly, and he'd promised himself he'd never be trapped by another. But here he was—in love again. It had happened before he'd had time to squash it like a bug under the heel of his boot. He tried to push her to the back of his mind as he drove.

Lance continued north through Jay and turned back east, still on Highway 20. In less than twenty minutes he was in Sycamore Springs, the place where he'd become a seasoned police officer under the guidance of Charlie McCord.

The population of Sycamore Springs had been shrinking for the last several years, and he guessed it was now home to no more than a couple thousand people, some white, some Hispanic, with a large number of Indians mixed in, mostly Cherokees. Poverty had overtaken the small town. The main industry was simply chickens—chicken houses and one large chicken processing plant.

Lance drove through the main part of town and parked next to four other farm trucks in front of the Waffle House. He had fond memories of the small restaurant, a daily meeting place of the local police officers. This would be where his friend Charlie McCord said he'd be, waiting for retirement day to arrive.

Lance got out and went into the restaurant and scanned the crowd for Charlie or anyone else he knew. No luck. He sat at the end of the counter where he could see the entire restaurant without effort.

"Eating or just drinking, honey?" The middle-aged waitress looked as if she'd lived a harsh life, one where hard work had stolen her youth sooner than it should have.

"Coffee. Black."

She slid a mug in front of him and filled it with steaming coffee. Lance turned and surveyed the parking lot again.

"Male or female?" she said.

Lance grinned. "Charlie McCord said he'd meet me here."

"Oh, honey, you're going to have a long wait." She wiped the counter with a wet cloth. "He stormed out of here over thirty minutes ago. Turned on those flashing lights of his and tore off toward the chicken plant. Doubt he'll be back very soon."

A bell dinged in the kitchen window and the waitress turned to retrieve a plate of food and deliver it to a corner booth. Lance sipped his coffee for a moment, then dropped a couple of bills on the counter and left.

⁜

Before Lance arrived at the Sisson Farms chicken plant at the south edge of town, he could see the flashing lights in the distance. He pulled in, parked near the gate, and got out of his truck. He could see Charlie leaning against his cruiser, writing on a clipboard. The strained buttons on Charlie's shirt indicated he'd been spending a little too much time at the Waffle House, and Lance thought he could detect a short-timer's attitude in the expression on his face. He knew Charlie's approaching retirement couldn't arrive soon enough.

Charlie looked up and grinned when he saw Lance. Lance walked over and shook hands with his friend. "Hey, Keem-o-sabi, how goes it?"

"Good to see you, Tonto. This is your lucky day."

Lance laughed at the familiar exchange while Charlie opened his car door and dropped the clipboard on the dashboard.

"Oh, yeah? Lucky how?" Lance said.

"You said you were looking for someone named Skinner. Right?"

"That's right. Ben Skinner. Goes by Buck. Only been missing for a day, but his niece is pretty worried about him."

"Well, I've got bad news for that little niece of his. I've got me a dead man in there and his killer has been identified as one Benjamin Skinner."

"No way." Lance couldn't hide the surprise in his voice. "What happened?"

"Evidently, he showed up here early this morning ranting about something, got into a scuffle with one of the workers, and instead of gutting a chicken, he gutted one of the employees."

Lance realized his mouth was gaping. "Are you sure we're talking about the same Buck Skinner?"

"Come on into the main office with me. The woman who identified him on the security camera videotape says she knows him pretty well."

Lance followed Charlie into the office, where two women sat hunkered around a small desk, gripping coffee cups. Their ashen faces reflected shock. A man stood looking through a huge plate-glass window at the interior of the plant, where two conveyor belts continued to move without a chicken in sight.

Charlie introduced Lance, then turned to one of the women and spoke.

"Ma'am, we're going to need to get your statement. Do you want to come down to the office or do you want to do it here?"

"I've already told you everything I know. An employee noticed the side door was ajar. When she tried to get in, she found the body. Several people heard her scream."

The woman hesitated and Charlie urged her to continue.

"I was standing outside the office door on the ledge that overlooks the workers." She pointed through the large window at a catwalk that encircled the large room. "It was just as the morning shift was coming on. I heard a ruckus and then I saw Benny running out the back door. Right over there." She pointed through the window again at an exit on the opposite side of the building.

"Benny?" asked Lance.

"His name is Ben Skinner, but everyone calls him Benny."

"How do you know Benny?" Lance asked.

The woman looked surprised at the question. "Everyone knows Benny. He used to work here and comes around all the time."

Charlie stepped in. "Do you know where we can find him?"

The woman let out a long sigh. "He hangs out with a woman who lives in the Vista Trails Trailer Park over by the river."

Lance looked at Charlie as they moved quickly toward the door. "Mind if I ride along?"

Chapter 7

Sadie began to feel a sense of urgency, with the small voice in the back of her head churning out thoughts of home. Even in this magnificent place, she would never be able to relax and enjoy herself if she couldn't let go of the events going on back in Oklahoma.

When she reached Haycraft Park, she stood under the open shower and allowed the cool water to run over her body, rinsing the sand off her legs, feet, and rubber flip-flops. Water squished onto the pavement with each step until she reached her condo and parked her slippers by the front door. She let herself in and immediately peeled out of her bathing suit, leaving it where it fell on the bathroom floor while she hurriedly took a shower.

Less is more, she thought, as she dressed in a plain pink summer dress and a new pair of white sandals, and then sat down on the couch to detangle her long black hair. The walk had revived her spirit, brought things into focus. As soon as she finished her meeting, she'd see if she could catch an earlier flight home.

After securing her hair at the nape of her neck with a beaded clip, she picked up her cell and flipped it open. The battery had regained enough life to tell her she had missed another call from Lance. She hit the speed dial for Lance's number and waited. A mechanical-sounding voice announced that all circuits were busy and she should try her call again at a later time.

She sighed, dropped her phone into her purse, and walked out into the late morning sunshine. With map in hand, she was on her way to Kihei, which on the map appeared to merge into Wailea, that magical-sounding place on the other side of the bay.

She drove her rental car out of Maʻalaea, winding around the south-central part of the island, hugging the beach where she had walked earlier that day. Following the instructions the nice lady at the lobby reception desk had written down, she drove through an area identified on a sign as the Kealia Pond National Wildlife Refuge. The flat, muddy terrain triggered a childhood memory of an awful drought that had caused both her dad's ponds to dry up to little more than mud puddles. She remembered watching as her dad tirelessly pumped water from an underwater spring so the horses would have fresh water to drink.

The memory quickly faded as she turned right onto South Kihei Road and continued close to the shoreline, where she passed a fruit stand and noticed a man sitting on a mat carving huge wooden totem-like pieces. She made a mental note to return this way so she could take a closer look at his work. Carefully, she dodged a group of young surfers who had congregated near the road, making their way from their cars to the water.

Before long, she arrived at her destination, the Azeka Mauka Shopping Center, where she easily spotted Playin' in Paradise Travel nestled in the corner of the L-shaped cluster of stores. She parked, checked her looks in the rearview mirror, smoothed a few loose strands of hair behind her ears, then got out and went in.

Pua, the helpful woman from the airport, sat at the front desk. Under the office's fluorescent lights, she appeared to be somewhat older than Sadie had first thought—in her fifties, Sadie guessed—yet her flawless toffee-colored skin, accentuated by a colorful floral, slim-fitting dress, gave her a youthful appearance.

"Miss Walela, it is so nice to see you again," she said. "I trust you've been enjoying our island so far?"

"Oh, yes." Sadie beamed. "And now I know where you got the name for this company. This place truly is paradise."

The two women visited for several minutes before a young, good-looking man wearing a Hawaiian shirt and khaki slacks joined them and introduced himself as Richard Yamaguchi. In a few short minutes, the trio was walking across the parking lot to Stella Blues Cafe. Once again, Hawaiian music filled the air. Sadie loved the warm hospitable feeling it created.

The hostess ushered them through the busy restaurant, walls covered with Grateful Dead and Jerry Garcia memorabilia, to an outside patio table where they all three indulged in the day's special—Caesar salad with grilled monchong, a fish Sadie had never heard of—and discussed Sadie's future as a travel agent. By the time they got to the mango ice-cream pie for dessert, Sadie felt so comfortable with her new business associates that she would have taken the job even before they offered the free bonus trip to Maui once a year. She was in. They returned to the travel office, where they sat and leisurely talked the afternoon away. Finally, Sadie signed a six-month agreement with an option to renew based on the original agreement she'd made with Jan.

"Here's the orientation book," Richard said as he smiled and they shook hands. "It will give you something to put you to sleep on the plane back to Oklahoma."

Pua stood and embraced Sadie with the customary hug of aloha.

"If you have no other plans for today, I'd love to invite you to join me. My daughter is dancing hula at a nearby hotel in a few minutes. It's not far. I think you would enjoy it."

"I would love to."

Sadie left her car parked in front of the travel agency and rode with Pua. They traveled down South Kihei Road until the shops, restaurants, and condo buildings gave way to luxury homes and lavish golf courses, all lined with majestic palms and blooming flowers.

"Is this Wailea?" Sadie asked.

Pua looked at Sadie and smiled. "Yes," she said. "Lots of expensive property here."

Sadie acknowledged with a nod and continued to absorb the passing scenery.

Pua turned into the driveway of an extravagant hotel and pulled up to the front door, where two men in matching flowered shirts opened the car doors for both women and placed flower lei around their necks.

"I could get used to this flower thing," Sadie said as one of the attendants whisked Pua's car away to the parking area.

Pua guided Sadie through an open-air lobby, across cool marble floors, and past towering exotic flower arrangements. Sadie tried not to gawk at what she was sure she would never in this lifetime be able to afford. A pang of guilt hit her as she thought of her modest home and her missing neighbor. Instead of enjoying paradise, she thought, she really should be making arrangements to get back home and help Lance find him.

She followed Pua outside onto a manicured lawn where an area had been roped off and a long line of people waited for their turn at a buffet table covered with food. At the edge of a stage, between the lawn and the beach, Sadie saw a group of beautiful young women wearing white ankle-length dresses and long purple lei. Each girl had a large white flower over her right ear.

Pua found two chairs at the edge of the crowd. "Wait here. I'll be right back."

While Sadie waited for Pua, she soaked in the beauty of the place. Out in the ocean, she could see the small horseshoe-shaped island, much closer than the view from her room, as well as the island behind it, whose name she still couldn't pronounce. Boats of all sizes floated by, and a few surfers sat on their boards waiting for the perfect wave to transport them to shore. Across the bay, the sun had begun to descend toward the ocean, something she hadn't been able to see the night before from her condo. Someone played a ukulele and sang a Hawaiian song in the background. The air had begun to cool, intensifying the fragrance of the nearby flowers that enveloped her senses. She loved this place.

Sadie visually searched for Pua and found her in the midst of the young ladies near the stage. Pua stood out among the others, with a stately presence. One of the dancers turned and looked directly at Sadie, smiled, and waved. Her facial features, regal posture, and friendly smile bore a striking resemblance to Pua, convincing Sadie that the young girl must be Pua's daughter. These had to be the nicest people on earth, thought Sadie. A few minutes later, Pua returned and the rest of the crowd began to take their seats.

A young man took the stage and sat near the end with a drum cradled between his knees. As the drummer played and chanted, the dancers filed across the stage with elegance and poise. They began to sing, chant, and sway in unison. Sadie had never seen hula dancers in real life, only those who appeared in movies with grass skirts and coconut bras. This was so much different. Their movements mesmerized her. The dancers epitomized beauty and grace, so unlike what she had imagined they would.

Pua translated the Hawaiian words and the meaning of the movements for Sadie. The performance ended after four short numbers. As the crowd dispersed in all directions, Pua said, "Come with me. I want you to meet my daughter."

They walked across the lush grass to the smiling dancers. As Pua started to introduce Sadie, one of the young girls interrupted.

"Oh, I'm so happy to meet you. My name is Usi." She hugged Sadie and kissed her lightly on the cheek. "Mom told me all about you. She said you're Cherokee. Is that right?"

Sadie smiled. "Through and through."

"We have Cherokee blood, too," the girl continued. "My great-grand-mother was a Cherokee princess."

"Oh, really?" Sadie tried to keep a straight face. While it was true that Usi could easily pass as American Indian with her latte-colored skin and dark brown eyes, high cheekbones, and black hair, she thought if she heard that fraudulent claim from one more person she would scream. She wanted to sit down and explain to this sweet young lady that the Cherokee people had neither kings nor queens, therefore there had never been any princes or princesses. Instead she smiled and quietly said, "That's nice," then turned the conversation. "Usi is a beautiful name. Is it Hawaiian?"

"Oh, no. It's the name my grandfather used to call my grandmother. Her name is Lehua, but that was his pet name for her—Usi." She looked at Pua. "It's Mom's middle name, too." After a moment, the girl returned her attention to Sadie and added, "He died in the war."

"Oh, I'm sorry to hear that," Sadie said.

The girl continued. "I know Tutu Lehua would love to meet you."

Sadie nodded. "I would be honored, but I only have a couple of days, and I may have to go home early—that is, if I can change my ticket. A friend of mine is missing, and I may need to help in the search. I'll be in touch with your mom, though."

Usi looked disappointed. "It was nice to meet you," she said, then turned and rejoined the other dancers.

"Well, that's about it for tonight," Pua said. "I'll take you back to your car. I'm sure you're dying to start reading that orientation manual."

"If I'm not able to change my ticket right away and have time, I'd like to do some research about what it was like on Maui during World War II," Sadie said.

"Really?" Pua smiled. "Then how would you feel about a boat ride to the island of Lāna'i?"

"Lāna'i?" Sadie looked surprised. "Why there?"

"That's where Tutu lives. My mother," she explained. "She's the best resource I can think of. She lived on Maui during the war. That's when she met my father." Pua looked at Sadie. "Usi is right, you know. She would love to meet you."

"No kidding? How old is your mother now?"

"She will be seventy-eight years old in a couple of months, but you'd never know it. She still teaches hula at the senior center once a week. She says it keeps her young. It's very good exercise, you know."

Sadie smiled. "She sounds delightful. Okay, I'll call you in the morning as soon as I find out about changing my flight."

The two women left the hotel and drove off into a starry night, leaving a tiny portion of paradise behind. Sadie was already in love with Maui.

Chapter 8

Lance ran to his truck, retrieved his Smith and Wesson, and jumped into Charlie's cruiser. They tore out of the chicken plant parking lot and back to town. They streaked down Main Street, then Charlie quickly turned west onto Creek Street, a short street that ended at the entrance of the Vista Trails Trailer Park. Charlie came to a stop next to a dirt path marked with a small arrow that read "office," where he calmly rolled out of the cruiser, lumbered up to the front door of a small cottage, and rapped on the door.

A woman appeared in a pink housecoat, holding a small brown dog under her arm. Lance could see her shrug her shoulders and point into the small park that held no more than a half dozen dilapidated trailers.

Lance got out of the car, clipped his badge to the front left side of his belt, and wedged his firearm between his jeans and the small of his back. At the rear of the trailer park, Lance could see a bluff on the far side of a dry creek bed. It wouldn't be easy for anyone to escape in that direction. The only escape routes would be over the stockade fence on either side of the park, or out the front entrance.

"The manager says she doesn't know anyone by the name of Skinner," Charlie said as he returned to the vehicle, "but she says there's a dark-skinned fellow who spends a lot of time at that last trailer on the right. Says the renter's name is Cynthia Tanner."

Lance nodded. Tanner was a Cherokee name and Buck Skinner was also a full-blood Cherokee. Lance guessed that in some circles a Cherokee could pass as "dark skinned."

The two men walked the short distance to the Tanner residence. An old beat-up Ford truck peeked out of a carport attached to one end of the trailer. A rusted lawn mower sat in the middle of the yard surrounded by tall grass, as if it had stopped working and no one ever bothered to move it. Lance walked to the rear of the truck and made a mental note of the combination of letters and numbers on the plate.

While Lance waited near the truck, Charlie climbed up three wooden steps and knocked, rattling the glass of the storm door. Nothing. Charlie knocked again, harder. Still no answer.

Lance surveyed the area, sweeping every inch with his eyes, including the truck. He stopped when he got to the driver's door and nodded to Charlie.

"Looks like blood on the vehicle."

Charlie looked at Lance and then back through the glass door at the doorknob.

"Yeah, I think we've got the same thing here and the main door is ajar. Looks like probable cause to me." He drew his weapon, pulled open the storm door, and pushed the heavy door open with his foot. Lance followed him in.

"Cynthia?" Charlie called out. "Cynthia Tanner?"

The small trailer creaked as the two men walked across the threshold. Other than that, the place was deadly quiet.

Lance waited in the small kitchen area while Charlie walked down the short and narrow hallway, calling out the woman's name again. Charlie leaned over the bed and cursed, and then called out to Lance, "Well, if this is our perp, he isn't going to be killing again anytime soon."

Lance let out a long sigh. Surely this couldn't be the end of a Cherokee warrior like Buck Skinner.

Charlie pulled a cell phone out of his pocket with his left hand and dialed with the click of one button.

"I need an ambulance at the Vista Trails Trailer Park, stat. Last trailer on the right. Gunshot victim. Barely alive."

As Charlie called it in, Lance tried to force himself into the small bedroom behind Charlie.

"Is he still alive?" Lance asked.

"Not really, but the medics get paid to determine that. Not me." Charlie replaced his phone.

Lance looked at the huge "dark-skinned" man lying face down on the bed as Charlie lifted the dead man's head enough to expose an exit wound in the middle of his forehead.

"I guess we can rule out suicide," Lance said in a matter-of-fact tone.

"Do you think this is your missing man?"

"Negative. I've met Buck Skinner and this isn't him. Buck is close to eighty years old. This man can't be a day over forty." Then, a horrible thought crossed his mind. If the dead man wasn't Buck Skinner, it was possible this poor guy had died at the hands of one very angry old Cherokee. Surely not, he thought to himself, and then said, "Charlie, do you see a weapon?"

As both men looked around and under the bed for a gun, the truck outside roared to life and gravel sprayed the side of the trailer. Lance ran back into the living room and looked out the window just as the truck spun around Charlie's cruiser and left rubber on the pavement of Creek Street.

"Secure the scene!" yelled Charlie, as he ran out the door to his police car. In seconds, the blaring siren and flashing lights of Charlie's cruiser careened down the street behind the fleeing truck. Lance could hear the ambulance coming in the distance.

Lance returned to the victim and checked for a pulse. The man was definitely dead. When the ambulance pulled up outside the trailer, Lance met the medical personnel at the door and flashed his badge.

"I hope one of you boys is the medical examiner," he said. "Otherwise, it was a wasted trip."

One of the paramedics rushed past Lance, spent a few seconds in the bedroom, and then returned. "We'll give him a call."

While the paramedics stood outside, Lance returned to the dead man and quickly fished a billfold out of his back pocket. What he saw gave him a start. The name on the Oklahoma driver's license read "Benjamin Skinner."

✤

Charlie almost crashed into another vehicle as he turned north off of Creek Street onto Main in pursuit of the Ford truck, veering onto the shoulder of the road and then fishtailing back onto the highway. The truck was getting away. He slammed the accelerator to the floor and climbed the hill leading northeast out of town. The runner was headed for Arkansas or Missouri.

Charlie picked up his radio and gave the information to dispatch to contact both state agencies. Just as he replaced the transmitter, Charlie topped the hill and saw the truck clip the front of an eighteen-wheeler, causing the semi to jackknife and spill its entire load of live chickens across both lanes of the highway. Charlie screeched to a stop and watched feathers fill the air as the old Ford disappeared around a curve in the distance.

✠

The fleeing driver jerked the steering wheel from one side to the other, causing the truck to slide wildly across the highway. The truck careened around the semi and almost ran headlong into an oncoming car. The driver watched in the rearview mirror in horror as the semi jackknifed, and then looked up too late to see the sharp curve rising out of nowhere. The driver punched the brakes hard, causing the wheels to lock and the tires to screech against the asphalt just before the truck left the road, bounced across a steep ditch, and plowed through a barbed wire fence. The driver's head hit the windshield as a cottonwood tree that must have been at least a hundred years old stood firm against the crashing blow.

After losing consciousness for just a moment, adrenaline kicked in and supplied enough awareness and strength for the driver to force open the passenger-side window to escape. The fall from the truck onto the ground hurt, but the cold water from the creek brought everything back into focus— the heart-thumping fear, the sight of blood, and the reality of death. Panic pushed the driver, hobbling, disoriented, into the cover of the woods.

✠

While Lance waited for either Charlie to return or the medical examiner to arrive, he carefully nosed around the crime scene. He didn't want to disturb any evidence, but he thought there might be something there that would tie the victim back to Buck Skinner. After all, his search for Sadie's neighbor was the reason he'd ended up here in the first place.

He found two letters that had fallen on the floor near the bed. Using his pen, he turned them so he could read the return address. One was from Hawai'i. Lance looked at the dark-skinned man again and realized maybe he wasn't Indian at all. Could he be Hawaiian? The other letter had a foreign address on it. He pulled his small spiral-bound notepad from his shirt pocket and copied the return addresses. He couldn't risk getting his fingerprints on the envelope, so he would have to wait for the lab to arrive before he could learn the contents of either letter.

Seeing the Hawai'i address made him think about Sadie. She wasn't going to believe the strange turn of events that had taken place in the search for her neighbor.

Lance's thoughts returned to the victim. He was relieved to know that Ben Skinner, the murderer who had "gutted a man like a chicken" and then escaped through the back door of the chicken processing plant earlier that day, was not the Buck Skinner he was looking for. Instead, the chicken plant murderer, who had become a victim himself, had most likely been the thorn in Buck's side, the thief who had stolen Buck's social security number and used his name as well. Stealing Buck Skinner's identity had been a big mistake on the murdered man's part, and Lance hoped that mistake hadn't been the reason this big guy had a bullet hole in his head.

Lance knew Buck Skinner was capable of killing, just like he and all the other veterans who had served in combat, and he surmised that under the right circumstances, everyone had it in them to kill. Lance thought about the truck Charlie was chasing. He pulled out his cell phone and dialed Maggie.

"Maggie, can you look up a vehicle license plate for me?"

"Well, it's about time. I've been trying to get hold of you all morning." Maggie sounded as if she had had one too many cups of coffee. "Figured you were out of cell phone range, but—"

Lance cut her off. "I've been a little tied up, Maggie. I need you to look this up for me." He rattled off the combination of letters and numbers as he remembered them from the truck's license plate and waited.

After a few moments, Maggie returned to the phone. "I guess you found your man."

"Not sure. What'd you come up with?"

"Benjamin Skinner, of course."

"Of course." Lance said in disgust. "Address?"

The address matched that of the Vista Trails Trailer Park.

"That's all I've got on Benjamin Skinner. Have you talked to Sadie?"

Lance's phone beeped in his ear. "Hold on, Maggie. I've got Charlie trying to get through." Lance switched lines on his phone, but all he could hear was a lot of static and the sound of Charlie talking on his radio to someone else. "Charlie, did you get him?"

Charlie came on the line. "No, lost him in a hail of chicken feathers, but just got word from a state trooper that they've found the truck wrapped around a tree. Suspect's disappeared. Search is under way. I'm on my way back to you now. ETA fifteen minutes."

Charlie had already disconnected when Lance switched back to the other line. "Maggie, are you still there?"

"Yeah, Chief, I'm here. If you need anything else, just holler. Have you talked to Sadie?"

"No, we seem to be playing phone tag." Lance could hear someone driving up out front. "I've got to go, Maggie. I'll get back with you as soon as I get rid of this dead body." Lance slammed the phone shut and crammed it in his pocket.

Chapter 9

Cynthia Tanner stood in front of the meat counter, trying to choose what to prepare with her morel mushrooms. For weeks she'd been craving the delectable treats that grew in the woods close to the creek not far from her home. She considered them a gift from the Creator to the Cherokee people, and she'd loved them ever since she'd first tasted them as a child.

The mushroom crop had been plentiful for only a few weeks in April, immediately after a week of cool showers had passed through the county, so she'd picked as many as she possibly could and stored them for future use. After she thoroughly shook them in a paper sack to remove the dirt and debris, and dunked them in a cool bowl of water, she'd threaded each mushroom on a piece of heavy thread, using a sewing needle to pierce through the stem just as her Cherokee grandmother had taught her. Then she'd hung them to dry for almost a month before placing them in airtight plastic bags and stacking them above the refrigerator, where she thought they'd be good for at least six months. If there were any left after that, she would carve out a spot in the freezer for them.

Cynthia grinned inside when she thought about her sister, who had never acquired a taste for morels yet had spent most of the day helping Cynthia with the harvest, all the time complaining about shuffling through dead oak leaves for what she referred to as "icky fungus." Cynthia had always tried her best to instill in her sister some of the lessons she'd learned from her grandmother. Someday she might be thankful for a meal provided by the earth, she'd told her.

Refocusing on the meat cooler, Cynthia finally made her choice. It would be chicken again, not only because it came from the local processing plant, but because it cost a lot less than beef or pork. She would bring the mushrooms back to life with bacon grease in a saucepan, brown the chicken in the skillet, and pour the mushrooms on top. It would be delicious.

After choosing the cheapest package of chicken legs available, she dropped it next to two bags of potato chips on top of the other items in her grocery cart, and headed for the beer section in the refrigerated aisle with guarded anticipation. Did she have enough to pay for all this food?

Benny had called from the Northwest Arkansas Airport to let her know he was almost home. He'd been visiting family in Hawai'i, and she knew he would be famished after the long plane ride. She'd never fixed mushrooms for Benny before, but she knew he'd like them.

Guiding her cart down the beer aisle, she picked up a six-pack of Benny's favorite—Pabst Blue Ribbon—and pushed her cart toward the checkout lane. Coming to a halt in the middle of the aisle, she counted the number of items she had. No express lane for her today.

She waited patiently behind a young mother who balanced a toddler on one hip as she placed items on the conveyor belt for the cashier. The other child, a preschool boy, ran around the entire group of checkout lanes, stopping each time he circled to pull on the toddler's shoe and provoke an ear-splitting shriek.

Cynthia tried to focus. She studied her grocery cart and made another attempt to mentally add the cost of the contents. She thought she had enough balance left on her food stamp debit card for the groceries, but she would have to pay cash for the beer. The cashier would never let her slide on the beer, even though she'd seen her do it for others. Cynthia heard a siren and watched through the grocery store's large plate-glass window as a truck flew by, followed shortly thereafter by a police car.

A jolt of adrenaline shot through her. The truck looked just like Benny's truck. She tried to think. It couldn't be. He hadn't had time to get from the Arkansas airport to Sycamore Springs. Then another thought entered her mind. Unless he had lied about where he was when he called. Suddenly, her face felt hot. There were other things that had taken place while Benny was gone, personal things she'd prefer he didn't find out about.

She'd made no promises to Benny before he left two weeks ago. She was still a single woman, one that a lot of men still found attractive, including Tomas Hernandez. She might not look like the fashion model on the front of the magazine in the nearby rack, but nobody did. She looked down at her clothes, cotton pants and tee shirt, plain but clean. She pulled in her stomach momentarily, trying to hide the muffin-top bulge that showed through her knit top. She pushed her straight hair away from her face with the back of her hand, wishing she had the money to get a real haircut at a beauty salon. The last time she'd trimmed her hair with the sewing scissors her sister had laughed nonstop for a week before finally helping her clean up the uneven edges.

At the age of thirty, Cynthia felt her youth slipping away and rationalized that no one could blame her for having a little fling while Benny was gone. And, no one had to know. Especially Benny.

Benny had a terrible temper, but that certainly wasn't anything new to her. She had grown up in a household full of hotheads. She knew how to duck and block a punch, something she'd learned early on from her mother.

She had met Benny in a bar south of town almost a year ago, where she'd seen his rage on full display, with plenty of strength and machismo. She thought he was gorgeous—a big man with coffee-colored skin and thick black hair. The attraction was mutual.

He never talked much about his past or his family, or if he had either. She knew he mailed most of his money to a foreign address in envelopes displaying long words that she couldn't understand or pronounce. She never asked questions and he never offered any information. If he had a wife and family somewhere else, she figured the less she knew about it, the better.

He'd lost no time making himself at home at her place, where they'd fostered an on-again off-again relationship. On, when he was working and sober; off, when he shoved her against the wall and blackened her eyes.

"Are you ready?" The cashier's voice pierced her thoughts.

Cynthia moved her cart forward and lifted her items onto the conveyor belt with shaking hands. A glass bottle of picante sauce slipped from her grip and crashed onto the concrete floor, sending tomatoes, onions, and peppers in all directions and onto her white sneakers. "Oh, no. I'm so sorry."

Tears spilled off her face as the realization flooded her body. She was afraid of Benny.

The cashier picked up the receiver of the phone that hung on the wall near her register and spoke into it. Her words echoed across the grocery store. "Clean up at front register, please. Clean up at front register."

"Can you hurry?" Cynthia blurted. "I've got to go."

The cashier made a face, hung up the phone, and started flinging Cynthia's groceries into paper sacks. "You got money for the beer?" she asked.

"Forget the beer," she said. "I don't really want it anyway."

The cashier finished deducting the groceries from Cynthia's food stamp card, and Cynthia quickly rolled the cart to her car, where she loaded the sacks into the backseat and tore out of the parking lot.

When Cynthia reached the entry to the trailer park and saw the ambulance sitting by her trailer, she gasped and slammed on the brakes. She swallowed, drove forward, and parked behind the EMS vehicle. A man she'd never seen before walked out of her trailer and stood on the top step. When she got out of the car, she could see his badge on his belt.

"What's going on?" She directed her question first to the paramedic who was leaning against his vehicle.

He shrugged his shoulders and nodded toward the man who quickly descended the steps.

"Lance Smith," the man said, as he offered his identification for verification. "Are you Cynthia Tanner?"

She stared at his badge before reluctantly answering. "Yes, I'm Cynthia. Who's hurt? Why is this ambulance here and who are you? I've never seen you before."

Her thoughts began to swirl as the man named Smith began to explain to her how he had come to be in charge of securing a crime scene out of his jurisdiction, that he and Sergeant Charlie McCord of the Sycamore Springs Police Department had entered the premises only after blood had been found on the doorknob of her place and the door handle of a vehicle that had since been driven off by an unknown person at a high rate of speed.

"So who is the ambulance for?" she insisted.

"Unfortunately, there is a deceased person in your residence, and we have reason to believe foul play was involved."

"Deceased person?" Her voice rose in pitch. "Let me in."

He held her as she tried to push past him. "I'm sorry, ma'am. I can't let you go in right now."

"This is my place!" she screamed. "Let me in. Who's in there?"

"Ma'am, do you know anyone by the name of Benjamin Skinner?"

Cynthia jerked her head around the trailer looking for Benny's truck. "He called me this morning and said he was on his way home from the airport, the Walmart airport in Bentonville, Arkansas."

He nodded.

"That's why I stopped at the store on my way home from work," she continued, "so he'd have something to eat when he got here." She looked back toward Creek Street. "I saw a truck a while ago being chased by police. At first, I thought it was Benny, but it couldn't have been. He hasn't had enough time to get here."

"What time did he call?"

"I don't know. An hour ago, maybe longer." Cynthia thought for a moment. "I work the night shift at the nursing home and usually get off at seven. But I had to work overtime this morning because one of the day-shift girls called in sick. I had to help with breakfast." She rubbed her forehead with her forearm. "So, I'm not sure what time it was. It wasn't that long ago, though."

"It would only take about an hour to get here from Bentonville. Are you sure he hadn't already left the airport? Maybe he'd planned to arrive early, you know, surprise you. Women like surprises, don't they?"

"Not necessarily," she snapped. It occurred to her that she had no idea where Benny had been when he'd called. He'd lied to her before. Why would this time be any different?

"Why are you asking all these questions about Benny? His truck isn't here." She swallowed hard and then realized what had happened. He'd been snooping on her. He'd seen her with someone else, waited for her to leave, and then probably beat her newfound friend to death. Now he was running from the cops. After a few seconds, she backed up and leaned against her car. "This cannot be happening to me," she cried.

"Do you know anyone who would want to do harm to Benny?"

She watched the lawman's eyes travel to the red spatters on her white shoes and she panicked.

"Are you trying to tell me Benny is dead?" Fear turned to hysteria. "No, no, no! Don't tell me something happened to Benny. It can't be him. It can't be him!" She began to beat on the officer's chest and scream until he held her with his strong arms. Finally, she collapsed against him.

After she had calmed down, he repeated his question. "Do you know anyone who would want to hurt Benny?"

She moaned like a hurt animal and then stepped away. "I have a friend," she said in a quiet voice, "that I've been seeing while Benny was gone." She wiped at her nose with the back of her hand. "It wasn't anything serious. And I told him there were no strings and that when Benny came back, it would be over. Last night, he said he would fight for me to the death." She looked up at him. "I swear, Officer Smith, I thought he was kidding."

"What's his name? The man you've been seeing?"

"Tomas," she said. "Tomas Hernandez."

"Tomas doesn't happen to work at the chicken plant on the edge of town, does he?"

Cynthia nodded. "He works the early shift, has to be there before seven. Benny didn't even call me until after that." She looked up and saw a police car turn into the trailer park and roll to a stop behind her car.

"Fight to the death?" he said. "Well, unfortunately, I think Benny might've beaten Tomas to the punch . . . or maybe I should say 'to the gut.'"

Chapter 10

A day earlier, Sonny had watched his owner, Sadie, get into a car and disappear into the distance, leaving him alone at the farmhouse with only the horse for company. He walked over to the edge of the porch where she sometimes dropped extra food and found an extra-large hunk of half-frozen venison. Not knowing when she might return, he devoured the raw meat, and then slipped away to the top of a nearby ridge. He found a comfortable place under a shade tree where he could see anyone or anything approaching, and fell asleep.

When he awoke, he walked down the hill to a cold stream for a drink of water, and then trotted back to his perch and sat on his haunches. The valley below crawled with people, some on foot, some on horseback, and others in vehicles like the one his owner had gone away in. When he recognized one of the trucks, he stood and whined. Satisfied Sadie wasn't there, he lost interest and found a place under the low-hanging limbs of a cedar tree and lay back down.

When the heat of the day began to diminish, a field mouse caught his eye. He pounced on the rodent, played with it for a while without hurting it, and then let it go. Bored, he traveled down to the creek again for another long drink of water.

When darkness had overtaken the valley and the stars began to twinkle overhead, he decided to return to the house and look for his owner. He acknowledged the horse, and then moved silently past the barn and the gate. Standing in the shadows, he studied the dark farmhouse for several minutes before turning and disappearing into the night. He crossed the road and moved along a well-traveled path into the neighboring ranch to one of his favorite places. He curled up near the mouth of a cave and rested his muzzle on his paws.

In the early morning hours of dawn, a distant sound caught his attention. With heightened senses, ears at attention and nose twitching, he tested the night air. Then he tilted his head back and to one side, and began to softly howl. After a few moments, he rose and trotted toward the sound of human singing.

✥

Buck woke to a clammy darkness with the smell of damp earth surrounding him. Above he could see a few stars hanging next to an almond-shaped moon.

Where was everyone? He felt around for his M1, the rifle that had never left his side since it had been issued to him in California. He couldn't put his hands on it. Where was his sidearm—the government-issued Colt .45 that was a gift from his buddy who'd lost the use of his right hand in the last firefight? Without a weapon he'd be dead as soon as the Japanese found his hiding place. His head ached. Where was his helmet? Adrenaline raced through his veins the same way it had a thousand times before.

He tried to stand to assess the situation and pain shot though his body, shattering his illusion of war and slamming him back into the present. Damn, he thought. The war had been over for more than a half century, but the memory felt like it had been only yesterday. He would give anything if he could kill the part of his brain that held those memories the same way he had killed the enemy—up close and personal.

He knew he was in a dangerous predicament. He just needed to rest for a while, collect his thoughts, and figure out what to do next.

He closed his eyes, and the image of a red pincushion came into his thoughts. He reached for it, stretching as far as he could, but before he could make contact, he lost his footing and fell.

His eyes flew open and he blinked several times, as if doing so would clear his thoughts. Focus, old man, he thought. Focus.

Then he began to sing to calm his mind.

O ga je li ga
Ja gv wi yu hi
Ja je li ga hno
Ja gv wi yu hi.
O ga je li ga
Ja gv wi yu hi
Ja je li ga hno
Ja gv wi yu hi.

Chapter 11

Sadie awoke to a loud rumble, a sound like a train barreling down its tracks. She could hear dishes rattling in the cabinet and objects falling, crashing onto the floor. The bed began to shake, and she gasped as an uncontrollable feeling of vulnerability washed over her. "No!" she yelled, as she jumped out of bed and pushed her hands against the wall for stability.

The shaking felt like it had gone on forever, but then she realized it had probably lasted about thirty seconds. She ran into the living room for her purse and cell phone. A bookshelf had tipped over, its contents strewn across the ceramic tile floor. Her phone rested under a pile of broken glass, cracked open like an egg.

"Damn! This can't be happening." Her words had barely left her mouth when it all began again. She quickly moved away from the broken glass and to the bathroom door, hanging onto the jamb until the quaking of the after-shock stopped. The only thing she could remember about earthquakes was that standing in a doorway afforded extra protection. That sounded good in theory, she thought, but it offered little consolation to her at the moment. She looked at the concrete walls and wondered how long it would take for the entire building to crash down on top of her.

Everything—the lights, the ceiling fans, the clock radio—all came slowly to a halt. She swallowed hard, pushing down the queasiness in her stomach.

She pulled on a pair of shorts and a tee shirt, took her room key, and ran out the door, letting it slam behind her. She stopped at the top of the stairwell and peered down, half expecting the stairs to be covered with debris. They were clear except for a young couple who had just passed her doorway on their way down. Quickly, she followed.

At the bottom level, she stepped out into the morning sunshine. A group of people stood about ten feet from the building, coffee cups in hand, engaged in casual conversation. Sadie realized her knees were shaking and steadied herself against a nearby parked car. She looked around expecting to see huge gaping cracks in the parking lot. Surprisingly, everything looked the same as it had before. No cracks in the sidewalk, no downed trees, no chunks of concrete falling from the building. Nothing.

The friendly woman who had welcomed her two days before came out of the lobby, barefoot, with a flowered towel piled on her head and another wrapped around her body. She smiled at Sadie and the others.

"Everyone okay?" she giggled. "The manager is checking the outside of the building for cracks right now, but everything appears to be fine. You can go back in when you are ready." She smiled again. "It may take a little while for the electricity to come back on, so be patient. We'll be on Hawaiian time for a little while." With that announcement, the woman and her flowered towels returned to the lobby, acting as if this happened on a regular basis.

The others, who were standing nearby, meandered back toward the building. Sadie's knees felt like Jell-O when she tried to walk, so she moved to a nearby bench and sat. A young boy in the crowd of bystanders stopped and looked at her. He appeared to be about ten or twelve years old, slender and well tanned, with thick, unruly brown hair that fell across the top of his eyebrows.

"You okay?" he asked.

Sadie nodded. "I'll be fine."

"Your first quake?"

"That apparent, huh?"

He laughed. "Yeah, you look a little scared. We live in California, so this is no big deal to us."

"Well, California, go ahead and try to convince me this is no big deal."

"My name is Bobby." He sounded offended.

Sadie smiled. "Have a seat, Bobby. My name is Sadie."

The boy sat on the far end of the bench. "Where are you from?" he said.

"Oklahoma."

"Oh, tornado alley." He scrunched his nose. "That's worse."

Sadie shook her head. "I'll take a tornado any day over this," she said. "At least you know when a tornado is coming and you can take shelter. Not always, but normally," she added as a disclaimer.

"How do you know when a tornado is coming?" The boy seemed genuinely interested.

"Well, first of all, the weather people in Oklahoma live for tornado season. They break in every five minutes on television and tell you exactly where the rotations are and which way the storm cells are headed. They project the time and direction and tell people to take cover when it gets close. Then, if you live near a town or a community that's in the path of the tornado, the sirens wail."

Sadie stopped for a moment and thought about her grandmother. "But before weather forecasters came along, the old people taught us how to distinguish the odor of ozone in the air before and after the rain falls, how to read the sky when it turns a greenish black, what a wall cloud looks like, and to take cover when your surroundings go deadly quiet. No wind, no birds chirping, no dogs barking. Nothing. Dead still. That means a tornado is very close."

The young boy's eyes widened. "And you think that's better than a little shake, rattle, and roll?"

Sadie laughed and began to relax. "Yes, yes, I do."

A woman called to the boy from the second-floor walkway.

"I have to go." He quickly jumped up and disappeared into the building.

Grateful for the young boy whose conversation had helped calm her nerves, she returned to her condo and surveyed the damage. It wasn't nearly as bad as it had first appeared. She pushed the bookshelf back up and against the wall, and returned the books and other items to its shelves. Inside a closet, she found a broom and dustpan and swept up the broken glass. Then she fished parts of her phone out of the sharp slivers.

She wanted to call Lance and tell him what had happened, but that would have to wait. She glanced at her destroyed phone and then read the note posted above the telephone in the living room: No long distance service provided. She picked up the handset and listened anyway. No dial tone.

She put the phone down, walked out onto the patio, and stared at the lush pink-and-orange flowering shrubbery that bordered the landscaped lawn between the building and the ocean. Two children splashed water at each other in the pool while their mother kept watch from a nearby lounge chair. The ocean continued to roll, waves slapping at the rocks and sand. The perfectly blue sky provided a clear backdrop to the island in the distance with the name she still couldn't pronounce. Thoughts of the earthquake returned to her and a chill ran down her spine. The power of the earth, and everything in it, overwhelmed her. She wanted to go home.

She threw her purse over her shoulder and descended the stairs once again to the lobby, where the flowered towels had been replaced with a flowered strapless dress and flip-flops. A battery-powered radio sat on the counter buzzing with white noise.

"Is everything okay?" the woman asked.

"Yes," Sadie laughed. "Except that my cell phone is a victim of the earthquake. Do you have a phone I could use?"

"Aw, I wish I did. But there's no phone service anywhere on the island right now. Don't worry. It'll be back up soon." The woman's smile seemed to make everything okay. "See?" she said, nodding toward the radio. "The radio station is not even broadcasting yet. But they will." The woman walked out from behind the counter and pointed toward the ocean through the open doorway. "I've been watching the ocean. It's been over thirty minutes, so I'm pretty sure we're out of danger. If the water recedes, it means a tsunami is coming."

Sadie's heart jumped into her throat. "Oh, my gosh. What do we do?"

"Oh, don't worry." The woman's smile had returned. "I didn't mean to scare you. The emergency people will blow the sirens before that happens. We'll have plenty of time to evacuate. The information is in the front pages of the phone book in your room."

"Do you have any idea when we will have power again?"

Suddenly, the tinny speakers of the battery-operated radio came to life. A woman's voice, full of confidence and authority spoke.

"Aloha, everyone. Nice little alarm clock wake 'em up, yeah? No worries. You can relax. We got all the info. There is no tsunami warning at this time. Repeat. No tsunami warning. However, the Maui Police Department is asking everyone to please stay where you are until they can move one big boulder from a rockslide on the Honoapiilani Highway near Ukumehame Beach. The folks are out there checking all the roads, but if you get on the highways, you'll just get in the way. The airport is closed until they can get some backup power going out there, so if you've got a flight going out, well, it ain't going out. There will be a few more planes landing, so if you need to pick up someone at the airport, just chill out. They'll still be there when you get there. Keep it tuned here, and we will keep you updated." Hawaiian music immediately took over the airwaves.

Sadie sucked in a gust of air when she realized she had been holding her breath. "Oh." The realization had just struck home. She was stranded in the middle of the Pacific Ocean, three thousand miles from her home, her dog, her horse, and her family, with no means to let them know she was okay. But most of all, she was light-years away from the man who held the keys to her heart, Lance Smith.

"Do you need a book to read until we get some power for TV?" asked the woman in the flowered dress. "There's a whole cabinet full behind you," she said, pointing with her finger.

"I need to go home," she blurted. "I've got to see if I can change my ticket."

"I think you'll have to wait until the airport reopens for that, probably tonight or tomorrow. Is something wrong? Can I help?"

"No, I guess you're right." Sadie turned and almost ran headlong into Bobby.

The young boy bounced away from her and pulled an earphone from his right ear.

"Sorry," he said, and then continued across the lobby, through the open doors, and down the steps onto the front lawn. He found an empty table and plopped his backpack in the center. In a few short seconds, he had pulled out a laptop, turned it on, and begun to type.

"Thanks for your help." Sadie waved to the flowered dress and hurried after the young boy. She pulled out a chair and sat across the table from him. "Say, is your computer working?" she asked.

The boy removed the headphones again. "Yeah. Why?"

"Are you able to get on the Internet?"

"Yeah, weird, isn't it?" He shrugged his shoulders. "Different satellites, I guess. Why?"

"I need you to do me a favor."

"This is my dad's computer," he said. "You're not going to get me in trouble, are you?"

"Of course not. I need to let someone know I'm okay and the phones won't work. Can you send an e-mail?" She recited an e-mail address and watched the young boy type into his father's computer. At that moment, his mother called to him from the open lobby.

"I'm coming," he yelled, as he continued to type. Then he slammed the laptop shut.

"Wait!" Sadie cried. "Did you send it? What did you say?"

"I said 'everything is okay' just like you wanted," he said, as he ran toward his mother.

Chapter 12

A sharp pain rocked Buck into consciousness, where he found himself in a precarious position. His backside felt like a bullet had ripped through it, and his head hurt. He took inventory of his body parts by starting at his head and moving down. He could taste blood, he had a bump on his head, and his lip throbbed. His arms were both all right, but when he tried to move his legs a burning sensation shot through his bad knee. "Damn," he said, and gingerly poked at his kneecap with his thumbs. It wasn't broken, he thought, just worn out. It'd come around in a little while. It always did.

He brushed dirt from his face and looked up, sizing up the extent of his predicament. He had fallen into a sinkhole—a deep one—and landed on a narrow shelf. Even if he could stand up, there didn't appear to be any easy way to climb out.

How did he fall into a sinkhole? He couldn't remember. "Think, old man. Think," he said to himself. Eventually, bits and pieces began to form in his memory. The IRS. Someone screwed up his income tax return. He could lose his ranch. He tried to remember the rest, but it wouldn't come. They could call it old age if they wanted to, but he knew the truth. He couldn't remember half of what he did because his brain had been shook up in the war. Shook up the way his mother used to shake up a pint jar of cream, turning it into butter. He knew it and the government knew it, he thought angrily.

But the government was unwilling to admit the truth. If they claimed responsibility, they might have to pay him some money. Buck didn't want their money. He just wanted to be left alone.

He shifted his weight and focused on his current problem. How in the world had he ended up here? He'd seen plenty of the cylinder-shaped holes in and around the county, but he never dreamed he could ever be so unaware as to fall into one.

He could hear rushing water and realized he'd landed above a stream. It must have taken decades to create the cavity that might end up being his grave if he couldn't get out. He supposed the ancient limestone that was so prevalent in the area had simply given way when he stepped on it. For now, the hole seemed to be stable, for which he was grateful.

He leaned his head against a rock and assessed his situation. He estimated the distance to the top of the sinkhole to be about fifteen feet. The void beneath him was too dark to determine how far it was to the bottom, so for now, he would concentrate on the top.

He called out for help. Nothing. Where was he, anyway? Was he on his own property or somewhere else? He couldn't remember seeing any sinkholes on his land. He knew his voice would never carry far enough to get someone's attention unless they happened to be fairly close to the hole. It would take more than a miracle for someone to find him.

Without food and water, he guessed he might last a week. He tried to relax and overcome the sharp pain in his knee. He wiped his face on his shoulder and tried to adjust his sitting position. Somewhere down below he heard a bullfrog bellow.

"How in the hell did you get down there?" His voice echoed in the empty space between his ledge and the bottom of what he surmised might be his final resting place.

The bullfrog bellowed again.

Buck realized there must not only be a large air cavity, but also a pool in the underground stream for a frog to sit around and call out to other frogs. He thought about it for a minute and then dismissed the idea. If he was ever to get out of this sinkhole, it was going to have to be from the top. He hadn't quite figured out how that was going to happen yet, but if he could climb out of as many foxholes on as many islands as he had in the Pacific, then this shouldn't be that big a deal. The memory of floating on a stretcher to an awaiting ship entered his mind, and he quickly squashed it.

"Hey, Bullfrog. Come on up here and fight like a man. I might get hungry later and frog legs sound pretty good." Buck glanced toward the sky. "Of course, they'd taste better if I could build a fire to toast you on."

The frog bellowed again and Buck laughed at the idea of carrying on a conversation with a frog. At least he hadn't lost his sense of humor.

He rested his head against the wall of earth and felt the pain, thankful he was still alive. He didn't relish dying in this hole, but it would be better to meet his Creator here instead of waiting for medical care in an Indian Health Service hospital. He thought about the emergency-room doctor who had given his cousin two pills and told her to come back if her side didn't quit hurting in a couple of days. Buck watched her die the next morning. Later, they said her appendix had burst.

Buck rummaged in the pockets of his overalls and found the venison jerky he'd put there before he left the house. "Hallelujah!" He had forgotten he had it. He pulled out a piece and bit off one end. The jerky would sustain him for a few days, but he was going to have to devise a way to access the water below too. Maybe if he tied the laces of his work boots together and attached his handkerchief to one end, he could dip it into the stream below.

He worked for several minutes putting together his small rope. He made a loop at one end and secured it to his finger so he wouldn't accidentally lose it, then reached over the side of the ledge and lowered the shoelaces and handkerchief as far as he could. He could feel the flow of the water tug at the string. He quickly pulled it up and slapped the cold, wet cloth across his face, sucking as much moisture out of it as he could with his mouth. He repeated the process several times and then stowed the device in his pocket. He couldn't afford to let it slip away in the darkness. He felt better after another bite of jerky and several hankies of water, but he knew this would keep him alive for only a few days.

Buck stared at the sky. At least he would die peacefully. He would become a part of the earth forever, and neither the IRS nor anyone else could remove him from the land. He closed his eyes and drifted back to the war.

Suddenly, Buck could feel dirt and pebbles falling around him. Then the sound of a wounded comrade came from above. Why was he hiding in a foxhole when someone needed help?

"Hang on, man, I'm coming," yelled Buck. He raised his head to assess the position of the Japanese. Once again, the pain in his knee shattered his dream and he cursed.

He wiped dirt from his face and several small rocks fell from above onto his hand. Was someone up there?

"Down here!" he yelled. "I'm in the sinkhole. Can you hear me?"

Something large and furry appeared in the moonlight at the top of the sinkhole, and a loud bark echoed in the cavern.

"Oh, hell, Sonny," Buck exhaled loudly. "You damn near scared me to death." Then realizing someone might be with the wolf-dog, Buck yelled again. "Help! Anybody hear me?"

The sound of Buck's voice excited the dog and he dug at the loose rocks, causing more dirt to fall. Then he whimpered and stared down at Buck as if wanting Buck to come out and play.

"Go get help," Buck commanded.

Sonny barked.

"Go get Sadie."

Sonny barked louder and Buck cursed again. He was trying to talk to a dog. How stupid was that? After a few moments, Sonny relaxed, lay down, and placed his muzzle between his paws where Buck could see him in the moonlight.

Buck thought for a moment, then pulled out the handkerchief he had been using to gather water and untied it from the rope he had made from his boot strings. Then he dug in his pocket for his truck keys and tied the handkerchief to the leather fob. He could use the handkerchief to swing the keys up on top. He contemplated giving up his only means of accessing water, but if Sonny attracted enough attention maybe someone would see the white handkerchief and come to his rescue.

He swung the handkerchief and keys hard into the air. He heard them land nearby. Sonny disappeared for a few moments before returning to the edge of the sinkhole with the handkerchief in his mouth.

"Good boy, Sonny." Buck used the best dog-communicating voice he could muster. "Take it to Sadie," he said. "Take the keys to Sadie."

At the sound of Sadie's name, Sonny promptly dropped his prize, keys and all, into the sinkhole and barked. Buck grabbed the keys right before they fell into the oblivion below.

Buck studied the situation for a few moments. Maybe the dog was smarter than he was. He untied the handkerchief and put it back into his pocket to use later for water. Then in a desperate, angry move, he threw the keys as hard as he could. Once again, Sonny disappeared and returned with the keys. This time the dog gripped the leather fob tightly in his teeth.

Buck didn't want to expend his last hours of energy playing fetch with a wolf-dog. He decided to ignore Sonny, and as soon as he did, the dog disappeared in the moonlight.

All the movement had stirred up the pain in his back. He retied his drinking apparatus fashioned from his handkerchief, soaked it in the fresh springwater, and splashed his face. He rested his head against the dirt wall and closed his eyes. A voice came to him—a soft, female voice—reciting a story:

> *One day, the goddess of the volcano met a handsome young man. She desired to have him as her sweetheart, but alas, he confessed that he loved another. This enraged the goddess, and she used her magical powers to change the young man into an ugly, twisted tree. His lover pleaded with the gods to return the young man to her, so the gods transformed the woman into a flower and placed the bloom on the tree so they could be together forever.*

Buck could feel a tear slip down his cheek as the voice gradually faded into the emptiness below.

Chapter 13

Lance had decided to spend Sunday night at Sadie's house. He wanted to be there in case Sonny decided to come back home. He was beginning to lose patience with both Sadie and her dog. What was he? A dog sitter, a house sitter, a finder of lost neighbors? Why hadn't she called? It wasn't like her to not be in contact. An uneasy feeling crept into his thinking and he brushed it away. He wished he could just go back to work and forget about all this. But of course he couldn't. To rid himself of Sadie or anything that had to do with her would be like chopping off his hand. Way too painful.

He sipped morning coffee and thought about Buck. Nothing so far made any sense. Sure, Buck was capable of killing, but Lance knew in his heart that wasn't the case.

He walked to the kitchen sink and looked out the window. There he was. Sonny stood at the edge of the yard staring at the house. Quickly, Lance opened the door and called to him. Sonny turned and walked away for a short distance, then turned back around and sat down. Lance called to him again, and Sonny repeated his routine.

"Damned dog," Lance muttered to himself. He pulled his cell phone out of his pocket and dialed Maggie. "Good morning, sunshine," he said in a friendly voice. "I've got something else I need you to look up for me," he said as he pulled the small spiral-bound notebook from his front shirt pocket. "Got a pencil and paper? I'm going to have to spell it for you."

"From the tone of your voice, I'm going to guess you don't know about the earthquake."

"We had an earthquake?"

"They had a 7.1 earthquake off the shore of the Big Island in Hawai'i this morning."

"What?!" Panic struck.

"The news says that all the airports are shut down on all the islands. When I heard, I tried to call you, and then I tried to call Sadie. All I got was voice mail from both of you."

Lance could feel the muscles tighten in his neck and back.

Maggie continued to talk. "The news also said that the phone service was out, but I can't imagine why her cell phone doesn't work unless the cell towers were damaged." Maggie paused for a moment. "And there's another thing. I got a really strange e-mail from someone."

"What's that got to do with Sadie?"

"I think it was the only way she had to communicate with you to let you know she was okay." Maggie paused again. "The only thing the message said was 'Everything is okay.' The e-mail came from someone by the name of Robert Walters III."

Lance stood motionless, holding the cell phone to his ear. No words would form.

"You still there, Chief?"

"Yeah, I'm here. Let me give you this information. It's an address." When he was finished spelling long unpronounceable words to her, he continued. "Listen, I'm going to do a little more work on this missing neighbor of Sadie's. Let me know what you find out and . . . keep me updated, will you?"

"Sure thing."

Lance immediately clicked on Sadie's television with his right hand while dialing Sadie's number with his left. He waited until the sound of her voice on her voice mail prompted a smile. At the signal, he left a short message. "Please call me," he said, then closed his cell phone and dropped it in his shirt pocket. He clicked from one news station to the other, mesmerized by the video of the earthquake damage, most of which was coming from the Big Island. He turned off the television and walked outside. He called for Sonny, but the wolf-dog had disappeared again.

He walked down the stairs and sat on the bottom step. He thought he would try one more time to make friends. "Come on, you goofy thing." He spoke partly to the wolf-dog and partly to himself.

On the ground next to his foot, Lance noticed something he hadn't seen before. It was a key ring holding two generic-looking keys and a leather fob displaying the U.S. Marines insignia. Lance picked it up, turned the well-worn piece of leather over in his hand, and frowned.

Who did these keys belong to and how did they get here? Why hadn't he noticed them before? Maybe Sadie had dropped them on her way out the day before.

He got up and tried both keys in Sadie's door. Neither worked.

Another thought struck. Maybe someone had been snooping around and accidentally lost them. He sat back down on the bottom step. The next thought that crept into the back of his mind gave him an uneasy feeling. Maybe Sadie had a friend he didn't know about, a male friend, a Marine friend.

He began to think about all the Marines he knew in Delaware County, too numerous to count. From young to old, Indians loved to join the Marines, including himself. Even Buck is a Marine, he thought, as he remembered the old trunk in the abandoned house. His mind began to race. Maybe Buck was running from the law after killing the identity thief, came looking for Sadie, and discovered she was gone. He rubbed his face and dismissed thoughts of a murdering Buck. He couldn't buy that argument even from himself.

He looked up long enough to see Sonny appear and disappear again. Maybe if he waited, the dog would return.

Then his thoughts shifted. Who exactly was Robert Walters III?

He spit in the yard and looked closer at the keys. The leather piece looked like it had canine teeth imprints on the corner. Maybe the unknown Marine had a stupid dog too. Well, Lance allowed, Sonny wasn't stupid, just independent and stubborn, like his owner. Was he rationalizing? Maybe the dog had found the keys and brought them home as a gift for Sadie.

He called again for Sonny. No movement. No sound.

He bounced the keys in his hand and shoved them in the pocket of his jeans. His next stop would be a restaurant for some bacon and eggs and strong coffee. He could always think better on a full stomach and a double shot of caffeine.

Chapter 14

Dee Dee Skinner pulled her black Cadillac into Buck's front yard and stared. "This house is going to fall in on your head, old man," she mumbled.

The grueling, two-day drive from California to Oklahoma had left her cranky and stiff. She slid out of the car, stood up, and stretched her long legs and lean body. She looked around the yard and shook her head, then walked up onto the porch and pushed open the front door.

"Uncle Buck, are you here?"

Dee Dee wrinkled her nose at the stale air in the quiet house. She walked into the kitchen and caught her stiletto heel on a small hole in the linoleum flooring, causing her to trip and fall toward the kitchen sink. As she banged her hand against the counter, one of her long, candy-apple red fingernails snapped off and bounced onto the floor. She cursed loudly, and then jammed her finger into her mouth. After she regained her composure, she retrieved the piece of acrylic and held it in her hand before forcing it into the pocket of her skin-tight jeans. Maybe she could pick up some nail glue later and fix it.

Perspiration had already popped out on her forehead and upper lip. She gathered her fiery red hair in her long fingers and lifted it off her slender neck, then pushed open the window above the sink, allowing a small, stifling breeze to enter the room. Knowing her uncle had no air conditioning, she would need to work fast. She couldn't stay trapped in this house for very long, she thought, or she would pass out right on the spot.

She pushed the button on the answering machine and listened to her own voice, the message she'd left two days earlier, then began to search through the drawers and cabinets. When she got to the kitchen table, she fingered the envelopes from the IRS. She read the top letter, cursed again, and spoke aloud. "Oh no, you don't, you old coot. You better not lose this place to back taxes. This place is supposed to be mine." She dropped the letter back onto the table and had just decided to move her search into the rest of the house when a knock at the door caused her heart to jump.

She peered through the screen door at a handsome Indian man holding his cowboy hat in his hand. "May I help you?" she asked as she smoothed her hair behind her ears and smiled.

"Name's Lance Smith," he said. "Just driving by and thought maybe Buck had turned up. I've been helping search for him."

Dee Dee walked out onto the porch and shook his hand. "I'm Dee Dee Skinner. Nice to meet you. I'd invite you in, but that house is filthy," she said. "Not to mention it's hotter than a pizza oven in there." She smiled again to deliberately reveal her straightened teeth.

"Oh, you must be his niece. I noticed the California plates on your car."

"Yes, that's me. It's a shame there's no one to take care of my uncle but me. Now he's gone and disappeared. Do you have any idea where he is?" She didn't wait for a response before she continued. "I've been trying to get him to put his affairs in order before something dreadful happened to him. I don't think he takes very good care of himself, and now he's up and disappeared. If he doesn't show up pretty soon, I'll probably have to go to court to gain control over his property. No telling how much that's going to cost. I'm his only heir, you know."

"No, ma'am, I don't know too much about that kind of stuff."

She watched him as he nervously bounced his hat in circles in his hands.

"But you're saying you haven't heard from him in the last couple of days?" he asked.

Dee Dee shook her head. "No, and I knew in my heart there was something wrong. That's why I called Sheriff O'Leary. He told me if they couldn't find him and if there was no sign of foul play, there was nothing he could do. You'd think the law around this hick county could do something."

"Yeah, you'd think." Lance turned toward his vehicle.

"Wait," she said and reached for his arm. "Can you help me out? I don't come here very often. Do you have any idea where I can spend the night?" She wrinkled her nose. "I can't stay here."

"I'm sure you can get a room either in Jay or Sycamore Springs," he said, pulling his arm away. "I doubt there's anything in Eucha that would meet your expectations." He walked into the yard. "You be sure and let the sheriff know if you hear from your uncle, you hear?" He climbed into his truck and drove off.

"Well, thank you, Mr. Smith," she said aloud. "I think I'll remember you. You're kind of cute." Dee Dee pushed her bangs off her sweaty forehead and returned to the sweltering house to continue her search for anything of value, anything she thought she might want, just in case her uncle never returned.

✢

Lance drove, silently evaluating what he'd just seen and heard. Dee Dee Skinner's appearance and attitude weren't exactly what he'd expected. From what little he knew about Buck and the simple life the old man lived, it was apparent that he and his niece were about as diametrically opposed as they could possibly be. Lance could visualize the places and people in Dee Dee's life, and they weren't even close to the area and folks in Delaware County.

No wonder the old man hadn't returned the woman's calls. They couldn't possibly have enough in common to make a conversation last more than thirty seconds.

There was no denying the attractiveness of Buck's niece. Based on his lawman's intuition, he guessed her to be close to his own age—about fifty. She must have inherited her red hair and fair complexion from one of her parents, he thought, and it wouldn't have been the one related by blood to Buck. The shape of her face and her high, chiseled cheekbones reminded Lance of some beautiful Indian women he'd met over the years, but her freckled skin and green eyes screamed Anglo descent. The intense hue of her hair appeared to have been helped along chemically, but it obviously wasn't that far off from her natural color—red.

Red hair meant she was probably part Irish. Lance chuckled. An Irish-Cherokee woman could be a very stubborn, strong-willed woman, and he thought it would be best if he steered clear of this one.

After all, he was already wrapped up emotionally with Sadie. With her coal-black hair and intense blue eyes, she'd captivated him from the first time he'd ever laid eyes on her. It wasn't her outward appearance alone that had stolen his heart, but her unparalleled inner grace and strength. She was all woman. He was crazy about her and already missed her terribly.

As Lance traveled the gravel road a couple of miles past Buck's house, he noticed a man sitting on the porch of his house. He decided to stop and see if he could find out anything about Buck.

Lance turned into the yard, parked, and let the dust settle before getting out of his truck. Two bluetick hounds rose from their shady spots at the base of a tall elm tree, stretched, and welcomed him with a duet of howls. One short word from the man on the porch and the dogs' suspicious barks immediately transformed into wagging tails and slobbery snorts.

Lance introduced himself from a distance. The man silently nodded an invitation to join him on the porch before speaking. "Jeremiah Hart," the man said. "You can call me Jelly."

"Hello, Jelly." Lance removed his hat and shook the calloused hand of a man who appeared to be in his mid- to late sixties, with a friendly face and fair skin that had been weathered to a soft tan by the constant and unrelenting Oklahoma sun.

"Have a seat," Jelly said, as he ran his fingers through his thick, unkempt salt-and-pepper hair. "It's cooler out here than it is in the house."

Lance settled into a nearby folding lawn chair, the kind of lightweight portable chair Indians typically carried to powwows all over Indian country. Jelly handed him a metal ladle and nodded to an aluminum bucket sitting on the porch railing.

"Want a drink of cool water?" he asked. "Just filled it up from the springhouse."

Lance got up and dipped the ladle into the water and took a long drink, then thanked the man, handed the dipper back to him, and resettled in his chair. After the customary small talk about the heat and the lack of rainfall ruining everyone's gardens, Lance began to talk.

"We've been looking for your neighbor, Buck Skinner," he said. "You haven't seen him in the last day or two, have you?"

Jelly looked off into the distance. "No, can't rightly say that I have. But whatever he decides to do is all right with me."

"Decides to do?"

"The last time I saw Buck, he was pretty riled up at the government. Can't say that I blame him." He shifted uncomfortably in his chair. "I've got my own bone to pick with the likes," he whispered.

Lance waited in silence for Jelly to continue.

"You know, you spend your whole life doing what you think is right by others, and most people give it right back. But those big shots, they don't care nothing about nobody. They take your money and that's it. They don't care nothing about you as a human being." The man spit into the yard.

Lance sat forward in his chair and frowned. "You think Buck might've been up to something?"

Jelly laughed quietly. "Maybe old Buck decided to chuck it all in." He paused for a moment and then continued. "Maybe he decided to walk off into the sunset and call it good." He turned and looked at Lance. "That's what I'm going to do. When they come and try to throw me off my land, I'm going to set this place on fire, walk off into the woods, and call it good."

"Why would anyone want to throw you off your land?" Lance asked, realizing the conversation had taken a turn in the wrong direction.

"Just 'cause they can," he said, and then repeated, "Just 'cause they can."

"You live here by yourself?" Lance began to feel concern for the man.

Jelly looked down at his feet. "I lost my wife about six months ago. Everything's been all messed up ever since she died." The words seemed to catch in his throat. "And it's been real lonely around here without her."

"You got any family close by?"

"Nope," Jelly answered sharply.

Lance decided to let the man's answer go, allowing it to evaporate into the stifling air between them. "So you think Buck is okay, maybe just went off somewhere?"

"Probably."

"You don't think Buck would want to go off and hurt anybody, do you?"

A raspy chuckle rose slowly out of Jelly's chest. "I wouldn't want to make Buck Skinner mad at me."

"So, you're saying he could be violent if he wanted to?"

Jelly grinned and swatted at a fly, caught it in his fist, then slowly opened his hand and let it go. "Nah, Buck Skinner wouldn't hurt a fly."

Lance stood, pulled a business card from his billfold, and handed it to Jelly. "If you see Buck, would you mind giving me a call?"

Jelly took the card, slid it into his shirt pocket, and nodded one time. Lance got back into his truck and headed toward his original destination— Sycamore Springs.

Chapter 15

Back in her condo, Sadie quickly lost interest in the paperback the woman had insisted she take from the bookcase in the lobby. She dropped the book on the coffee table and walked to a CD player near the television. She hit the play button and waited to see if the batteries would work. They did. A pleasant ukulele melody filled the air, and then a pleasant male voice began to sing.

Sadie picked up the CD case and sat on the nearby sofa. The haunting words of the first song struck at her heart. She rose, went back to the player, and started the CD over and turned up the volume.

The lyrics told a story of ancient Hawaiian ancestors, wondering what they would think if they saw the changes to their sacred land. Tears came to Sadie's eyes as she listened to words written about the Hawaiian experience that echoed the struggle of all Native people, including her Cherokee ancestors.

Goose bumps ran up Sadie's arms when the chorus began. The emotional song described the pain associated with the loss of land and how Hawai'i would never be the same. She turned the CD case over in her hand and read the credits. The song, "Hawai'i '78," had been recorded by Israel Kamakawiwo'ole.

She allowed the CD to continue playing through two more songs before starting it over and listening to the first song again. Finally, she returned to the CD player, punched the off button, and stared at the ocean. The sad music caused her to think about Lance and her situation. She felt conflicted. This place seemed to hold a magical spell over her, yet she had never felt so unsettled, having lost contact with the rest of the world, especially Lance. If she could just hear his voice, she would feel better.

A loud knock caused her to jump. She approached the door and stood on her tiptoes to eye her visitor through the peephole. It was the flowered dress.

"I brought a friend to see you," the woman said through the door.

Sadie unlocked the deadbolt and opened the door to discover Pua standing behind the receptionist.

"Oh, how nice to see a familiar face," Sadie said, genuinely pleased to see her. "Please, come in."

The flowered dress nodded and disappeared down the hall as Pua stepped out of her sandals and left them beside the door, then followed Sadie into her vacation rental. "I would have called first, but none of our phones are working."

Sadie pointed to the pieces of broken cell phone lying on the kitchen counter and laughed. "I know the feeling."

"I'm on my way to Lāna'i to check on Tutu. I'm sure she's okay, but I'll feel better when I see for myself. I thought you might like to go with me." She looked at her watch. "It's not yet ten o'clock. If we hurry we can catch the noon ferry, spend a few hours with her, and then come back on the last sailing of the day at six forty-five."

"Oh, I was going to see if I could catch an earlier flight home."

Pua sounded sympathetic. "I have a feeling they're going to have their hands full, with canceled flights and all, and you mentioned you had an interest in island life during the war. Tutu might be willing to talk to you about it. I just don't know."

Sadie thought for a moment. "You're right. No point in hanging around here when I could be out sightseeing."

"Let's hurry then."

Sadie pulled on a pair of sneakers, grabbed her purse, and followed Pua down the stairs to her car.

"How far is it?" Sadie asked. "The woman on the radio said to stay off the roads."

"The ferry is in Lahaina Harbor. If the road is completely closed, we'll have to come back. But I think we can get through."

The two women climbed into Pua's small and well-used Toyota and took off. They traveled an almost deserted highway around the island in the opposite direction from the one that Sadie had driven the night before.

"How do you know the ferry will be running?" Sadie said. "Isn't everything shut down? What if there's another earthquake?"

"Mother Earth is pretty unpredictable, but after she lets out a good burp like she did this morning, she's usually okay for a while." Pua looked at Sadie and smiled. "Besides, my cousin is the boat captain, and he says the safest place to be is on a boat in the water. We'll be okay."

Sadie nodded, accepting her new friend's rationalization.

Pua drove carefully, dodging several small and medium-sized rocks that had fallen into the road. As they approached a road crew moving a large boulder to one side, Pua slowed the vehicle and came to a stop, then leaned out her window.

A heavyset, dark-skinned worker wearing a fluorescent orange vest bent down to Pua's window. "Hey, Sis, what you doing out on the road?" He glanced through the driver's window toward Sadie with a look of concern.

"Got to catch the next ferry to Lāna'i and check on Tutu."

The road worker nodded. "Okay, you be careful. One big rock in the road down there." He pointed with his head in the direction they were driving.

"Will do, Lui," Pua reached out to the large man and touched his arm with her hand and offered her thanks. "Mahalo," she said.

Before Sadie knew it, Pua had maneuvered around "one big rock in the road," sailed past miles of vacant coastline, and parked at their destination—the Expeditions Ferry's loading pier in Lahaina Harbor, across from the Pioneer Inn. Pua got out of the car, gathered two large paper sacks from the backseat, and approached the ticket booth, where she pulled something from one of the sacks and gave it to the woman selling tickets. The woman smiled, looked at Pua's driver's license, and sold her two tickets.

Pua hurriedly ushered Sadie onto the nearly empty vessel to a seat at the front of the enclosed cabin. Pua placed the two sacks on the seat next to her and began to rummage through one. She pulled out a box that read Home Maid Bakery on the top.

"How about a little snack for the road," Pua said, and handed Sadie a napkin and a pastry that looked like a fried doughnut without a hole.

Sadie graciously accepted the treat and took a bite. "Oh, my gosh." Sadie tried to speak with her mouth full. "What is this? It's delicious."

"*Malasadas*. They're best when they're hot, but Tutu will appreciate them no matter, hot or cold." Pua poked around in the sack again. "Tutu loves anything from Home Maid Bakery. Besides *malasadas*, I've got some crispy *manju*, too. They're filled with *imo*, purple sweet potato," she explained, "and some peanut butter *mochi*. *Mochi* is pounded rice cake." Pua looked at Sadie. "Want one?"

"Ooh, I'd better wait. We don't want to eat all of Tutu's goodies before we get there."

"So true," Pua said, laughing. "It's customary to take gifts when traveling from one island to another. We call it *omiyage* in the Japanese culture— a gift to share, something to eat."

Sadie smiled, thinking about the similarity between island culture and her own Indian ways. The ferry began to move, and the two women settled into their seats.

The captain skillfully nudged the ferry out of the slip and moved it into open waters, where they set sail for the island of Lāna'i. The front of the ferry rose and fell as water sprayed both sides of the boat. As the women talked, sharing things about their lives with one another, Sadie began to feel a kindred spirit in Pua.

"You mentioned Japanese culture a while ago," Sadie said. "Is your mother Japanese?"

"Japanese Hawaiian. My grandfather was Japanese. His name was Kichiro Takahashi, but he changed it when he moved from Japan to the islands. He was about twenty years old and wanted to begin a new life working in the pineapple fields." Pua bit her lower lip. "It was a new life all right, a very hard life."

She stopped for a moment and then continued. "He took the name Keola, which means 'life,' and then Kichiro morphed into Kimo. Kimo is a familiar Hawaiian name for Jim, or James," Pua explained again and smiled. "I think he thought he fit in better as Kimo Keola, but let's face it," Pua laughed, "once Japanese, always Japanese."

"Tutu's mother was Hawaiian," she continued. "Her name was Leina'ala. They were married in 1926 not long after my father arrived in Hawai'i, and Tutu was born the next year. Tutu was only seventeen when her father, my grandfather, joined the army. Even though he was thirty-seven years old by then, he was so distraught about what was going on with the war and all, he joined the 442 in 1943. I was actually born the following year."

Sadie did the math silently. It was hard to believe that Pua was sixty years old.

"We don't know if he ever got the letters telling him he was a grandfather," Pua continued. "We never heard from him again. He died in 1944 fighting the Germans in Europe." Pua's voice wavered for the first time. "He never even got to see me."

"What is the 442?" Sadie asked.

"U.S. Army 442nd Regimental Combat Team, made up entirely of Japanese Americans, the most highly decorated unit in U.S. military history." Pua stared straight ahead and spoke as if she were reciting a story she had memorized as a child. "They fought in Italy, France, and Germany. They lost eight hundred men in one battle trying to rescue two hundred Texans who were surrounded by Germans and cut off from their unit." Pua looked down at the limp hands in her lap. "Eight hundred for two hundred. Doesn't seem right, does it?"

Sadie remained quiet and waited for Pua to continue.

"On the mainland, they rounded up all the Japanese Americans and put them in internment camps, but they couldn't do that in Hawai'i because there were too many. The 442 came from Hawai'i." Pua finally looked at Sadie. "After all that, the other soldiers still called them 'Japs' and 'Pineapples.' You'd think giving your life for your country would afford a little more respect than that."

After a long pause, Pua continued. "My father was from the mainland and stationed at Camp Maui." Pua looked at Sadie. "Cherokee, you know. He died fighting the Japanese before he even knew I existed."

"Do you mind if I ask your father's name?"

Pua shook her head. "I do not know it."

Sadie tried to hide her surprise, but doubted her success.

Pua continued. "It is not spoken. They were not married. I do not bear his name. It caused great embarrassment for Tutu and her mother. There's a lot of hurt and pain associated with the war for Tutu. She may or may not want to talk to you about it. Just don't push her, okay?"

Sadie nodded.

Before they realized it, their destination island grew larger and larger as the forty-five-minute, nine-mile ride across the Auau Channel neared an end. Sadie fished a small camera from her purse and clicked photos of the lush coastline. The island, with its steep cliffs leading into Manele Bay, looked deserted. She could see no tourists whatsoever as the captain guided the ferry into the tiny harbor and moored the boat with heavy ropes against a wooden walkway. They grabbed the bakery goodies and disembarked onto the island of Lāna'i.

Chapter 16

Lance parked his truck next to Charlie McCord's cruiser, got out, and walked into the Sycamore Springs Waffle House to the welcoming aroma of freshly brewed coffee and fried bacon. He immediately spotted Charlie pouring syrup on a stack of pancakes at his favorite booth in the far corner of the restaurant.

Before he had settled across the table from Charlie, the waitress plopped down a mug for him and filled it to the brim with steaming coffee. "Eating or just drinking?" she asked as she placed the coffeepot on the table and reached for a plastic menu she held under her arm.

Lance looked up at her and waved off the menu.

"I'll have two eggs over medium, bacon, hash browns, and biscuits and gravy." He looked wistfully at Charlie's pancake. "Bring me a pancake, too," he added.

"You got it, honey." She picked up the coffeepot, turned on her heel, and stopped at every table to top off coffee mugs on her way back to the pass-through window to order his food.

"You must be on a diet," Charlie said with a chuckle.

"Just hungry, I guess."

"Missing your little lady? Trying to replace her with food?"

Lance ignored Charlie, took out his cell phone, looked at it, and then put it back in his pocket.

"Take it from me, my friend," Charlie continued. "It only tastes good for a little while. Then you get to where you can't run down crooks on foot anymore without stopping to catch your breath, and the first thing you know your job's in jeopardy and they want to retire you to a desk, then you got to starve yourself and start exercising every day to get back in shape before they'll put you back out on the street. It's a vicious cycle, Smith. Don't go there."

Lance watched Charlie smear more butter on his pancakes and saturate them with syrup. "I see you're a man of great wisdom and experience. I'll take all that under consideration." Lance took a sip of coffee. "In the meantime, you got anything on the dead guys?"

"The dead guy at the chicken plant is Tomas Hernandez. He's got a green card that says he's from somewhere in Mexico. The folks at the chicken plant say he's been there about a year and was a hard worker. Hasn't caused any problems in the past. The security tape clearly shows the man everyone knew there as Benny Skinner stabbing him. He dropped the knife and split."

"Sounds like Benny didn't much like Cynthia's new boyfriend, Tomas."

"Guess not." Charlie sipped coffee and continued to eat.

"What about the dead guy in the trailer park?" Lance asked. "And the one that got away?"

Charlie took another bite of pancake. "Well, let's see. The dead guy in the trailer park." He wiped his mouth with a paper napkin and leaned back in his seat. "Seems as though everyone thinks he is, or was, one Benjamin Skinner. He's got an Oklahoma driver's license that confirms that. The woman at the Department of Motor Vehicles in Oklahoma City says he turned in an out-of-state license two years ago and the local driver's examiners issued him an Oklahoma license based on that information. They did a background check and nothing unusual came up. Someone's supposed to be running his fingerprints today. Maybe that will turn up something."

The waitress zipped by, sloshed some more coffee in both mugs. Charlie took a sip and went back to work on his pancakes. In a few short seconds, the waitress returned and slid two plates of food and a small bowl of gravy in front of Lance. Lance rubbed his belly and dug in.

"What state would that be?" Lance asked.

"State of confusion, mostly." Charlie laid his fork on the table and pushed his plate aside.

"No. What state driver's license did he turn in for the Oklahoma license?"

"I'm working on that. The little lady at the DMV said they shred all those licenses and since that was two years ago she'd have to do some research. She ought to be calling back any time now."

Lance nodded and continued to shovel food into his mouth. "What about the woman at the trailer where we found the body?"

"Cynthia Tanner. Interesting young lady. She works the graveyard shift at the nursing home. Been there about six months. The woman at the nursing home says she hasn't had any complaints on her. Shows up on time, doesn't call in sick, keeps her nose clean. Says she shows up ever' once in a while looking a little beat up, but she figures what the employees do on their off time is none of her business."

Lance took a bite of biscuit and washed it down with coffee. "Really."

"I hear she's a regular at the Back Alley Bar on the south side of Sycamore Springs. I plan on doing a little investigating down there when I get a chance."

"So, she's a local."

"Talk around town is she grew up across the line in Arkansas, raised by her grandmother. She's got a younger sister—she took over the parenting when the grandmother died. I hear the sister is a lot younger. Don't know how old she is. The manager at the trailer park says her name is Becky Tanner, a good kid, goes to school in Fayetteville at the University of Arkansas, and she's a regular visitor at Cynthia's place."

"Wonder if she can shed any light on this situation?"

"I doubt it, but you never know."

"What about the runner?"

"That would be the major part of the confusion. So far, I don't have a clue on him. I never got close enough to get a description. I couldn't tell you if he was white, Indian, or alien. The state trooper who worked the accident said there was a little dab of blood on the windshield, so I'd say wherever he is, he's got a headache. We checked all the hospitals with no success. If he's hiding out in the woods in this heat, I'd think the ticks and chiggers would chase him in pretty soon. I can tell you his blood type is O positive and that's about it."

Lance lifted his lips in a smirk. "Well, that narrows it down to about ninety-five percent of the population. What about the gun? Did they find it in the vehicle?"

"Yeah, and it was registered to Cynthia Tanner. She says she keeps it for protection. Her work alibi holds up, so my assumption is that the killer used it on Benny and then ran like hell when we showed up. Shouldn't take long for the ballistics tests to tell us if it's the weapon we're looking for, but I'm guessing it is."

"Prints on the gun?"

"None that can be used."

"I noticed a letter on the floor. Did that tell you anything?"

"Came from a foreign country. Lab's still working on it. But I can tell you one thing."

"What's that?"

"It isn't looking too good for the old man you're looking for."

"Why's that?" Lance pushed his plate to the side.

"I had one of my junior officers pulling prints off the wrecked truck. I'm guessing those prints probably belong to the deceased, and if we're lucky, maybe the runner." Charlie finished off his coffee and wiped his mouth.

"Come on, Charlie. Don't make me drag everything out of you."

"Like I said, we should have reports on the fingerprints later, but if your assumptions are right about the old man, and he was ticked off about someone stealing his social security number, it could be he just got pissed off enough to shoot the old boy in the head."

Lance rolled his eyes. "That doesn't make any sense, Charlie. If he'd found the culprit, why not just turn him in? He could take him to court and straighten everything out with the IRS."

"You tell me." Charlie chuckled. "Is that the Indian way?"

Lance frowned at his friend. "I guess shooting him in the head would be the best way to expedite justice in today's world. It would take years to get anything accomplished through the courts." He pulled his phone out of his pocket again and stared at it.

"What's up with you and that darned phone? Someone sending you secret messages?"

"Maggie told me there was an earthquake in Hawaiʻi this morning, and I haven't heard from Sadie since yesterday."

"Hmph." Concern crossed Charlie's face. "Come on," he said as he pulled himself out of the booth. "No point in sitting around here. Let's go see what we can find out."

The two men paid for their food and headed to their vehicles. Lance locked his truck and opened the passenger-side door of Charlie's cruiser. Charlie was already on the radio barking orders to someone. In less than a minute, Charlie's cell phone rang. He dropped the radio transmitter in his lap and answered.

Since Charlie seemed to be doing more listening than talking, Lance took the opportunity to try to call Sadie again. He stood beside the police car and dialed her number. When her voice mail clicked on, he hung up and dialed Maggie. Maggie answered on the first ring.

"Got any news for me?" Lance asked.

"CNN says all lines of communication are still out across Hawaiʻi."

"Okay. What about the foreign address?"

"It's from Samoa."

"Samoa?" Lance said, with surprise in his voice. "Hmm. I can't say that I know much about Samoa. Do you, Maggie?"

"Not really, Chief. But I'll see what I can find."

"Okay, thanks. Let me know. I'm going to be riding with Charlie McCord for a while this morning. Stay in touch." Lance didn't wait for Maggie to acknowledge before snapping his cell phone shut and dropping it into his pocket.

When Charlie had finished his conversations on both the radio and the phone, he barked another order to Lance. "Get in, Smith."

Lance climbed into the front seat of Charlie's cruiser and buckled up. "Maggie says the address on the letter is Samoan."

Charlie raised his eyebrow. "We need to hire her in Sycamore Springs. I don't think we knew that yet."

"Well, you can't have her. What's the rest of the scoop?" Lance asked.

"The county boys searching for the runner just found something interesting. Let's run out and see."

Lance nodded as Charlie nosed the cruiser onto the highway.

"Tell me something, Smith," Charlie said. "If you were going to send a bomb threat to a bank, would you send it through the U.S. mail?"

"Uh, probably not," Lance said. "But, of course, I've never considered sending a bomb threat before."

"Remember the branch where Sadie used to work? The one where that old boy tried to kill her?"

Lance nodded.

"Evidently, the manager there got a real strange letter. The bomb techs went out and checked out the building. Didn't find anything, but the letter mentioned a future event. Guess I'll have to go by and give them some pointers on what to look for. You know, community service."

Uninterested, Lance glanced out the side window.

Charlie continued. "The official info on the earthquake is there were only a few minor injuries, phone lines are overwhelmed, and the airports are closed until they can get the power back up. They're not going to allow planes to take off until they can x-ray everyone's underwear," Charlie chuckled. "So I'd say your little lady is going to be stuck for a couple of days. When is she scheduled to head back home?"

"Couple of days," Lance said, and then shifted his gaze back out the car window.

Chapter 17

The sun climbed higher in the sky and Buck wrestled with his predicament. He pulled a piece of venison jerky from his stash, tore it in half, and returned the rest to his pocket. He chewed it slowly, allowing the salty taste to linger in his mouth.

His father had taught him well. He'd taught him how to survive—a lesson that had served him well in the war and every day since. It was as if he had an extra sense, an intuition of survival in battle. Buck, always prepared, gained the respect of his Marine buddies, who looked to him for strength, instruction, and advice, even though he was younger than all of them.

Buck relived the war every day, but he hadn't thought about the days leading up to it in a long time. It was strange to him that he couldn't remember how he'd got into a sinkhole the day before, but he could remember his childhood, when he was known as Ben instead of Buck, and he could remember the days of war as if they were yesterday.

In the summer of 1942, a few months after the Japanese bombed Pearl Harbor, the war had begun to affect everyone, including the Skinner family. News from the front lines arrived slowly to the rural areas of northeastern Oklahoma, but when it did, the stories of combat, carnage, and deadly sacrifice cast a pall over the community.

Times grew tough, but the Skinners knew how to survive. They and their Cherokee ancestors had been living off the land for centuries. This was no different. Ben and his older brother Jake stopped going to school and started hunting every day to help provide food for the family.

They harvested every kind of meat they could find for their mother's cast-iron skillet—rabbits, squirrels, venison, and even an occasional raccoon. They made jerky out of the extra venison and stored it for those winter days when they returned from hunting empty-handed.

When the fishing was good, the brothers came home from nearby Lake Eucha with a stringer full of catfish, perch, crappie, and anything else that would bite. Their mother and younger sister took turns tending the garden, which provided an abundance of vegetables for both eating and canning. Ben gathered eggs every evening from a few hens, and the Jersey cow provided rich milk that yielded both butter and cream. They shared what they had with their neighbors and traded for what they could at the Eucha General Store.

Jake had been born with a clubfoot. Though he walked with a limp, he could move as fast as anyone, even when challenging his brother in a game of stickball. When he reached the age of eighteen, he tried to enlist, but the U.S. Army rejected him and his clubfoot. He sulked for weeks.

Ben didn't want to be in the U.S. Army; he wanted to be a Marine. Only sixteen, he might have to lie about his age, but he knew he could fight just as well as, if not better than, the rest of the eighteen-year-old boys. He believed when the Marines found out how well he could shoot a rifle they wouldn't care how old he was. He was right.

Two weeks later, his mother stood beside their farm truck in front of Kirby's Service Station wringing her hands. Buck remembered how uncharacteristic it was for her to show much emotion, but he could see the pain in her eyes.

He put his arm around her shoulders and kissed the top of her head. "I have to go," he'd said, hugging her again. "It wouldn't be right for me not to go, and you know it."

"I don't know why you can't stay here like your older brother."

"Jake's got a clubfoot, Momma. He limps."

He let go of his mother and turned his attention to his father.

"You be careful, son. Keep your head down when the bullets start flying."

Ben shook his father's hand. "Don't worry. I know how to take care of myself."

"We'll be here when you get back," his father said.

Ben turned and walked to the waiting bus. He took the steps two at a time and grabbed the first empty seat. He knew his momma was waiting for him to wave, but he didn't look back at her. He was afraid she would see the fear in his face, so he stared straight ahead and thought about the adventure of going to war.

It took almost a week to get to California. He had lied to the recruiter, told him he was eighteen, and he worried they might find out. But they didn't care. Instead, the U.S. Marines welcomed him with open arms and made him one of their own.

In basic training he learned to walk like a Marine, talk like a Marine, and, most important, he learned to fight like a Marine. The food didn't taste as good as his mother's, but he learned to adapt. His muscles grew hard and taut and his feet grew by one size. He looked good in his uniform and had a picture taken to send to his mother.

He missed his thick black hair, but his closely shaved head was a time-saver when he had to roll out of bed before dawn every day. He knew it would make his mother feel better to get something in the mail from him, so he tried to get a letter mailed to her at least once a week.

Buck could remember the dates with uncanny accuracy. On August 16, 1943, his company became part of the newly formed 4th Marine Division in Oceanside, California. Less than six months later, Ben got his orders. He was going to be part of a secret mission—Operation Flintlock.

He had never seen a vessel bigger than the flat-bottomed boat he and Jake used to fish from on Lake Eucha, but on January 13, 1944, he climbed aboard the mammoth USS *LaSalle* and set sail out of the harbor at San Diego for the worst nightmare of his life. He had no idea this ship would take him and the rest of the 4th Marines straight into battle in the middle of the South Pacific. He was seasick for days.

After what seemed like an eternity, but was in actuality only a couple of weeks, the ship anchored at Maui to stock up on provisions. Forbidden to disembark, he could only gaze with wonder from the ship nestled between one large and two small islands. He'd never seen anything like it and wished he could tell everyone back home about it. More than anything, he wished he knew exactly when he was going to be allowed off this gigantic ship. He hadn't signed on to be a sailor, and now he knew for certain he didn't like sailing. He sat on his bunk and wrote his folks a letter that night expressing those very sentiments as the ship quietly sailed toward the front lines. He hoped he would get to see those beautiful islands again.

The next day, Ben and the other Marines finally discovered their destination—the Marshall Islands. They landed at Roi-Namur and went straight into battle. They fought for nine endless days before taking the islands and handing them off to the U.S. Army. Ben came away unscathed, which couldn't be said for everyone. He had watched Marine after Marine fall all around him, but they had won the battle. He knew the Japanese had suffered the bigger loss.

He was glad the fighting was over for now. The bitter taste of death clung to the back of Ben's throat and stole his breath away. He didn't know how many men he had killed at Roi-Namur, but the trauma of trying to stay alive had changed him in a way he didn't like.

Ben and the rest of the Marine Division returned to Maui in February and began to set up camp. According to the sergeant major, they would live there in their pup tents until the war ended or they were killed in battle, whichever came first.

In an effort to shake off the effects of war, Ben volunteered for every work detail offered. Then he joined the baseball team. Every chance he got he hitched a ride to the Kahului USO show where the local girls danced hula on the weekends. Anything to take his mind off the war.

Four months later, he was digging foxholes and trying to survive again. This time on the island of Saipan. He lost track of time. He fought past the point of exhaustion, when adrenaline took over. Finally, waiting for the next round of fighting, he'd collapsed in a foxhole and nodded off.

A pebble bounced off Buck's arm, thrusting him back into the present. The humidity and the damp earth in the sinkhole seemed to intensify Buck's memories of war. At least no one is shooting at me here, he thought. Another pebble fell from above and Sonny's head appeared, partially blocking the sun.

"You again, huh?" Buck called out for help just in case someone had followed the dog. Sonny stood up and barked. "Go get Sadie, Sonny. Go get

Sadie." The dog barked again and disappeared. Buck decided relying on a wolf-dog to save him deemed his situation pretty grim.

He tried to remember again how he had ended up in this hole in the ground. He remembered getting out of bed and going to the creek, where he'd performed the traditional purification ceremony of prayer, and going to water just as he'd done every morning for as long as he could remember. When he'd returned to the house, he remembered stopping by the mailbox, something he did at least once a week. That's when he'd found the letter from the IRS. He couldn't remember what happened after that. He knew he didn't want to lose his land. Thinking about it now caused anger to well up inside him.

He loved his two-hundred-acre ranch, there was no denying that. The land had started out as Indian land, part of the original land allotted to his Cherokee ancestors when the U.S. government divided up Indian Territory and parceled it out to tribal citizens when Oklahoma became a state. In his opinion, the land allotments had been a sorry pittance for the thousands of acres stolen from the Indians by Andrew Jackson in the 1800s. The corrupt U.S. president had single-handedly forced the Cherokees and the other tribes from their homelands in the southeastern United States, mostly for the rich gold reserves they had found.

He knew the story well, as told to him by his father and his father's father. Their ancestors had made the long walk from Georgia to Indian Territory on what had become known as the Trail of Tears. His people had starved, frozen, and died along the way in unbearable conditions. But that was in the distant past, and he couldn't focus on that right now. It made him too angry.

After Buck's father died, his mother had sold the land to a white man and moved to California with Buck's older brother. When Buck discovered what his mother had done, he'd tried to stop the sale from going through, but he was too late. A decade later, when he drove by and saw a "For Sale" sign nailed to the front gate, he almost wrecked his truck before he screeched to a stop. He pulled the sign off the gate, walked up to the front door, and handed it to the owner.

It took every penny he had, including all the money he'd sent home from the war, but the land was finally back under the name of Skinner where it belonged—free and clear.

Once he'd secured the old home place, he added another forty acres on the southwest side of the property to make an even two hundred acres. To some, the land might have seemed useless, with rocky soil, high ridges, and deep valleys making it unsuitable for growing crops, but for Buck it meant everything. It was a magical place that held memories of his ancestors and his childhood deep in its earthy grasp.

Buck's thoughts moved to his horses. No man should be without a horse, he thought. He'd acquired six mustangs—two brown-and-white paints, a red roan, and three buckskins—and he'd turned them loose to run free on his land. The wild horses had never been ridden, not even by him. They're just horses being horses, he thought, and he loved to sit on his back porch every evening and watch them graze on native grass.

His thoughts returned to his predicament with the IRS. If his mother hadn't sold off the land to a white man to begin with, the federal government wouldn't be able to put a lien on it because it had been Indian land. But she had—it wasn't Indian land anymore, and that was that.

Buck squirmed in an effort to release pressure on his back. None of this would matter soon. He'd be dead and a part of the land forever. And how ironic was that? A warrior should die in battle, he thought, not holed away like a chipmunk in the ground.

Chapter 18

Sadie followed Pua as they disembarked and walked to a waiting van.

"Aloha, Makani." Pua handed the driver a couple of bills. "All day for both of us," she said and nodded toward Sadie.

"Howzit, Pua? Just here for the day?"

Pua smiled. "Yes, just for the day. Want a *manapua*?"

The driver, a big man in an even bigger blue-and-white Hawaiian shirt, shoved the bills into his pocket, made a check mark on his clipboard, and smiled. "Thought you'd never ask," he said.

Pua dug into her paper bag and handed the driver a pastry and a napkin. He carefully laid his prize on the dashboard and kissed Pua on the cheek. "Mahalo," he said.

Sadie smiled at the driver and took the empty seat in the van beside Pua. "How many of those things do you have in there, anyway?"

"Enough," Pua laughed. "Say, Makani, was there any damage on the island? The phone service is out. I couldn't get in touch with Tutu."

"Not much. My brother said the shaking knocked his Jeep out of gear and it rolled into the ocean, but I think that story is suspect. My brother drinks a lot."

Pua smiled. "Did you lose power?"

"Of course not. We got one big extension cord here on Lāna'i. It runs on the bottom of the ocean all the way to Honolulu. We always got power." Makani grinned and flexed his upper arm.

"That's good to know, Makani." Pua shook her head.

A man with a golf bag slung over his shoulder walked off the ferry, climbed into the van, and took a seat in the rear.

"One lonely tourist," Pua whispered. "That's okay. By tomorrow they will have forgotten all about the earthquake and everything will be back to normal."

"Is there a lot of tourism on Lāna'i?" Sadie asked.

"Ever since Dole shut down the pineapple fields, the only thing keeping this island alive is tourism. We have three hotels and two championship golf courses. Everything else relates to those places in one way or another. Either that, or the folks are retired from Dole."

Makani climbed back into the driver's seat, closed the van's door, and picked up his pastry. He took a bite and began to speak.

"Looks like you wahines get special treatment today." He gestured with the *manapua* in his hand. "Got to make one stop at Manele for the gentleman, but if no one gets on then I can take you wherever you want to go." He finished off the *manapua*, wiped his hands on the napkin Pua had given him, and began to guide the van up the hill and away from the harbor.

Sadie stared out the window at the lush palms and brilliant tropical flowers that lined the road. She felt like she had entered another world, a world a million miles away from her little place in Eucha, Oklahoma. Her thoughts turned to Lance. She wondered what he was doing and whether or not someone had found Buck. She frowned as she thought about the old man and wished she could help search for him. But she was so far away, so helpless. Thinking of Lance again, she wished he was with her to see this magnificent place.

Her thoughts about home were cut short when Makani turned the van off the road and down a long driveway toward a luxurious hotel. The sign at the entrance read "Manele Bay, a Four Seasons Resort." The manicured grounds were exquisite, picture perfect.

Makani pulled the van up to the front door and parked under the canopy. The golfer stood and hurriedly exited the vehicle. He turned and offered Makani a dollar bill and walked away without saying a word.

Makani shoved the bill in his pocket and turned toward Pua. "We will be here for fifteen minutes if you want to get out and walk around. I'll stay with the van, so your things will be safe." He smiled broadly. "That is, unless I locate the rest of those *manapuas*."

"Can we?" asked Sadie. "This place is gorgeous."

"You keep your hands off these pastries, or you'll have to answer to Tutu," Pua warned.

Makani looked like a scolded youngster and then laughed. The two women joined in his laughter as they climbed out of the van and entered the resort.

Sadie found herself lagging behind Pua, staring at her surroundings, knowing she would never be able to absorb it all. She reached for her camera and snapped a few photos of the exotic Asian-themed decor before Pua took her arm and pulled her forward.

"Let's hurry," said Pua. "I want you to see the view from the terrace."

The view turned out to be one of the most beautiful sights Sadie had ever seen. The unique shape of the pool, the bright yellow umbrellas, the bright pink shrubbery that gave way to the white sand beach and azure ocean below all came together to create a stunning sight.

"That's Hulopoʻe Beach below," Pua said, "and you can't see it from here, but the golf course is over there." Pua pointed to their right, past flower gardens filled with exotic plants and waterfalls. "People come from all over the world just to play golf here. Jack Nicklaus designed it. It's called The Challenge at Manele."

"Wow, how do they keep from hitting their balls into the water?" Sadie asked as she continued to view the area through her camera lens.

"Oh, I'm sure there are a lot of balls in the ocean," Pua said, "but it's kind of hard to climb down a cliff to retrieve a golf ball."

Sadie watched as a waiter delivered umbrella drinks to a group of women sitting near the pool.

"This is the hotel where Bill Gates got married in 1994," Pua continued. "He rented the entire island, every room on Lānaʻi. Can you believe that?"

Sadie shook her head. "Wow, not really."

"Hurry," Pua said, "get your pictures. Time's up."

Sadie clicked her camera as fast as she could before Pua pulled her away and guided her back through the hotel to the van, where a grinning Makani stood tapping his foot and pointing at his watch.

The two women quickly climbed into the empty van.

"Are my *manapuas* still safe, Makani?" Pua teased.

"Safe for now," he said. "Let's go."

With that statement, Makani nosed the van out of the hotel driveway and back onto the paved road leading away from Manele Bay. Sadie watched from her window as the vehicle moved around first one curve and then another, switchbacks that continued to climb higher and higher. She could see the ocean in the distance and the hotel they had just left grow smaller behind them.

After only a few minutes, they reached the top of a plateau. Makani turned right at a T intersection, onto a road lined on both sides with giant Norfolk pines. Beyond the pines, there was nothing but vacant land.

"All of this used to be pineapple fields," said Pua. "Lānaʻi is known as 'The Pineapple Island.' Tutu worked for Dole until they shut down. Makani, we'll get off at the Blue Ginger."

Makani nodded to her in the mirror.

Pua turned to Sadie. "We're almost there," she said. "Lānaʻi City is only a couple more miles. Tutu lives in town. We'll check at her favorite café first, and if she's not there, we can walk on over to her house."

Lānaʻi City turned out to be a small community filled with petite, colorful wooden homes and not a single stoplight. Dole Park, full of more giant Norfolks, sat in the middle of town, surrounded on three sides by local businesses—gift shops, cafés, a post office, and a bank. The Blue Ginger was a café, painted bright blue, of course.

The folks inside the Blue Ginger welcomed Pua like a long-lost family member, offering hugs and food. Tutu had not been there that morning, according to the teenager behind the counter, so after introducing Sadie to everyone and spending a few customary minutes to visit, the two women left for their next stop—Tutu's house.

Sadie and Pua took Ilima Street, the side street next to the Blue Ginger that looked more like an alley than a city street, and walked two and a half short blocks. Suddenly Pua gasped, dropped her bag of pastries, and ran toward a pink frame home. A tall ironwood tree had fallen onto the house, leaving the front window shattered and the front door blocked. Sadie ran with Pua to the back of the house, where they found the back door standing wide open.

"Tutu! Are you okay?" Pua called out to her mother as they entered the empty house. After searching every room with no success, they returned to the back porch.

"I can't believe no one at the Blue Ginger said anything about this," Pua said. "Surely someone would have known."

"Do you have any idea where your mother would have gone?" Sadie asked.

Pua thought for a moment. "I'm not sure. Maybe the senior center. Let's go."

After retrieving the pastries and stowing them inside Tutu's kitchen, the two women walked with urgency back toward the town square.

They returned to the Blue Ginger, then turned right on the sidewalk and walked to the end of the block. The senior center turned out to be no larger than anything else in town. The door to the center was locked and the building appeared to be deserted. Pua turned and looked across the street. "Let's try the church," she said.

When they got closer to the Lāna'i Union Church, they could hear the unmistakable sound of a ukulele and someone singing.

Pua laughed. "I'd know that voice anywhere. We've found her."

They entered a side door into what appeared to be a fellowship hall and found Tutu sitting on a folding chair, strumming her ukulele, singing and shouting commands to five gray-haired ladies as they danced hula together. Tutu stood and placed her instrument on her chair.

"Please ladies," she said, "watch me." Tutu's slender hips swayed and her arms moved gracefully above her head as she showed the women the correct moves.

Pua clapped for her performance and the old woman let out a shout. "Ah, come, come. Show them how it's done, Pua."

Pua stood in place and copied her mother's moves to the delight of everyone. Sadie stood in awe at Pua's graceful movement.

"That's it for today, ladies." Tutu's voice was strong. "Same time, same place, next week."

The women gathered their things and left as Pua and Sadie made their way over to Tutu. Tutu embraced Pua and kissed her cheek.

"Are you okay?" Pua couldn't hide the concern in her voice. "The ironwood tree made a hole in your house."

"I'm fine. You should have called," Tutu said. "What on earth are you doing here? Aren't you working?"

"The phones are out of service because of the earthquake. How else would I know if you were okay?"

"That's silly. I've lived through more earthquakes than you'll ever know. I've been trying to get rid of that tree for years. Just hacked on it in the wrong place, I guess. Someone's coming tomorrow to fix everything up."

"You tried to cut down an ironwood tree?" Pua sounded angry. "Why didn't you tell me? We could have made arrangements and had it removed."

The elderly woman turned her attention to Sadie. "Aren't you going to introduce your friend?"

"This is Sadie Walela. She's one of our new travel agents from Oklahoma. I asked her if she wanted to come along today because she's doing some research on one of her relatives who was stationed in the islands during World War II. We thought you might be willing to share what it was like on Maui during the war."

Sadie moved forward to shake her hand, but the woman ignored her gesture and instead gave her a hug and kissed her on the cheek.

"What was your relative's name, dear?" she asked.

"Andy Walela."

"Was he Hawaiian?" Tutu asked.

"Oh, no. Cherokee. Walela is a Cherokee name."

Tutu's eyes sparkled. "Cherokee? Really?"

To their surprise, Pua's cell phone rang. She dug in her purse, turned her back to the others, and answered. Her voice sounded like a mother calming a daughter. "I'll be home this evening, honey. We'll talk then. Yes, Tutu's fine. I will. Love you, too."

"Is everything okay?" Tutu sounded concerned.

"Usi sends her love."

Tutu smiled and nodded.

"And," Pua continued, "the good news is that phone service is working on all the islands now." Pua turned to Sadie. "I can help you change your flight if you still want to do that."

Sadie nodded. "I need to get back home as soon as possible."

"I'll work on it while you visit with Tutu." Pua handed her phone to Sadie. "Do you want to call your friend in Oklahoma and let him know you're okay?"

"Oh, yes. Thank you." Sadie walked away and dialed Lance's number. After a few seconds, she returned Pua's phone to her. "Thanks. No answer," she said.

"Come on," Tutu interrupted. "Let's go to the house. I'll make you something to eat and we can talk before you have to catch the ferry." Tutu moved toward the door, and then turned. "You didn't happen to bring dessert, did you?"

Chapter 19

Cynthia Tanner didn't want to go back into the trailer. It would never be the same knowing what had happened to Benny there. How could she ever sleep in the same bed where his life had been snuffed out by some deranged person? Then a scary thought occurred to her—what was stopping that same person from coming back and doing the same thing to her? She didn't know where she would go, but it would have to be somewhere she could start over. It wouldn't take long to stuff everything she owned into a few boxes. If she had to, she'd live in her car for a while.

She'd lost both Tomas and Benny in one short morning. The craziness of it all engulfed her. As her thoughts wandered to Benny, she realized she knew very little about him. It was by choice, and now she wondered why. She'd always thought the less she knew the better off she was. Now she felt the loss of a man she didn't even know and wondered why it hurt so badly.

She thought about the unknown person, or persons, Benny had been mailing letters to regularly, wondered who they were, and what their reaction would be when the letters stopped coming. Cynthia was glad they would never know about her, about the tumultuous life she and Benny had lived, hoping they would never know how he'd died. She didn't want anyone to know that she was the reason he'd lost his life.

Cynthia wiped her nose with the back of her hand, went inside, and began to throw clothes and shoes into boxes. Everything should fit in the trunk of the car. There wasn't that much to take.

She still had the groceries she'd bought the day before, except for the chicken legs she'd finally tossed into the dumpster behind the grocery store when they began to smell. She would gather as many nonperishables as she could, leaving the food in the refrigerator behind. Climbing on a kitchen chair, she reached on top of the refrigerator, scooped up the plastic bags of morel mushrooms, and tossed them into her box. One bag was missing, and she lamented the thought that it had probably fallen behind the refrigerator, but there wasn't time to worry about a couple of mushrooms. The old woman who managed the trailer park could have everything else.

Once she had packed her things and loaded the car, she returned for one last check. She shrugged her shoulders and walked out of the trailer for the last time.

✣

When Lance and Charlie arrived where the abandoned runaway truck had been found, the only thing left was a badly scarred tree and two young officers walking around carrying large plastic bags.

Charlie got out of the car and chuckled. "How're you boys coming along with roadside trash detail?"

Lance winced at Charlie's comment as he rolled out of his side of the vehicle, hoping the other officers appreciated Charlie's humor as much as he did.

"That's about all we've got is trash," commented the youngest looking of the two as he used his forearm to wipe sweat out of his eyes. "As you already know, we can tell that the driver escaped from the passenger's side of the vehicle and, based on the way the grass was beat down, made a beeline to the creek. But that's all we can find. He must have walked in the creek bed for quite a ways before moving back onto land again. And we can't find where that was. Sarge says if we don't find anything by noon, that's it."

"I thought you found something interesting. None of this sounds too interesting to me," quipped Charlie.

"No, sir. It doesn't. The only thing we've found so far is this baseball glove." He walked over to his car, popped the trunk, and held up a leather baseball glove encased in one of the large plastic bags. "It's pretty dirty and looks like it belongs to a kid. I don't think it has a thing to do with this runner we're looking for, and Sarge says I can have it if you don't want it for evidence."

"Let me see that," said Lance, reaching for the glove. "Where'd you find it?"

"South of here." The young man pointed with his head. "It was in the ditch halfway between the road and the fence line."

"I think I'd have to agree with you, young man." Charlie sounded disgusted. "It's highly unlikely it flew out the window of a crashing vehicle and traveled that far."

"Agreed," Lance said, nodding his head. "A more likely explanation would be the town park that's not far from here. The Little League and junior high teams play ball there all summer, and this glove looks like it used to belong to a kid. No telling how they lost it." Lance turned the glove over in his hands and then passed it back to the officer. "I know from experience that it's virtually impossible to get any fingerprints off of leather unless you can see them, and I don't see any blood on it. Besides," he said, "it looks kind of girly. Someone drew roses on it with a red ink pen."

The young officer nodded in agreement.

"I'd say the evidence question would be up to you and your supervisor," Charlie said. "What other trash have you come across?"

Lance and Charlie followed the young officer over to the trunk of his car and began to inspect several clear plastic bags that held an array of items, including discarded drug paraphernalia, beer bottles, soda cans, cigarette butts, paper cups, fast food restaurant sacks, a condom, and one child's tennis shoe, all of which Lance assumed had been pitched out of various vehicles as they sped by.

"Thanks, son," Charlie said, and walked off.

Lance climbed back into Charlie's cruiser, and together the two men headed south.

"That was a waste of time," Charlie muttered.

The conversation between the two men waned, and Lance became lost in his own thoughts as they drove back to Sycamore Springs. He began to worry about Sadie; he didn't know what to do. He didn't want to overreact, but he felt like he needed to do something. How could he protect the woman he loved, if he couldn't even talk to her?

Finally Charlie spoke, bringing Lance back to the present. "You ever play baseball, Lance?"

"Of course." Lance grinned. "Best short stop in Delaware County. Everybody plays baseball."

"Not me," Charlie said. "Just wondering if your man Buck Skinner ever did."

"During the war." Lance scrutinized every passing car as if it carried someone he was looking for. "He played baseball during the war."

Charlie maneuvered a right turn to the Waffle House where Lance had left his truck. "Oh, yeah? How on earth would you know that?"

"He wrote about it in a letter he sent home to his mother." Lance began to tell Charlie about the letters he'd found in the dilapidated house on Buck's property.

"Damn, Lance. Your stint in Liberty turning you into a thief?"

"I'll give them back to him when he finally turns up. Or, I guess I should say if he turns up. If not, then I'll give them to his niece. She showed up from California, you know. I don't know much about Buck, but she's not exactly what I expected." Lance pulled out his cell phone, looked at it, and let out a grunt. "Women. They drive me crazy."

"Ah, ain't love grand?" Charlie said, as he parked next to Lance's truck.

Lance got out and slammed the car door without saying a word.

✛

Charlie parked his cruiser in front of the main door of the Sycamore Springs branch of First Merc State Bank, and although he often used this branch to transact personal business, memories of the deadly bank robbery always seemed to lurk in the back of his mind. He sat for a moment, scrutinizing every car and person in sight, before getting out and lumbering into the building.

After the teller counted out his cash, he secured it in his money clip and shoved it in his pocket as he headed for the door. The manager appeared out of nowhere with a worried look on her face.

"Mr. McCord, do you have a moment?"

"Yes, of course." Charlie nodded and followed her into her office.

She closed the door behind them and Charlie remained standing. The nameplate on her desk read "Melanie Thompson."

"Is everything all right, Ms. Thompson?" Charlie couldn't decide if bank managers were getting younger or he was just getting older. This woman couldn't have been a day over twenty-five years old, he thought, and what would she do if she suddenly encountered a murdering thief the way Sadie had? He decided not to bring it up. "What can I do for you?"

"I know you're a regular customer," she said, "and I thought you should be aware of the bomb threat we got in the mail, you being a police officer and all."

Charlie nodded as she spoke. "Yes, ma'am. I'm aware that you received a letter and I understand the bomb squad has already been here and determined that the building was clear."

"Yes, yes. That's true. They took the letter, said they'd give it to the FBI, but I kept a copy for myself, and I'd like for you to see it." The manager opened her top drawer, pulled out a sheet of paper, and handed it to him. Charlie read silently to himself.

God tells you what to do. He even tells you exactly how to do it. Figure it out by Friday or the place will be destroyed.

The note had been handwritten in childlike print. "Do you have a copy of the envelope as well?"

"No, but it was postmarked in Sycamore Springs on last Friday."

Charlie chewed on the inside of his cheek and thought for a moment before handing the paper back to Melanie. "Can you make a copy of this for me?"

Melanie nodded, placed the paper in a nearby copy machine, and hit a green button. When the machine spit out the copy, she handed it to Charlie. Her hands were shaking.

"You know, Ms. Thompson, it doesn't exactly say anything about a bomb."

"What else could it mean?" Fear crossed her face and her voice rose in pitch.

"Well, it could mean anything, I guess." Charlie folded the note and put it in his shirt pocket. "I'm sure they've already asked you this," he said, "but do you have any idea who might've sent this to you, ma'am?"

"No. Not really. Almost every customer we have is mad about something or another these days, especially since the new management implemented higher fees on everything you can think of. I wish they had to listen to these whiny customers all the time the way I do and maybe they'd do things differently." She plopped into her chair and shoved the copy of the note back into her desk, and then slammed the drawer shut.

"Don't worry." Charlie tried to sound reassuring. "I'll check with the officer in charge. I'm sure they already have someone watching the bank, and I'll drop by myself on Thursday night and Friday morning. Most of the time, people are all talk. They rarely follow through on threats like this. Whoever sent this letter has probably already cooled off by now."

"Well, if that's the case, they owe me an apology." Anger swelled in her voice. Her smile appeared forced.

"I doubt they're going to do that, since making a threat like this is a federal offense, regardless of whether they do anything or not, and they probably know that. Heck, I bet they wished they had that letter back as soon as they dropped it in the mailbox." Charlie pulled a business card out of his pocket and handed it to her. "This is my direct number. I can usually get here pretty fast. Just give me a call if you see anything out of the ordinary or anybody acting suspicious. Okay?" He gave her a fatherly pat on the shoulder, checked the lobby, and left.

Chapter 20

Sadie and Pua sat on wooden chairs in the shade of a giant mango tree in Tutu's backyard, drinking mint-flavored iced tea, nibbling first on fish and rice and then on Home Maid Bakery pastries, listening to Tutu talk about the hardships of living on Maui during the war. Pua looked surprised when her mother opened up so easily to a complete stranger, revealing secrets Sadie imagined she must have been holding in her heart for many years. It was like watching the pain flow freely from an excised sore. The longer she spoke, the stronger her voice became.

Pua listened silently, as if she were afraid a whispered word might break her mother's train of thought. Sadie absorbed every word.

"It was hell," Tutu said. "When the Japanese bombed Pearl Harbor in 1941, we lived in fear they would do the same thing to us on Maui. A week later, they tried. A Japanese submarine fired ten or so shells into Kahului Harbor. Half of them didn't even go off, a couple hit the pineapple cannery, and a couple fell into the harbor. I think the only casualty was a chicken." Tutu clapped her hands together and laughed, and then became quiet again. "It sounds funny now, but we lived close to the beach and after that attack we were afraid. We moved further inland.

"About two weeks after that, I think it was on New Year's Eve, another submarine tried the same thing, but we had Navy men here by then and they returned fire and scared them off." She grinned. "I guess they learned their lesson because they never came back after that.

"About three months later, we had over thirty thousand army and air force troops. They came in and took over the island, which was all right with me because it made us feel safer from a Japanese invasion." Tutu stopped for a moment and sipped tea. "And sure enough, in May or June in 1942 the rumor was that they intended to invade the whole state, but then the U.S. stopped them at Midway." Tutu lowered her eyes. "I heard that was an awful battle."

The mynah birds called to each other in the tree above the three women as they sat in silence. Finally Tutu continued.

"We couldn't go anywhere at night because no lights were allowed. It was too hard to see to get around. We couldn't even drive cars with the headlights on. We covered our windows so not one bit of light escaped or the military men would come to our doors and threaten us. I did my homework with a flashlight under the sheets on my bed.

"We couldn't go to the beach because the military men had put barbed wire all along the shore, and we couldn't go anywhere without special identification and a gas mask. We had food ration cards and gas ration cards. For years, it was as if the whole island was one big prison.

"The Marines came in February of 1944." Tutu's face brightened momentarily. "That's when I met Pua's father," she said, and then became silent. She shifted in her chair and took another sip of iced tea.

"How old were you?" Sadie finally asked.

"I was a teenager, seventeen. I met Pua's father right after my father joined the army and was shipped off to Europe to fight with the 442. My father was killed in Germany, you know." Tutu looked at Pua and smiled. "He died in 1944, but I received the best gift of my life the same year." She patted Pua's knee. "I'm thankful for my baby girl. I was so distraught when I heard her father, my Ohia, had been killed, I almost took my life. But her presence inside my belly stopped me. I could have taken my life, but not hers."

With tears in her voice, Pua said the words to her mother she'd apparently wanted to say her entire life. "Please tell me about my father."

"He was a handsome and brave soldier, a Cherokee warrior, and he was strong as a tree." She smiled. "I called him my Ohia."

"Ohia?" Sadie asked.

Tutu ignored Sadie's question and continued.

"We had been in a car accident in Kahului, another girl and me, and out of nowhere came these two American boys. They stayed with us and helped get us to the hospital. My friend died and I was in the hospital for a week. It was horrible." She looked into the distance before she continued. "I couldn't understand why I survived and she didn't. It didn't seem fair." The sadness faded from her voice. "Then out of nowhere, there he was again. He showed up at my hospital room with a bouquet of flowers he'd picked along the road. The next thing I knew, we were in love.

"He was stationed with the others at Kokomo. Marines. They had these little tents on the ground, in perfect rows, as far as you could see. The men would train almost every day, but some days they could leave the camp. That's when we would sneak away to our special place, a place near the north shore where, hidden in the tall grass high above the cliffs where no one could see or hear us, we would make love as if there was no tomorrow. And then one day, tomorrow never came."

Pua winced and squirmed in her seat. Tutu stared at the ground and paused as if calculating what she would say next.

"He would never tell me when they were going into battle. I'm not sure he even knew." She shook her head. "Then one day he was gone."

"A few weeks later I went to our secret place where I could watch for the ships to come into Kahului Harbor and dock. I thought he and the other boys would be on one of them. I knew the boats were coming in that day because two of the men from the camp had come into the USO the night before and told me so."

Tutu smiled and talked with her hands. "I danced hula at the USO shows. It made me feel good because all of the boys clapped and whistled when our hālau performed. I don't think they understood we were telling a story with our hands. They just wanted to watch us move our hips. But it made us happy, anyway."

"I saw two boys with the same emblems on their uniforms that he had on his, so I asked them if they knew him and when he would be back from the war. They said they didn't know him personally because they had just arrived from the States, but they knew about the battle that was raging in the ocean somewhere between Hawai'i and Japan. They wouldn't tell me exactly where he'd gone, but they said it had been a terrible battle. They said thousands of our men had died. What they told me scared me, but I was young and never dreamed that he wouldn't return to me.

"I spent that morning making lei for us. I gathered flowers from the plumeria trees in our front yard and picked ti leaves from down the street. The plumeria flowers were beautiful—huge, white, perfect blossoms with yellow centers. I put the flowers and the ti leaves in a sack and carried them to the place where I planned to watch for the ship. When I got there I found a shady place under a monkeypod tree where I sat on the grass and began to thread the blossoms together on strings. Then I tore the ti leaves into strips and began to weave them together. I thought the plumeria was too girlish for a man without weaving in some ti leaves. I made a regular lei for him and a *haku* lei for me." She gently touched the top of her head with both hands and looked at Sadie. "A *haku* lei is a head lei," she explained, and then continued.

"The intoxicating fragrance of the plumeria blooms matched my spirits. I was so happy. I could hardly wait to tell him the news. He didn't know that I was expecting our child. I was scared to tell him, but I hoped he would be just as excited as I was.

"Just as I finished tying the last lei, I could see the boats approaching the harbor. My heart pounded in my chest. I put on the *haku* lei and then found a place so I could watch every man get off of each boat. There were so many men it was impossible to see him. Some of them took off walking and others climbed onto trucks that would carry them back to camp.

"I raced to the road and stood there watching as the trucks flew by. I knew if he was on one of them, he would make the driver slow down when he saw me so he could jump off. I waited for all the trucks to pass, but not one slowed down.

"When the last truck rumbled by, my heart sank. The only thing I could think of to do was to walk to Giggle Hill."

"Giggle Hill?" Sadie asked.

Tutu smiled. "That's what the local folks called the camp. It was located at the bottom of a large hill that the men used for jungle training. But at night, a lot of girls would meet their boyfriends at the bottom of the hill and, as the story goes, you could hear the girls giggling for miles."

Tutu laughed and Sadie smiled.

"So, I gathered my things and started walking toward Giggle Hill. Before long, a truck full of cane-field workers came by and offered me a ride. I just had to see him, no matter how long it took. I had to tell him the good news about the baby.

"By the time I reached the camp, the trucks had unloaded and the men had disappeared. I waited at the gate until I saw someone who looked familiar and then called out to him. I asked him if he could help me find him.

"The man was a tall and sturdy fellow. I don't know what he thought about me. My plumeria blossoms were wilted by then. I must have looked like a mess. He said, 'What can I do for you, little lady?' Then he winked at me and said his name was Roy something or other and wanted to know mine.

"I pleaded with him to help me find my man. I told him he had been away at war and would have been on the ship that just came in, but I didn't see him get off the boat. He mocked my speech and laughed. Then he told me if my 'man' didn't get off the boat, then that meant he wasn't there at the camp either. And furthermore, he wasn't ever going to be there. He spoke with anger, telling me how many men had died at Saipan. He called it a godforsaken island in the middle of nowhere. Then he said if he didn't make the boat, then it was his guess that he was still on that island. Dead."

Tutu raised her left hand to her forehead. Tears fell off Pua's cheek.

"Suddenly, I felt weak all over and I thought I was going to faint," she continued. "I sat on the ground. My heart was pounding and my head was spinning."

She moved her hands together and rested them on her chest.

"The man offered to get a Jeep and drive me home, but my world was such a blur, I just ran. I dropped my things and ran as hard and far as I could before I stopped and vomited in the pineapple field. Then I guess I just walked."

She dropped her hands to her sides.

"I was in a daze when I reached Ho'okipa. That's where the waves sometimes reach fifteen or twenty feet high. It was as if I was under a spell, or in a trance."

Tutu stared at the ground and her voice sounded as if she had returned to that same trance.

"I climbed down from above to where the huge black boulders were wet from the high surf. I stood on the edge of the rocks and turned my back to the water." She looked directly at Sadie. "I broke the number one rule of the ocean. My father taught me when I was a small child that one should never turn their back on the ocean, for to do so would show disrespect for the power of the surf, and the ocean would knock you down and gobble you up."

Tutu's voice regained its strength.

"The ocean has a rhythm all its own," she explained. "If you count the waves, you will discover that the waves come in sets. There will be several small waves and then there will be a big wave. Since the rocks where I stood were wet, I knew that the big waves had been hitting there. I didn't care. I stood there anyway with my back to the water, arms outstretched, and waited for the next big wave to take me, to wash me away.

"Then, as if sensing danger, the life inside me cried out. I rubbed my belly and wept. Suddenly, the numbness turned into a hot, aching pain in my chest. If I let the ocean take me to its depths, I would be killing the only thing I had left of him—his child. I stepped quickly and climbed out of the ocean's reach only seconds before the waves crashed against the rocks. I fell to my knees and wept. I was exhausted. I didn't wake up until the next morning."

Tutu stopped speaking and slumped in her chair, as if the story she'd just related had drained her of her spirit. Then the silence began to fill with the sounds of the island. A skylark landed and picked at the ground. A car traveled down the street. Children's playful laughter floated in the air from a nearby yard. Pua wiped tears from her face and took another sip of tea. She appeared to be gathering courage to speak, but remained quiet.

After a few moments, Sadie spoke. "Tutu, you said Pua's father was Cherokee. What did you say his name was?"

She looked down at her hands. "He was my Ohia, my Peniamina. He—"

Suddenly, the sound of a vehicle's blaring horn pierced the air. Pua looked at her watch and gasped. "Oh, no! It's Makani. We've got to go or we'll miss the last ferry." She quickly kissed her mother on the cheek. "I love you," she said. "I'll call you." Then she grabbed her purse and ran to the street. "Hurry, Sadie. I'll hold the van for you."

Realizing she had learned more about life during the war in the islands than any book at the library could possibly tell her, Sadie took Tutu's hands and looked into her eyes.

"Thank you," she said. "I can't tell you how much meeting you and hearing your story has meant to me."

"No. I am the one who is thankful to you," she said. "I've needed to tell that story for a very long time. It's just that no one ever asked me to tell it until now. Mahalo." She rose and kissed Sadie on the cheek, then pushed her away. "Go. You'll miss your boat."

Chapter 21

Sadie found her seat on the airplane, pushed her carry-on into the compartment above her head, and settled in next to the window. She was exhausted. She looked out the window at the nearby palm trees and the distant mountains as she thought about the day's events.

On the ferry ride back to Maui from Lānaʻi, Pua had made nonstop calls until she had rescheduled Sadie's flight back to Oklahoma. That left Sadie with only a few hours to pack and say her good-byes to the people she had met before rushing to catch the red-eye flight back to the mainland.

Pua saved precious minutes by helping Sadie return her rental car and then navigate the crowded airport. Using Pua's cell phone, Sadie called Lance and, just as she had been forced to do for the last three days, left him a message. This would be her last chance to call before arriving in Tulsa, she told him. She repeated her flight number and arrival time to him three times.

As her place in line approached the security checkpoint, Sadie turned and hugged Pua. "Thank you for everything," she said.

Pua pulled a lei out of her straw bag and placed it around Sadie's neck. "Come back soon," Pua said, "and next time, bring your fellow with you. There's so much you didn't have time to see. We will go back and visit Tutu Lehua. I think she liked you a lot."

"Thank you," she said. "I'll call you when I get to the office. Give me a day or so."

Sadie turned and placed her items on the conveyor belt and walked through the metal detector toward the escalator that would take her to her gate. Turning back, she saw Pua blow her a kiss. Sadie waved, blinking back tears. How could she become so attached to a place and people in such a short period of time? Then she remembered her grandfather's words. They call it the aloha spirit, he had said. She finally understood.

Once the plane was in the air, Sadie settled in and began to replay in her mind the events of the last few days. Losing touch with Lance unnerved her. She missed hearing his voice and longed to feel his arms around her. She continued to worry about Buck. Managing a smile, she thought surely he was home by now. He'd probably been out visiting friends or looking for horses. There were endless possibilities to explain his absence. At any rate, she felt better knowing she would be home by noon tomorrow in case she needed to help with the search.

Her thoughts turned to Pua and her mother. Visiting Lāna'i had turned out to be the best part of the trip. Learning about Tutu's life during the war and the loss of her lover, Pua's father, tugged at Sadie's heart. She couldn't begin to imagine how painful it would be to lose Lance like that.

She wished she could have learned more about Pua's father. Ohia seemed to be a nickname, and she thought it sounded Hawaiian. She tried to remember what Tutu had said his real name was, but she couldn't. She knew it didn't sound like a Cherokee name, even though Tutu had insisted he had been a Cherokee man. "Why does everyone want to be a Cherokee?" she muttered.

Everywhere she went, people, upon learning she was Cherokee, would launch into some story about a long-lost relative being Cherokee. When she would ask about tribal citizenship, they would always have some reason why none of their ancestors were on the rolls. In the end, none of them had proof of Cherokee blood, just something their great-great-whatever had told them. Everyone wants to belong to a tribe, even though they aren't Indian, she thought. At that rate, practically everyone alive would be Cherokee. The nonsense annoyed her.

Before long, the flight attendant dimmed the lights in the cabin for the movie. Sadie gave in to exhaustion and fell into a deep sleep. She dreamed first of hula dancers and soldiers at war, then she dreamed of her home, her horse, her wolf-dog, and then she dreamed about falling into the arms of the man she so dearly loved.

✤

Lance decided to drive by the baseball park to see if he could find any players who might be missing a glove. Finding the owner of the glove found near the wrecked runaway truck was a long shot, he thought, but then again, maybe he'd get lucky.

As he turned off the highway, he could see several cars parked near one of the baseball diamonds. He would start there.

Zeroing in on a man unloading baseball gear from the back of his SUV, Lance parked behind the man's vehicle, got out, and introduced himself. The man identified himself as Chet Turner, the coach for the Sycamore Slammers, a coed Legion League team.

"You mean you have girls playing on a boys' baseball team?" Lance sounded surprised.

"You take what you can get around here," Chet said. "It's hard to get kids interested in baseball these days. Most of them are off doing other things in the summer—going to summer school or working, or drinking and getting into trouble." Chet shook his head. "You'd be surprised. Some of the girls can play better than the boys."

"Really?"

Chet returned his attention to unloading his vehicle. "I've got a dandy pitcher and she's all female."

Lance grabbed a couple of bats and a catcher's mask and followed the coach into the enclosed bench area.

"Just stack them over there," said Chet, as he dropped three baseball gloves next to the bats.

"Do you supply gloves for the players?" Lance asked.

"Sometimes," he said. "Most of the kids have their own, but there's a few who can't afford a decent glove, and there's some who can never find their own."

"Anyone lose a glove lately?"

"Not that I know of. Why?"

"We found one today about five miles north of here, near the scene of an accident."

"Accident? Anyone get hurt?"

"No, they left the scene. Just doing a little follow-up."

Chet rubbed his chin. "Could be anybody's, I guess. I'll be glad to ask around when the kids get here."

Lance retrieved a business card from his billfold and handed it to the coach. "If you come up with any information, could you give me a call? Then I can get the glove to the rightful owner, provided they can describe an identifying mark on it."

Chet took the card and shook Lance's hand. "Will do," he said as a car full of teenagers parked nearby and the occupants swarmed onto the baseball diamond.

Lance climbed back into his car and frowned. "Girls are not supposed to play baseball with boys," he grumbled.

He knew girls could be just as tough as boys, but he hated the thought that they might get hurt playing ball with boys who weren't smart enough to know their own strength. The thought of Sadie being elbowed by some catcher as she tried to score caused him to cringe. He'd met plenty of strong women throughout his life; Sadie was one of the strongest. But at the same time, she was the classiest lady he'd ever known. The rare combination of beauty and strength was what he loved about her.

As he drove into the city limits of Sycamore Springs, his cell phone beeped, signaling that he had a voice mail he'd missed while out of the service area. He pulled it out of his pocket and flipped it open. The name and number were both unfamiliar. He'd wait and return the call as soon as he made it back to Sadie's house. He wanted to check on Sadie's dog one more time before heading home to Liberty. He needed a good night's rest.

The landscape disappeared from Lance's mind as he drove toward Sadie's house. In a few more days she would be home and he could rest easier, but not before she answered some questions. Who did the keys he'd found belong to? Who was this mysterious man who'd sent an e-mail saying she was all right? Did she meet someone there? Why couldn't she keep calling until they made contact instead of only leaving messages? As Lance drove past Buck Skinner's house, he noticed the black Cadillac parked in the front yard and curiosity overrode his better judgment. He pulled in and parked behind the car, then walked to the front door and knocked on the edge of the screen door. Dee Dee appeared a few seconds later in short shorts and a skimpy tank top, drying her hands on a dish towel.

"Mr. Smith," she said, "what a nice surprise. Won't you come in?"

"No, thanks. I was just driving by and wondered if you'd heard anything from your uncle."

She pushed the screen door open and walked onto the front porch. "No, and quite frankly I don't expect to."

Lance frowned. "Oh, really? Why is that?"

"He always said when it was his time to go he planned to just walk off into the woods and die, and I think that's exactly what he did." She pushed her hair behind her shoulders. "And, just to irritate me, he never wrote his will like I asked him to, or if he did I can't find it. Now the IRS is breathing down my neck. Another letter came in the mail today . . . well, no need to go into details. I'll get it all straightened out in the next few days. I'm due back in San Diego by the end of the week." She stepped closer to him. "Are you sure you wouldn't like to come in? I just made a pitcher of iced tea."

Lance stepped backward and almost fell off the edge of the porch. "Better not," he said. "Got to check on a lost dog and . . . well, I'd better get going. Thanks for the information."

He walked quickly to his truck and drove to Sadie's house, feeling like a fly that had barely escaped the sticky web of a lethal spider.

❖

Buck's memory began to return, but only in disjointed pieces, like a puzzle that refused to make a complete picture. Nothing made any sense. He remembered splashing cold springwater in his face and walking through the woods, but that was about all. It was as if he'd been plucked from one dimension and dropped into another.

How long had he been in this sinkhole? Two days, maybe three, he thought. His supply of venison jerky was about gone, and even though his string and handkerchief still held together well enough to dampen his face, he knew he was extremely dehydrated. Lack of water, he thought, would be his demise. He could hear the stream just out of reach below, so near yet too far away to access the life-sustaining water he so desperately needed.

His present-day memories began to mingle with dreams of his past. He closed his eyes, and the red flower returned. He climbed, stretched as far as he could, but it remained out of reach.

Suddenly, the pumping of adrenaline in the heat of battle, men maimed and dying, screaming for their mothers, the deafening sounds of bombs exploding and bullets ripping through the air, good guys and bad guys—after a while it all became a blur. He began to get angry. Why couldn't he get that blasted war out of his head? Pain shot throughout his leg.

He relaxed and gave in to the ache until a feeling of peacefulness surrounded him with comfort. This is it, he thought. He prayed the Creator would be merciful and take him soon, and then he began to sing "One Drop of Blood," a Cherokee song his mother had taught him as a youngster, a song his ancestors had sung over a hundred years before on the Trail of Tears.

Ga do da jv ya dv hne li ji sa
O ga je li ja gv wi yu hi
O ga li ga li na hna gwu ye hno
Jo gi lv hwi sda ne di yi
Ga do da jv wa dv hne li ji sa
O ga je li ja gv wi yu hi
O ga li ga li na hna gwu ye hno
Jo gi lv hwi sda ne di yi

Chapter 22

Lance stopped at Sadie's mailbox and retrieved her mail before continuing up the lane to her house. He parked behind her Explorer, got out, and whistled for Sonny. There was no sign of the wolf-dog. Joe, her paint stallion, whinnied and began to walk toward the barn. "At least I'm not invisible to the horse," he muttered. He met Joe at the gate and stroked his neck. "Don't worry, big fellow, she'll be home soon." Joe nickered and walked away.

Lance let himself into Sadie's house through the kitchen door and dropped her mail on the table. He pulled out his cell phone, punched in the code for his voice mail, and listened. Sadie's voice caused his heart to jump. He looked at his watch. She was already in the air and on her way home. He popped his phone shut and shoved it into his pocket. Why was she calling him from an unfamiliar number? He would be glad when she got home and everything got back to normal—if that was possible. He opened her freezer and pulled out a piece of venison and dropped it by the back porch. Maybe he could lure Sonny back home with food. If not, Sadie was going to be one unhappy lady when she got here.

He left Sadie's house and returned home to Liberty, where he tried to get a good night's rest. Unfortunately, his mind wouldn't cooperate. After a few restless hours he cleaned up, downed a greasy breakfast of Spam and eggs, and then climbed back into his truck and headed for the Tulsa airport to pick up Sadie.

The mind-numbing drive up the Muskogee Turnpike invited an endless circle of thoughts. Sadie had been gone only four days, but it seemed like a month. Even after she'd protested, he'd promised to check on her house and animals while she was gone. Not necessary, she'd said, everything would be fine for only five days. But his macho, overprotective genes had kicked in and he'd gone anyway. What had that accomplished? Now he was caught up in the middle of a mess.

An old man was missing, accused of murdering an identity thief who had turned out to also be a jealous lover who, right before being murdered himself, had "gutted a man like a chicken." The killer had sneaked away undetected and escaped in a truck registered in the name of either the missing man or the identity thief, and it was hard to know which, since they were both using the same name. After crashing headlong into a very sturdy tree, the killer had escaped into the woods without a trace, which meant the culprit was either very savvy or incredibly lucky.

Charlie had already pinned the second murder on Sadie's missing neighbor. Losing one's beloved land to the IRS was motive enough, according to Charlie, but it didn't ring true to Lance.

Lance didn't know much about Buck, and he hadn't had time to read all the letters he'd found in the abandoned house on Buck's property, but the few he had read reflected a brave man who loved his family and the men he'd fought alongside, a man of character who had learned at a young age about life and death up close. While it was true that Buck had all the skills he needed to kill someone and escape without detection, and while no one knows what drives folks off the edge enough to commit murder, Lance just didn't believe Buck was a murderer. That thought led to another question—if he wasn't the murderer, then who was? And where was Buck? Either dead or dying somewhere in the oppressive Oklahoma heat, he supposed.

Lance winced at the thought and then switched to thinking about Sadie and her new adventure of becoming a travel agent. He wished she would settle down and get a regular job. Being a travel agent didn't meet his definition of "regular." Sadie meant everything to him. She'd burrowed under his skin and into his heart in a way he'd sworn he'd never let anyone do again, and now that he was willing to make a commitment to her, all these red flags kept popping up in his mind. Whose keys did he find at her house? Who had sent the e-mail? Why did she keep calling on someone else's phone? The news reports had said everything was back to normal after the earthquake, and he guessed the folks in that part of the world were used to having earthquakes all the time anyway. It couldn't have been that big of a deal. Lance squirmed in his seat as he drove through the turnpike tollgate near the edge of Tulsa. He hadn't been able to have a decent conversation with her since she left and that irritated him. Maybe he needed to back off.

Lance turned into the Tulsa airport and looked at his watch—12:33 p.m. If her flight was on time, she should be ready to go. He didn't want to have to go to the trouble of finding a place to park in the parking garage, so he followed the circular drive marked for arrivals and drove slowly, searching through the glass walls for the baggage claim area. He quickly pulled next to the curb, jumped out, and flashed his badge to a nearby security officer. "I'll just be a minute," he said, and disappeared through the sliding glass doors.

✢

Sadie smoothed her long hair with her hands and secured it at the nape of her neck with a beaded barrette, and then checked her reflection in the mirror of the tiny restroom of the plane. She looked terrible. What little makeup she'd applied that morning had disappeared hours earlier, and the dark circles under her eyes looked as if she'd been on a week-long drinking binge. She hoped Lance wouldn't notice. She couldn't wait to see him, smother him in kisses, and tell him all about her trip.

She returned to her seat and watched the trees and houses on the ground grow larger. What was she going to say, as a travel agent, when folks wanted to know how bad the flight was between Tulsa and Hawai'i? She couldn't say "awful," which was her present opinion. How would she sell any vacations to Hawai'i with that attitude? She'd have to come up with something that didn't sound quite so bad yet wasn't a blatant lie either. Maybe she could just say something like, "You can sleep on the plane. It'll be worth it." She hoped she could quickly get a handle on her new career.

The plane touched down and taxied to the gate while she and everyone else on the flight quickly grabbed their belongings and impatiently waited their turn to disembark. Excitement grew inside her as she hurried up the

Jetway and into the Tulsa airport. As she pulled her carry-on down the long corridor and then rode the escalator to the baggage claim, she searched for Lance, but couldn't see him anywhere. She parked her bag by the rumbling carousel and checked her watch. Where was he? What if he never got her message?

She slowly exhaled as she continued to scan the crowd and watch for her checked bag at the same time. Her bag slid down the chute and wedged itself against another black bag. She smiled and thought of Lance when she saw the silver duct tape on the handle. Just as she hoisted the bag over the lip of the carousel, Lance appeared out of nowhere and grabbed it out of her hands.

"Come on," he said. "I'm parked in a no-parking zone."

Before she could say anything, he turned his back and carried her bag out the door. Sadie quickly followed him out onto the sidewalk as the automatic door slid shut behind them. Lance shook hands with the airport security guard standing next to his truck and deposited Sadie's bag into the bed of the truck. What was wrong with him? He wasn't even glad to see her, she thought. Blinking back tears, Sadie opened the passenger door and pushed her things onto the seat, climbed in, and slammed the door. It was going to be a long ride home to Eucha.

Chapter 23

By the time Lance turned his truck off the highway and was heading up the lane to Sadie's house, the tension between them had grown into a green monster. Finally, Sadie spoke angrily.

"You act like you're not even happy to see me, Lance. What's the deal?"

"Sadie, why didn't you return my phone calls? I'm here doing the best I can and you are off having a good time with who-knows-who and won't even take the time to call."

"Good grief, Lance. We had an earthquake. My phone was destroyed, which didn't really matter because all the phone systems were down. Nobody could call until later in the day, and then I did call you from Pua's phone. Besides that, I sent Maggie an e-mail. Didn't she tell you?"

"Who exactly is the guy who sent that e-mail, anyway?"

Sadie frowned. "The 'guy' was a ten-year-old boy." Her eyes grew wide. "You're jealous, aren't you? You know, I asked you to go with me and you wouldn't have any part of it, and now you're jealous because I talked to a ten-year-old kid? Give me a break." She gathered her things to make an easy exit from the truck. "Sometimes you act like a pompous, male-chauvinist pig." She quietly swallowed her angry sobs.

As soon as the truck rolled to a stop next to the house, Sadie pushed her way out of the truck. Her carry-on hit the ground behind her. Lance got out and retrieved her other bag from the bed of the truck and deposited it on her porch.

"I don't know what is wrong with you," she said, wiping a tear off her cheek with the back of her hand. "I'm gone for four days and you go bananas. I don't know who you are anymore."

Lance dug into his pocket and pitched the keys he'd found into the air toward her, letting them fall next to her feet. "Here, maybe this guy will be glad to see you."

Sonny trotted from the barn into the yard and began to dance around Sadie and bark.

"I can't believe this," Lance mumbled as he shoved his hat down on his head, got back into his truck, thrust the transmission in reverse, and almost hit a tree before tearing off.

✛

When Lance reached the road, he let the truck roll to a stop while he tried to collect his thoughts, then he spit out the open window of the vehicle as if trying to get rid of a bad taste in his mouth. Why did she make him so crazy? He couldn't remember another person in his whole entire life that affected him the way she did. How could he love her one minute and loathe her the next? It didn't seem natural.

He shifted in his seat and then turned left onto the road. Maybe Charlie would have some new information on the investigation into the double murder. That was another thing he could blame on Sadie. He wouldn't be in the middle of this investigation if he hadn't been roped into looking for her neighbor—a neighbor that was probably out chasing horses, or women, or both.

As he drove past Buck's house, Lance noticed two vehicles parked in the yard. One he'd seen earlier—the black Caddie that belonged to Buck's niece—was parked beside the house. The other, an unmistakable rental car, sat behind it. Maybe someone had brought Buck home, he thought.

Lance slowly brought his truck to a stop, backed up, and pulled off the road next to Buck's mailbox just as a middle-aged man dressed in a brown suit and carrying a briefcase emerged from the house. Buck's niece followed him onto the porch. She wore an outfit similar to the one she'd had on the last time Lance had seen her—skimpy. The brown suit man put his hand on the woman's shoulder. She smiled, and he got into his vehicle and drove off.

Lance's lawman curiosity took over. He got out of his truck and approached the woman. He stood in the yard, keeping what he deemed to be a safe distance from her.

"Say," he said, "haven't heard from your uncle, have you?"

Her smile felt phony to Lance. "Why, no, Mr. Smith," she said. "Have you?"

Lance shook his head. "No, I was just driving by and noticed you had a visitor. I thought maybe you had some news about your uncle."

"No, but if you'd like to come in we could sure talk about that."

"I'd better not." Lance tipped his hat. "But you'll be sure and give someone a call if you hear something, right?"

She smiled, crossed her arms, and leaned against the porch railing. "Yes, of course," she said.

✣

After Sadie watched Lance drive off, she dropped her purse and hugged Sonny while he licked her face with enormous, wet canine kisses. After sufficient welcoming had taken place, Sonny ran to the edge of the porch and began to chomp on a hunk of venison Sadie assumed Lance had dropped there earlier. She smiled. At least the dog was glad to see her. She gathered her things and went inside.

She sat down at the table and shuffled through her mail. Then she stared at some unknown blank place in her brain and sulked. How could everything be wonderful one minute and a complete disaster the next? Her body ached with exhaustion, but her mind churned angrily. How could he question her like that? She got up, walked over to the kitchen window, and looked toward her uncle and aunt's house. She wished they were home so she could ride over and spill her worries to them. They were rock steady, and she could always count on them for support, no matter what. But she knew they wouldn't be home for another three or four days.

She decided to get out of the house and breathe in the countryside, take Joe and Sonny and check on her uncle and aunt's house. By the time she had changed into a pair of worn jeans and an old tee shirt, and pulled on her favorite and most comfortable boots, she felt better.

As she walked from the house to the barn, she saw the keys that Lance had thrown at her on the ground. She picked them up and turned them over in her hand. She couldn't remember seeing them before and had no idea how they had come to be in her yard, and she didn't have a clue who owned them. She shoved them into her pocket and then made her way to her horse.

Joe snuffled a soft greeting as Sadie placed her cheek next to his. There was nothing like the love and the smell of a horse, she thought. Joe nuzzled her shoulder as she ran her hand down his neck and over his back. She patted his rump and headed for the barn to retrieve his saddle. It was good to be home, she thought, even if Lance was being a jerk.

With Joe saddled and ready to go, she climbed on his back and whistled. Sonny came running and the three headed into the pasture. After making sure everything was secure next door, Sadie guided Joe back into the woods toward the creek to the special place where she had played as a youngster. Two crows called to one another and three young squirrels scampered up and around a huge red oak tree, bouncing from limb to limb. The repetitive sound of Joe's hooves on the ground calmed her soul. She felt alive on his back, aware of his muscular body as it moved beneath her. Her horse, her wolf-dog, and the land came together and reenergized her like nothing else in the world possibly could.

Once they arrived at the crystal clear pool, she slid off Joe's back and let his reins fall to the ground. She walked to the pool's edge, dipped her hand in the cool water and splashed her face, and then sat on a patch of grass in the shade of a huge sycamore tree to think.

She stretched out her leg, pulled the keys from her pocket, and looked at them. Who did they belong to? Where had they come from? And how did they come to be near her back porch? The key fob looked like a faded U.S. Marine insignia, but Lance was the only Marine she could think of. Now that she thought about it, how would she even know whether someone was a Marine or not? Nothing made any sense.

Sonny waded through the creek and nosed around the other side of the pool, then lapped at the water. A gray squirrel caught his attention and he stood motionless, watching the animal scampering first up and then down the tree as if it couldn't make up its mind which way to go. The squirrel disappeared and Sonny appeared bored as he plopped down in the shade beside the pool and panted. His eyes landed on Sadie, and suddenly his ears perked up and he barked. He jumped up and ran straight to her. He sniffed at the keys in her hand, grabbed them from her, and ran into the nearby meadow. Then he stopped, turned around, and looked at Sadie.

"What's with you, Sonny?" Sadie said, irritated. "Bring those keys back to me."

The wolf-dog dropped the keys and barked, then sat on his haunches and stared anxiously at her. After a few seconds, he turned and ran a short distance into the meadow, then stopped and looked at her again.

Sadie walked to where Sonny had dropped the keys and picked them up. Suddenly, an image flashed in her mind and she remembered where she'd seen the keys before.

"Oh, no!" She ran to Joe and grabbed his reins, stuck her boot into his stirrup, and mounted. The stallion snorted as she squeezed him with her knees and reined him toward Sonny.

"Let's go, Joe." Then she yelled to the wolf-dog, "Go find him, Sonny! Go find Buck!"

Sonny jumped and barked with excitement and then took off running with tremendous speed, with Joe and Sadie following closely behind. When Sonny slithered through the fence that separated Sadie's property from Buck's, Sadie nudged Joe with her boots and the horse easily cleared the wire. Sonny led them through a valley, past an abandoned house and along the bottom of a ridge. All of a sudden, he stopped, looked down, and barked. Confused, Sadie rode up beside Sonny. "Where is he, Sonny?" Then she saw it—a sinkhole. She slid off Joe and fell first on her knees and then onto her belly, peering down into the darkness at a lifeless body.

"Buck?" she called out as Sonny stood beside her and barked. "Can you hear me? It's Sadie. Are you okay?"

Buck slowly raised his head. "It's about time," he growled. "Get me out of here."

"Okay, hold on." Sadie's mind raced. How was she going to get this old man out of his predicament? She ran to Joe and returned with a soft rope, one she always kept attached to his saddle. Carefully, she fashioned a loop at one end. "I'm going to lower a rope for you, Buck. Put it under your arms and hold on. Joe will have you out of there in no time."

Buck shook his head. "I don't think so . . . I'm pretty weak and I've got a bum knee. Can't stand up."

Sadie secured one end of the rope to Joe's saddle horn and returned to the hole to drop the loop in for Buck. She knelt on the ground again to guide the rope close to him.

"Can you reach it?" she shouted into the darkness.

Nothing.

"Buck? Can you put the rope around your chest, under your arms?"

Silence.

"Buck. Talk to me, Buck. Can you hear me?"

A frog bellowed from far below and fear shot through Sadie's heart. After all this time, was she too late?

"Hang on, Buck," she yelled. "I'm going for help. I'll be back as soon as I can."

She dropped the rope on the ground in case she needed it when she returned, and then rode hard and fast back the way she had come.

Chapter 24

She rode Joe back to her house like a barrel racer on full tilt and dialed Lance's cell phone. When she heard his voice mail recording click on, she slammed down the receiver and let out a screech of frustration. Regaining her composure, she called 911 and instructed the first responders to meet her at Buck's house, where she promised she would lead them straight to the sinkhole that held her neighbor prisoner.

She ran back out to Joe, pulled the saddle off his back, and dropped it inside the barn. Praising Sonny for his good work, she threw him another piece of venison and commanded him to stay put until she got back. After grabbing her purse and keys, she jumped into her truck, arriving at Buck's house just as the paramedics drove up with sirens blaring. Ignoring a black vehicle parked on the east side of Buck's house, Sadie motioned for the emergency personnel to follow her as she pointed her truck through an open gate and down a nearly invisible path into Buck's property. Both vehicles creaked as they bobbed up and down over the bumpy terrain, finally arriving where Buck's truck sat in front of a rock springhouse. Sadie got out and ran, past an old abandoned house and for nearly a mile to where she'd found Buck. The paramedics followed closely behind carrying a portable stretcher.

Sadie fell on her knees at the edge of the hole. "Buck, I'm back," she yelled. "Hang on. I brought help."

Buck weakly raised his head and looked at her. "*Wado*," he said and smiled. "Thank you," he repeated.

Anchoring one end of a rope to a sturdy tree, the smaller of the two medics slowly lowered himself into the sinkhole. The rescuer steadied himself against the wall of the sinkhole and placed one foot on the ledge next to Buck. After assessing Buck's injuries, the medic looked at Buck with a sympathetic smile. "There just ain't no good way around this, old man," he said. "This is going to hurt."

The medic went to work, rigging a crude harness with Sadie's rope while the other medic ran back to the emergency vehicle. The returning medic pitched a blanket to Sadie.

"Here, give this to him." He pointed with his head at the sinkhole.

Sadie fell onto the ground at the edge of the sinkhole and dropped the blanket to the medic, who carefully used it to protect Buck while he wrapped the harness between Buck's legs and around his waist and shoulders. The other medic quickly attached a block and tackle to the same tree they had used to lower the first medic into the hole.

"Hopefully," he said, "the blanket and this pulley system will allow us to pull him out without causing additional injury."

With one medic supporting Buck from below, Sadie and the other medic pulled him onto solid ground. Buck grimaced but never made a sound as the two emergency workers placed him on the stretcher.

"You'll be okay, Buck." Sadie wiped dirt and perspiration off his face. "How'd you get this gash on your forehead?" she said.

One of the paramedics checked the head wound while the other started an IV, then together they carried him to the waiting ambulance. Once they'd secured the gurney for travel, Sadie climbed in beside Buck.

"Hang on, Buck," she said. "We've got cool air coming right up."

Buck smiled with his eyes. One paramedic nodded at Sadie as the other began to chatter on the radio.

"There's a shortcut back to the road," she said. "We don't have to drive back through the pasture to his house." She directed them to an abandoned road obscured by overgrown weeds. "This used to be the road to that old house back there," she pointed with her head.

The driver carefully nosed the ambulance in the direction Sadie had motioned, and in a few short minutes, with lights flashing and sirens wailing, they were on their way to the Memorial Hospital in Sycamore Springs. Buck didn't say much on the ride to the hospital. He only squeezed Sadie's hand a couple of times and whispered his thanks to her.

Once they arrived at the hospital, the paramedics swept him past the check-in desk and through the double doors into a restricted area, stopping just long enough to instruct Sadie to wait there. After a couple of unsuccessful tries to sneak past a very robust nurse, she gave up and staked out the corner couch, where she could keep her eye on the activity at the desk, the double doors, and the outside door.

After an agonizingly long fifteen minutes, one of the nurses emerged, recognized Sadie, and approached.

"Are you the one who came in with Mr. Skinner?"

Sadie jumped to her feet. "Yes, I am. Is he going to be okay?"

"Are you family?" she asked.

"No, I'm his friend . . . neighbor. He doesn't have any family around here. Can I see him?"

"I'm sorry, but we're running some tests and getting some x-rays. We don't think anything is broken, but we need to make sure. He's pretty bruised up, and he's got lacerations on his head and knee." The nurse smiled an optimistic smile. "He's a little confused, but I'm not surprised with the state of his dehydration. He seems to be pretty tough. I think he'll be fine."

Sadie let out a sigh of relief and began to blink back tears. "I've been gone for four days. If I'd been here I could have . . ."

"It's going to be a while." The nurse patted Sadie on the shoulder. "You might as well go get a sandwich or something." Then she turned on her heel and disappeared.

Thankful for the nurse's reassurance, Sadie sat back down on the couch to think. Why couldn't anyone else in Delaware County have found Buck? Did they even try? Another day and he could have died from exposure. There she was on Maui having a good time and her neighbor, lying at the bottom of a sinkhole, was about to die. Why couldn't Lance find him? None of it made any sense to her. Then she remembered Lance's condescending words on the phone: *You can't be in control of everything. . . . If he's out there we'll find him. . . . I was in law enforcement for a long time before I met you.*

Thoughts swirled in her head, stirring fiery anger. In an effort to redirect her thoughts, she turned to a nearby table and picked up the *Sycamore*

Springs Gazette. Settling in on the couch, she began to read about two recent murders. "Man," she muttered, "leave for a few days and all hell breaks loose." She dropped her nose into the paper, engrossed by the article.

> According to a spokesman at the Sycamore Springs Police Department, a worker was found dead early Sunday morning at the Sisson Farms chicken plant, the victim of an apparent stabbing. The investigating officers found another murder victim a short time later in a trailer at the Vista Trails Trailer Park on Creek Street. The source refused to confirm whether the two murders were connected due to the ongoing investigation. Identities of the victims are being withheld until next of kin can be notified.

A nearby presence startled her. Looking up, she found Charlie McCord standing with his hands on his hips, grinning at her.

"Oh, Charlie. It's good to see you." She rose and gave the big man a hug. "How have you been? I haven't seen you since you helped Lance with the murder investigation in Liberty—when the woman who owned the Liberty Diner was murdered."

"Lance told me you'd given up the restaurant business. Do you miss the café?"

"No, not really. It was hard work." She laughed. "My ancestors must have had more stamina than I do. Did Lance tell you I'm trying my hand at the travel business?"

"No, can't say that I've heard about that. What are you doing here, Sadie?"

"I came in with my neighbor," she said. "He fell into a sinkhole, of all things, and I don't know how long he'd been there, but he's not in very good shape. They're getting him fixed up right now."

Concern crossed Charlie's face. "That neighbor wouldn't be Benjamin Skinner, would it?"

"That's right," she said. "But most folks know him as Buck, not Benjamin." She wrinkled her forehead. "What are you doing here, Charlie?"

"Picked up the information on the radio. I'm interested in Mr. Skinner's whereabouts as it pertains to a murder investigation. Didn't Lance tell you about it?"

Sadie frowned. "No. He picked me up at the airport this morning and then accused me . . . well, let's just say . . . uh, no, he didn't tell me anything about anything."

Charlie looked surprised. "Oh." He rose and walked over to the check-in desk, flashed his badge, and spoke with the nurse before walking outside onto the sidewalk. Sadie watched as he made a call on his cell phone before returning to the waiting area.

"Is it about these murders, Charlie?" She pointed at the newspaper.

He ignored her question. "Listen, Sadie, they're slow as molasses in this emergency room, so it's going to be a while before anything happens around here. Lance is on his way."

Sadie frowned again.

"He's been working with me on this case. I'm surprised he hasn't talked to you about it. We're going to need to talk to Mr. Skinner when he can talk."

"Buck," she corrected him. "His name is Buck."

"At any rate, it's going to be a while. Do you want to get a bite to eat?"

"That sounds like a good idea." Sadie grabbed her purse and stood up. "I didn't know how hungry I was until you mentioned it." She looked at the clock on the wall. "It's almost five o'clock and jet lag is catching up with me. This has been a really long day."

The outside double doors slid open and Lance rushed through, zeroed in on Charlie and Sadie, and froze. Almost immediately, an attractive woman with long red hair, wearing short shorts and a tight tank top, ran through the doors behind Lance, latched onto him, and burst into tears.

Sadie felt like her heart might explode in her chest. *What's going on? Is this woman the reason Lance was in such a bad mood on the way home from the airport? Please, God, don't let this be happening.* She'd been treated badly by men in the past—physically and mentally abused by her first husband and then later almost murdered by a man she thought she loved—and even though she'd grown stronger after each experience, this strange woman had hooked an insecure spot in Sadie's soul and reeled it to the surface. She wanted to shrink into the corner and disappear.

Sadie watched Lance try unsuccessfully to free himself from the woman. Finally, steering the redhead to a nearby corner away from Charlie and Sadie, he pushed her into a chair.

Sadie grabbed Charlie's arm. "Please," she pleaded. "Get me out of here."

Confusion quickly spread across Charlie's face as he guided Sadie through the doors and to his cruiser. Together they drove away from the hospital, Charlie staring straight ahead while Sadie sat in the passenger's seat and sulked.

Chapter 25

After angrily detaching himself from Dee Dee Skinner, Lance watched as Sadie and Charlie drove away. He walked over to the check-in desk and spoke to the young nurse.

"Benjamin Skinner's niece is here," he said. "Can you let her know when Mr. Skinner can have visitors?"

The nurse raised her eyebrow and looked past Lance at the woman dabbing a tissue at the black eye makeup smeared on her cheeks, then shifted her eyes to the empty couch where Sadie had been sitting.

"He sure is a popular guy," she said. "I thought the other woman who came in with him said he didn't have any next of kin around here."

Lance transferred his weight from one foot to the other. "That was his neighbor. I don't think she was aware that Miss Skinner had arrived from California."

The nurse nodded. "Okay, I'll let her know." The phone rang and she disappeared behind a cubicle partition.

Lance reluctantly returned to where Dee Dee was sitting, but kept his distance and remained standing. Dee Dee stood and Lance took a step backward.

"Can I go in?" she asked.

"They said they'd let you know when he can have visitors." He took his cell phone out and looked at it as if it held the key to his escape. "I've got to go. You'll be okay here."

"Oh." Dee Dee lowered her eyes. "Sure."

"If you need anything, have the nurse contact the local police department and they'll send someone out." Without waiting for her response, he retreated out the double doors to his truck.

⁜

Charlie pulled into the parking lot at the Waffle House and took the last parking space. He shifted the cruiser into park, switched off the engine, and turned to Sadie.

"Let's get a bite to eat," he said. "Everything looks better over a plate of food."

Sadie managed a weak smile. "Yeah, a little comfort food might be in order."

They walked together across the parking lot and entered the restaurant. Charlie headed for his favorite booth in the back corner. Sadie followed. Charlie took the side against the wall and Sadie sat with her back to the door. They both ordered big—cheeseburgers, fries, and Dr Peppers.

"You want to talk about it?" Charlie asked.

She avoided Charlie's piercing eyes by turning her gaze out the window next to their booth.

"Not really," she said, eventually returning her attention to him. "Let's talk about Buck. Why do you want to talk to him?"

"It's pretty cut and dried." Charlie waited for the waitress to deposit their soft drinks on the table and leave. "The old man went missing. Someone stole his social security number, which had created a little problem with the IRS, which in turn kind of angered the old man Benjamin Skinner because it was going to cost him his ranch."

"Buck," she corrected him. "His name is Buck." She sipped Dr Pepper and waited for him to continue.

"Okay, Buck it is. Anyway, it appears that Buck found the guy causing all the havoc with the stolen social security number and popped him in his lover's trailer house right after one and the same—that is, lover and identity thief—carved up the other old boy his girlfriend was having a fling with."

Sadie felt confused as she chewed on the end of her straw.

"That part took place at the chicken plant at the edge of town," Charlie continued. "But the suspect Benjamin Skinner, or Buck I guess it is, got away from us. That is, until you carted him into the hospital today."

"What?" Sadie almost spit Dr Pepper across the table.

The waitress arrived and plopped down their food—two huge plates overflowing with burgers and fries.

Charlie began to assemble his burger, pulling off the lettuce and to-matoes and pushing them to the side. He replaced the top of the bun and smashed it down with his hand.

"For which I'm quite grateful, I might add. Thank you very much."

Sadie's food sat in front of her for several seconds while she stared at Charlie as if he were a madman.

"You've got to be kidding me," she said, drawing out each word for em-phasis. "That's ludicrous. Especially since when I found him he was about dead . . . in a sinkhole on his property . . . in Eucha."

"Yeah, but you don't know how long he'd been there. He could have been hiding."

Sadie rolled her eyes. "You don't know Buck. There's no way."

"Maybe he planned it that way, so he'd have an alibi. Sounds like the old 'I-can't-be-the-killer-because-I-was-stuck-in-a-sinkhole' excuse."

Sadie shook her head. "You're wrong, Charlie."

"It's not that far-fetched. There's been folks out there looking for him for days and couldn't find him. Then all of a sudden, when you get back to town, he's right where you go look."

"You make it sound like I was in cahoots with him or something." She took a bite of her burger and talked with a full mouth. "To which I take offense."

"Of course not." Charlie sounded apologetic. "I've been wrong before, but you've got to admit, I've got a pretty good theory."

"Well, you're wrong," she repeated. "Dead wrong. And if I have to, I'll prove it."

Charlie grinned. "That's what I'm afraid of."

They continued to eat in silence, each deep in thought. The incident at the hospital with Lance and the unknown woman hung like a ghost in the air between them, neither wanting to broach the subject.

Charlie broke the silence. "When you were working at the bank, did you ever have any bomb threats?"

"No. Thank goodness. Bank robberies were about all I could handle. I'm glad I never had to deal with a bomb threat. Why?"

"The branch where you used to work got one." Charlie hesitated for a moment and then added, "Through the mail."

"I heard about that." Sadie sat back in her seat, wide-eyed. "Was there really a bomb?"

"No, it was more like a threat of something in the future." He dug in his pocket and pulled out his copy of the threatening note and handed it to Sadie. "This note is official police business, so if you tell anyone I showed it to you I'll have to say you're a liar."

"Right." Sadie snatched the note out of Charlie's hand and studied it for a few minutes before handing it back to him. "It's kind of strange, isn't it?" she said. "And it doesn't really say anything about a bomb."

Charlie folded the note and replaced it in his pocket.

"Yeah, it is kind of strange. I told the manager I'd keep my eye on the place. Do you know the manager there? Name's Melanie Thompson."

Sadie shook her head. "No. They've added a lot of new people since I worked there." She pushed her plate aside, her food half-eaten. "When we get finished here, can you take me home? I rode in the ambulance with Buck, and I left my truck sitting in the middle of his property near where I found him." She paused and thought for a moment. "I'll walk over and get it later. It'll be all right where it is for now. What time is it?"

Charlie checked his watch. "Little after seven," he said, wiping his hands on his paper napkin.

"I'd like to get back to the hospital pretty soon so Buck won't be alone."

"What exactly is that old man to you, anyway, Sadie?"

"He's my neighbor. He's a good man who lives alone. He'd do anything to help me and I'd do the same for him. I feel bad because, obviously, if I'd been here he wouldn't be in as bad a shape as he is, because I could have probably found him four days ago." She grabbed her purse and scooted to the edge of the booth to signal she was ready to go. "I guess that would have been the easiest way to prove his innocence, as well. I can't change that, but I can stand by him now."

Charlie dropped several bills on top of the ticket the waitress had left earlier and together they headed for the door.

✤

Sadie could see Lance's truck sitting next to her house when Charlie turned off the main road and crossed the cattle guard onto her property. He was leaning against the driver's side, obviously waiting for her to return.

"Looks like you've got company," Charlie quipped. He looked at Sadie and grinned. "You want me to stay and referee?"

"No, thank you," she said angrily. "I can handle this by myself."

"Now don't be too hard on him. I'm sure there's a logical explanation for everything." Charlie guided his cruiser to a place behind Lance's truck and rolled to a stop.

"Yeah, right." Sadie climbed out of Charlie's car and slammed the door.

Charlie lowered his window and stuck his head out so both Lance and Sadie could easily hear him. "Don't you lovebirds be pulling any feathers out of each other. You all hear?"

Sadie waved as Charlie reversed his vehicle and drove away. Lance grimaced.

Sadie walked toward the back door of the house. "You're wasting your time, Smith. I don't want to talk to you."

Lance grabbed her arm as she walked past him, stopping her in mid-stride. Suddenly, Sonny appeared out of nowhere and headed straight for Lance.

"*Alewisdodi!*" Sadie screamed. "Stop, Sonny. It's okay." Lance instantly released her arm as Sadie reached out for the dog, grasping the back of his neck. "I'm okay, Sonny. Good boy." She stroked the dog's head and then turned to Lance. "I think your welcome is worn out here."

"Sadie, I need to talk to you. Can I come in so we don't have to deal with this crazy animal?"

Sadie let out a long sigh. "Oh, okay. At least this should be interesting." She turned on her heel and headed to the door.

Sonny followed her and Lance hesitated.

Sadie turned. "You'd better get in the house while the getting is good."

Together, they walked into the kitchen and Sadie dropped her purse on the table.

"You know, Sadie, that dog is dangerous. One of these days, he's going to hurt someone. Either that or someone is going to shoot him out of self-defense. And it may be me."

"Is that what you wanted to talk to me about—the dog?"

Lance put his hands on his hips. "Where did you find Buck?"

"I didn't find him," she snapped. "Sonny found him." She dug the keys out of her pocket and threw them at Lance. They hit him in the middle of his chest before falling to the floor and landing at his feet.

Lance picked up the keys and looked at them.

"Those are Buck's keys, Lance. They don't belong to some secret lover of mine like you seem to think they do. They belong to Buck Skinner." Sadie's voice grew louder with every word.

Lance looked confused.

"Tell me something, Lance. When Sonny brought those keys to you, did he by any chance try to get you to follow him?"

Lance closed his eyes and Sadie knew she was right.

"All I had to do was show these keys to Sonny and he led me straight to Buck. That was pretty damned simple, wasn't it? Too simple for you, obviously, since you're such a seasoned lawman and you've been in law enforcement for such a long time." Sadie wanted him to remember his own words, the words he'd told her on the phone.

"You're kidding me." Lance walked over to the kitchen table, sat down, and spoke in a quiet voice. "Where was he?"

"About a mile beyond the old springhouse. At the bottom of the ridge. In a sinkhole."

"In a sinkhole?" He sounded amazed. "How'd you get him out?"

"I called 911, since you wouldn't answer my call."

Lance ran his hand through his hair. "I'm sorry, Sadie."

"Is that all you came here to talk to me about?" she asked. "Where did I find Buck?"

"No."

"Well, I've got a question for you. Where did you find the lovely redhead that looked like a leech stuck to your arm?"

"Her name is Dee Dee Skinner. She's Buck's niece, and she came in from California because Buck was missing."

Sadie felt like the air had been sucked out of her lungs. "And you made friends with her that fast? Good grief, I was only gone four days."

"It's not like that Sadie. We are not friends. I questioned her about Buck when she arrived and she was clueless about her uncle and everything else around here. She's real citified and, I swear, she doesn't have the sense God gave a goose to come in out of the rain."

Sadie walked over and sat in a chair on the other side of the table.

"I was on my way back to your house," he continued. "I wanted to talk things out. But Charlie called and said he'd heard on the radio that Buck had been found and was being transported to the hospital. So, since I was so close to Buck's house, I stopped by to tell her. She followed me to the hospital. I have no idea why she acted the way she did there. I swear, Sadie, that's it."

Sadie dropped her head in her hands, fighting tears and exhaustion. Lance quickly moved to her side and knelt by her chair. He took her hands in his and pulled them away from her face.

"I'm so sorry, Sadie. I jumped to so many conclusions and I was wrong. Can you forgive me?"

Tears fell off Sadie's cheeks. "I guess I'm guilty of the same thing. I'm so tired, I can't think straight. I'm sorry, too."

Lance stood, pulled Sadie to her feet, and encircled her with his arms. She gave in to his passionate kisses until they could hear Sonny scratching at the back door. They began to laugh, and tension fled the room.

"I love you, Sadie. Let's not ever be apart again."

"You have no idea how scary that sounds. I'm not ready."

"That's okay." He pushed her hair away and kissed her forehead. "I'll wait," he said. "I don't care how long it takes."

"You would love Hawai'i." She rested her head on his chest. "It is too beautiful for words."

They could hear Sonny whining at the back door. Sadie looked at her watch and pushed Lance away. Grinning, she said, "Okay, I'll buy you a ticket next time so you can go too. I'm going back to the hospital. Want to go?"

He grinned and headed for the door. "I'll meet you there in a bit," he said, "if you'll call off your dog."

Chapter 26

When Sadie arrived at the hospital, the sun had already dropped behind the western treetops, tinting the sky pink. She parked and entered through the main door instead of going back through the emergency room where she had left Buck earlier in the day.

Recognizing one of the ladies at the information desk, she approached and decided to make small talk before trying to extract information about Buck.

"Hi, Hazel," she said.

The gray-haired woman looked over her glasses at Sadie and smiled. "Well, look at you." Her southern drawl sounded as if she had just arrived from south Texas. "I haven't seen you in a coon's age. How are you doing?"

The two women exchanged pleasantries, and before long Sadie had convinced the retired nurse that a Hawaiian vacation was exactly what she needed, and she highly recommended the island of Maui. Besides that, as the town's newest travel agent, she would be glad to give her a new-customer discount. Hazel laughed and agreed to come by and see her soon.

Sadie began to pry. "By the way, Hazel, I came by to check on my neighbor, Buck Skinner. I came in with him through the emergency room earlier today. Can you tell me if he's in a room yet?"

"Oh, my, what happened?" Hazel's face took on an animated air of concern.

"He fell into a sinkhole. Can you believe that?" Sadie exaggerated her words.

Hazel's lips formed a silent "Oh" and then she went to work. Without a blink, she tapped for several seconds on her keyboard with long, red acrylic nails, and then raised her nose so she could look through the bottom part of her glasses at the computer screen.

"I can't tell," she said. "Hold on and I'll call back to emergency and see where he is." She picked up the phone, dialed, and waited. After inquiring, she hung up and looked at Sadie. "They just moved him into a room on the fourth floor." She wrote on a small slip of paper and handed it to Sadie. "If they give you any trouble, just tell them you're family. They won't care."

"Thank you so much, Hazel. I know Buck will appreciate it too."

Hazel winked at Sadie. "You take care of yourself, you hear? And, don't be falling into any darned sinkholes."

Sadie smiled and was walking toward the elevators when Hazel called after her. "And I'll be in to see you pretty soon about the new-customer discount on a trip to Maui."

Sadie gave her a thumbs-up, got on the empty elevator, and after a quick ride found herself on the fourth floor. She looked at the paper Hazel had given her and quickly followed the signs to room 410. The door stood ajar, and she could hear the noise of a television coming from inside the room. She quietly knocked and pushed the door slightly open. She could see Buck lying in the far bed next to the window. He had an oxygen tube running to his nose and an IV running from a machine to his arm. Another elderly patient, snoring loudly, occupied the bed closest to the door, grasping a television remote in one hand and the bed railing with the other.

Sadie tiptoed into the room and approached Buck's bed. As she got closer, he opened his eyes, grinned at her, and then closed his eyes again. Sadie came closer and patted his arm. "Is there anything I can get for you, Buck?"

Buck raised his head and moved his eyes toward the insulated cup sitting on a nearby rolling table.

"Want a drink of water?" she asked as she instinctively reached for the cup and guided the bent straw to his mouth.

He sipped and then pushed the straw out of his mouth with his tongue. "I'm going to buy your dog a tube steak," he said quietly.

Sadie smiled at his reference to bologna.

"Me, too," she said. "Do you mind if I stay for a little while, or would you rather sleep?"

Buck nodded toward a chair in the corner. "Pull up a chair. Nobody can sleep in a place like this, except him," he said, nodding toward his roommate. "They come in here every five minutes and poke on me somewhere." His voice sounded surprisingly strong, considering the ordeal he'd been through.

Sadie pulled the chair from the corner of the room to the edge of the window and sat in it. Buck turned his head and looked at her. "*Wado*," he said. "I don't think I could have made it much longer."

"Don't worry about it. I'm sorry I didn't get there sooner. I was gone. But you're right about Sonny. He led me straight to you." Sadie settled back in her chair. "He brought me your keys, you know. I can't imagine how he got your keys."

Buck shook his head again. "A miracle, I guess. I got angry and threw them at him. Damned dog's smarter than I thought he was."

Sadie could hear heels clicking in the hallway a few moments before the door swung open and the redheaded niece marched through it. Her eyes zeroed in on Buck as she walked up to his bed. "Uncle Buck. I can't believe you don't take better care of yourself. Look at the mess you're in now."

Sadie sat up straight, bristling at the woman's lack of respect for Buck.

Buck looked at his niece without a hint of emotion in his face, and then looked at Sadie.

"This is my brother's girl. I guess she's come all the way from Cal-i-forn-i-a just to see if I am still kicking." He looked back at his niece. "This is my neighbor, Sadie."

"Charmed, I'm sure." Dee Dee managed to force a smile. "They told me only family was allowed in here. Do you mind leaving us alone so we can discuss some family business?"

Sadie started to stand.

"No," Buck said, his voice sounding even stronger than before. "Sadie *is* family. She saved my life. If you've got something to say, you can say it in front of her."

Dee Dee scowled. "Okay, fine. Did you draw up your will like I asked you to?"

"What's your rush? I've got a lot of good years left in me." Buck's voice trailed off as he mumbled something in Cherokee.

"Don't call me that," she snapped. "I changed my name to Dee Dee years ago, after I got tired of trying to explain such a stupid name. Dee Dee is my legal name now."

Buck turned his head and looked out the window into the darkness of the evening. "Your father would not approve."

"Yeah, well, he's dead, so it really doesn't matter what he'd think, does it?"

Sadie sat in silence, horrified by the conversation taking place, wishing she could speak her mind to this disrespectful redhead and knowing it was not her place to do so, especially now that she could see the woman looked much older than she'd first thought. *How could I have been jealous of her?* Sadie squirmed in her chair and pushed her hair behind her ears when she realized how irrational she'd been.

Buck spoke softly. "I swear there can't be a drop of Cherokee blood running through your veins. They must've got you mixed up with some *unegv*, some white baby, when you were born."

Sadie stifled a laugh.

Dee Dee let out a grunt of disgust as she rummaged through her large handbag and pulled out a legal-size piece of paper. "I need you to sign this power of attorney so I can take care of some things for you." She pulled the rolling tray near his bed, pushed his water cup aside, and laid the paper down next to it. She dug in her purse again and produced an ink pen. "Here," she said.

Sadie tensed again and stood.

Dee Dee looked at Sadie and said, "What?"

Sadie remained standing.

"What do you think you need a power of attorney for?" Buck asked.

Dee Dee glanced at Sadie before she continued, the tone of her voice suddenly taking on a childlike tone. "Uncle Buck, we've got a chance to make a lot of money. All we have to do is bottle and sell water from your spring. I had a man look at it and he says we can bottle up to two hundred thousand gallons a day. Do you have any idea how much money that will generate?"

Surprised, Sadie gasped.

Buck sneered at his niece and pushed the paper away. "You are not going to sell my springwater . . . at least not while I'm still alive. You can go back to your fancy city life in California, and then after I'm dead and gone you can do what you want with it. But until then, it stays just the way it is."

"Uncle Buck, I've got an investor willing to help us get the company up and running, and he isn't going to wait around for very long."

Buck began to get angry. "Go on. Go bother someone else for a while." Buck leaned back on his pillow.

A nurse flew through the door. "Mr. Skinner. Your blood pressure is going up on my monitor. Are you okay?" She looked at Sadie and Dee Dee. "You might want to wind down your visit. Mr. Skinner needs to get some rest."

Dee Dee grabbed the paper and pen and shoved it back into her bag. "That's okay. I was just leaving." She turned and left, leaving nothing but the sound of clicking heels behind her. The nurse frowned and followed her out.

Sadie touched Buck on his arm. "Is there anything I can get for you?"

Buck nodded his head. "Can you bring me a bologna sandwich? I'm hungry and I can't eat this stuff." He pointed with his head toward an untouched dinner tray sitting on a table next to his bed.

Sadie smiled. "Of course." She turned toward the door, pulled the remote control from the other patient's hand, and clicked off the television. "I'll be right back," she said, as she placed the remote on the man's bedside table and slipped through the door.

✤

Lance pulled into the hospital parking lot and immediately spotted Sadie's Explorer. As he parked next to it and started to get out, he froze. First he saw the Cadillac, and then, in the dimness of the parking lot security lights, he saw Dee Dee Skinner walking down the sidewalk, talking on her cell phone. He decided to wait for her to get in her car and leave so he wouldn't have to talk to her again. She had caused enough trouble for him already. A few seconds later, the rental car he'd seen leaving Buck's house a few days earlier pulled in next to the Cadillac and parked. Dee Dee got in the rental car and closed the door.

Lance remained in his truck, hoping they wouldn't recognize his vehicle, knowing they couldn't see him in the darkness. After a few minutes, he saw Dee Dee lean over and kiss the driver before getting out. She looked around, then walked to her car, got in, and followed the rental car into the night.

Suddenly, Sadie appeared next to his truck, giving him a start. He rolled down his window. "Get in and we'll pick up where we left off earlier."

Sadie laughed. "I'm bushed, Lance, and I've got to go over to the store and pick up something for Buck to eat, then I'm going to go home and get some sleep before I pass out."

"He must be feeling better."

"He is. How about lunch tomorrow?"

"Okay, I'll stop by the hospital and check on you two. I'm sure Charlie is going to want to question him about some things."

Sadie frowned. "I hope I'm there when he shows up."

"It'll be okay, Sadie. You want some help?"

"No, I'll see you tomorrow." She leaned through the window and gave him a kiss and then hurried to her car.

Sadie stopped by a convenience store about a block away, where she bought two preassembled bologna-and-cheese sandwiches. In less than twenty minutes she was back at Buck's bedside. She unwrapped the first sandwich and handed it to him just as a very large nurse's aide walked into the room and looked at Sadie.

"I'm glad someone finally got here who can translate for us. Trying to communicate by sign language isn't working too well for me." The nurse went into the bathroom and returned holding up a plastic container. "Can you tell him we need a urine sample?"

Buck looked straight ahead as if he didn't understand a word.

Still holding the bologna sandwich in midair, Sadie looked first at the urinal and then back at Buck, and then tried to stifle a laugh. "Sure," she said. "Leave it there and I'll take care of it for you."

Without a word of thanks, the nurse's aide quickly disappeared through the door.

Sadie retracted the sandwich just as Buck reached for it. "Have you convinced her you don't understand English?"

Buck grinned. "Works better that way," he said.

Sadie rolled her eyes and handed him the sandwich. "Well, eat up, my friend. Your secret is safe with me."

Buck ate quickly, his eyes laughing.

Sadie left the other sandwich next to his phone and picked up the plastic urinal. "Would you please pee in this thing before you go to sleep?"

Buck frowned.

"I'll see you in the morning," she said. "Is there anything else I can do for you?"

"Can you open the window?" he asked. "I might need an escape route."

Sadie walked to the window and slid it open about three inches. "They're probably not going to like you letting their refrigerated air out," she said.

Buck nodded in agreement and continued to eat. Sadie slipped out of his room, through the hospital, and into the night.

Chapter 27

Buck could smell alcohol before he opened his eyes. His body ached and his knee throbbed. He moved his left hand to his forehead and felt the bandage, trying to gather his thoughts. Oh, yes, he remembered, the military hospital. How long had he been here?

Then he remembered the man yelling for help. Buck didn't know if he'd been shot or what, all he knew was someone needed help. Buck followed two men out of the foxhole, all three running toward the sound of the injured comrade. It was a trap. The bomb blast blew Buck backward. He couldn't move, couldn't see, and couldn't hear. All he could remember now was the sensation of someone picking him up and carrying him away before he passed out from the pain.

A nurse walked into the room. "How are you feeling this morning, Mr. Skinner?" she asked.

"What about the other men?" he said. "Did they make it?"

The nurse straightened his bedding. "What other men are you asking about, sir? Your roommate has already checked out and gone home this morning."

"The men in front of me. Did they make it?"

"I think a young woman came into the emergency room with you, Mr. Skinner. Is that who you're asking about? She was here late last night, wasn't she?"

Buck blinked wildly and looked around at his surroundings. "Oh, that's right," he said quietly, and closed his eyes. "That's right."

✤

Sadie awoke later than she had planned. After quickly wrapping the brownies she'd baked the night before, she showered and dressed to return to the hospital.

As she headed toward her car, Sonny jumped up from his place at the bottom of the porch steps, raised his nose, and sniffed at the plate full of brownies in Sadie's hand. She patted his head with her other hand. "I'll be back later, Sonny," she said. "Stay here and stay out of trouble."

She deposited the brownies on the passenger seat, fastened her seat belt, and drove out of her driveway and onto the road to Sycamore. As she pulled onto Highway 20 and turned east, she reminded herself to stop by the phone store on the way home and pick up a replacement cell phone.

When Sadie pulled into the hospital parking lot, she saw a police car and then recognized Charlie McCord walking toward the front door. She knew he was on his way to talk to Buck, so she quickly parked and ran to catch up with him.

"Wait up, Charlie," she yelled.

The big man stopped and waited for her.

"Are you on your way to talk to Buck?" she asked.

"Maybe. What do you have there?" he asked, nodding at her foil-covered plate.

"Brownies for Buck. Can I bribe you with one of them?"

"Sure, I'm an easy buy."

Sadie pulled out a brownie and handed it to him. "Here, my hands are fairly clean."

Charlie shoved the whole thing in his mouth and began to talk. "Your friend's in more trouble."

Sadie frowned. "I don't know how, since you already think he murdered someone. Or have you found the real killer already?"

Charlie ignored her question as they entered the hospital and walked right past Hazel at the information desk. Hazel winked at Sadie as they passed and continued her conversation with another visitor. By the time they made it to Buck's hospital room, Sadie was almost out of breath trying to keep up with Charlie's long strides. Charlie pushed the door open and entered without as much as a knock. Sadie followed. The bed next to Buck was empty and Sadie wondered what had happened to the man who'd been watching television the night before. Buck sat in a wheelchair, holding onto his IV tower while the same nurse's aide Sadie had seen the night before changed his bed. His right knee had been wrapped in bandages.

"*O'siyo, tohitsu?*" Sadie greeted him and asked how he was doing.

Buck smiled and waited for the aide to leave before he spoke. "I'll feel a lot better as soon as they let me loose from this contraption so I can break out of here."

"How's your knee?"

"Sore" he said. "It's got a cut on it. Not sure how that happened."

"Well, I brought you sustenance," Sadie said. She pulled back the foil and held the plate so Buck could take a brownie, then placed the rest on a nearby table. "These will get you back on your feet in no time."

Buck took a bite and looked past Sadie at Charlie. "Who's your friend?"

Charlie stepped forward and offered his hand. "Sergeant McCord," he said. "Sycamore Springs Police Department. Mr. Skinner, do you feel up to a few questions?"

Buck looked blankly at Charlie. "Okay, if you'll call me Buck. I don't much go by Mr. Skinner."

"Okay, Buck it is. Do you mind if your neighbor, Sadie, is present while I question you?"

"Nah, if it weren't for her I don't think I'd be here, anyway. Go ahead. Fire away."

Sadie smiled. Charlie retrieved two folding chairs from behind the door, and they sat facing Buck.

Charlie leaned forward. "Okay, Buck, before I ask you any questions I need to advise you of your rights."

"Is that really necessary?" Sadie said, irritated.

Charlie nodded. "Yeah, I'm afraid so." He pulled a laminated card out of his pocket and started reading. "You have the right to remain silent. Anything you say can be and will be used against you in a court of law. You have the right to speak to an attorney, and to have an attorney present during any questioning. It you cannot afford an attorney, one will be appointed to represent you. Do you understand these rights I just said? And, are you willing to talk to me?"

Buck frowned and sat forward in his wheelchair. "I don't have much use for lawyers," he said. "There's nothing good about them. They're trying to take what little I have, and I don't like it. I have nothing to hide. Go ahead."

"There've been a lot of folks out scouring the woods for you, Buck. Can you tell us where you've been?"

"The earth just gave way," he said. "I fell into a hole and I couldn't get out, that is until this young lady came to my rescue." Buck smiled at Sadie.

"How'd that happen, sir? Didn't you know the hole was there? Hadn't you seen it before?"

"No, sir. It'd never been there before that I know of. The ground just gave way and the next thing I knew, there I was talking to a bullfrog."

"Where were you before you fell into the sinkhole?"

Buck frowned and looked at the floor. "You know, it's all kind of fuzzy." He wet his lips. "I get kind of mixed up sometimes. I remember getting a letter from the government saying I owed them money, and it made me real mad."

"What about Sunday morning? Where were you then?"

"In a hole, I guess. I don't rightly know."

"How about a woman by the name of Cynthia Tanner? Do you know her?"

Buck thought for a moment. "A lot of Tanners live around Old Eucha. Don't know if there's a Cynthia among them or not."

Sadie sat quietly, following the flow of conversation from one man to the other.

"Do you know anyone who works at the Sisson chicken plant here in Sycamore Springs?" Charlie asked.

Buck looked lost. "I don't know," he said.

"What about a gentleman by the name of Tomas Hernandez?"

Buck shook his head. "No."

"You didn't know that he was found murdered at the chicken plant? The workers say someone named Benjamin Skinner killed him."

Sadie sucked in a long breath.

"Did you know there's a warrant for your arrest?" Charlie asked.

Buck remained quiet for a moment and then said, "No, I don't guess I knew that."

Alarm filled Sadie. "For what?"

"For drunk and disorderly conduct in a bar on the south side of Sycamore Springs. It's about a month old."

Sadie's mouth flew open. "Oh, good grief, Charlie. Is this some kind of a joke?"

"No joke, Sadie," Charlie said. "Do you know anything about it, Buck?"

Buck looked past Sadie. "You know," he said. "I seem to be getting blamed for a bunch of stuff I haven't done. And I'm beginning to get real tired of it."

Sadie felt a presence behind her and discovered Lance standing silently inside the door.

"You know, Charlie," Lance said, "it doesn't take a rocket scientist to figure out that whoever stole Buck's identity is responsible for all these things you're accusing him of."

Charlie turned in his chair, acknowledged Lance, and then looked back at Buck.

"What about the old boy who stole your identity, Buck? Did you track him down to a trailer court over on Creek Street and put an end to him? We found him with a bullet in his head."

Sadie gasped. "That's enough, Charlie. Buck did not kill anyone. How could he? He was trapped in a sinkhole in the middle of his property."

Buck began to laugh. "Did you say he was dead?"

"Yeah, he's dead," Charlie answered.

Buck's laughter slowly transformed into a look of distress. "How am I ever going to straighten out this problem with the IRS if he's dead?"

"Did you kill him, Buck?" Charlie asked.

"Not that I remember," he said.

A nurse suddenly burst through the door. "Sorry to break up a party, but we need to get Mr. Skinner cleaned up so we can get him back in bed. You all can wait in the waiting room and we'll come and get you when we're finished."

"That's not necessary," Lance said. "We were just getting ready to leave, anyway."

Charlie looked at Lance and nodded. "Sounds good. I'll catch up with you later."

The trio walked out into the hallway, rode the elevator down to the lobby, and filed out the front door. Everyone seemed to be lost in their own thoughts. As they walked down the steps of the hospital, Sadie almost ran headlong into another one of her neighbors—Jelly Hart.

"Oh, Jelly, I'm sorry. I guess my mind is somewhere else. How are you?"

"Making it, I guess." Jelly looked embarrassed. "Heard they found Buck. Is he okay?"

Sadie laughed. "It's hard to keep a crusty old man like Buck down for very long. He'll be good as new before you know it. You ought to stop by and see him. I know he'd appreciate it."

Jelly nodded. "That's what I came for—to make sure he was okay." He acknowledged Lance and Charlie and then disappeared into the hospital.

When the three of them reached the parking lot, Sadie turned to Charlie. "I swear, Charlie, if you weren't my friend I think I'd punch you in the nose."

"It's just business," Charlie said. "Don't take it personal. But you should've noticed, he never denied killing anyone." Then he turned to Lance. "I'll call you later," he said. With that he got in his cruiser and drove off.

Sadie, full of sadness, looked at Lance and then leaned on his chest. "I cannot believe anyone would think that Buck Skinner could be a murderer."

Lance engulfed her in a bear hug. "Don't worry, Sadie. We'll figure it out. I haven't given up yet."

Sadie looked up at him and smiled. "That's what I like about you, Smith. You've got perseverance."

Together they walked to her car. "Come on," she said. "Let's get something to eat."

Lance held the door open for her and waited for her to get settled in her car and lower the window. "How do you feel about a hot dog?"

Sadie scrunched her face. "A hot dog?"

"Yeah, a hot dog and a little ice cream? They're playing baseball over at the park and I need to do a little investigative work on a baseball glove I found. Want to go?"

"A baseball glove?" Sadie tried to hide her amusement. "So this is a working lunch, then?"

"Well, sort of, I guess." His eyes sparkled. "No harm in taking your girl to work with you, right?"

"You are so romantic," Sadie giggled. "I haven't been to a baseball game since I can't remember when. But, I'm a working girl too. I'm supposed to be setting things up in my new office this afternoon. Remember? I have a new job as a travel agent, and I'm taking over next week."

"How could I forget?"

Sadie chewed on her lip for a moment. "If you'll go with me to replace my cell phone first. Then I'll finish up at the office later this evening."

Lance leaned over and kissed her through the car window. "Come on," he said. "Leave your car here and we'll pick it up later." A few seconds later they were on their way to the phone store, followed by a trip to a hot August afternoon baseball game.

Chapter 28

Sadie and Lance arrived at the ballpark just in time to see the ninth inning of a coed softball game between the Sycamore Sparrow Hawks and the Jay Bulldogs. Jay was ahead by two points and the Sycamore fans were doing their best to cheer the home team to victory.

They found good seats near first base, and Lance went to the concession stand to gather baseball food. Sadie saw several people she knew, waved to those at a distance and chatted with others nearby, talking up her new travel business at every opportunity. It felt good to be among so many friends.

She watched Lance from a distance. She loved the way he moved fluidly through the crowd with both respect and authority, and the way people reacted to him in kind. His coal-black hair and his handsome face stirred her heart. Any woman would be honored to have him look their way. Why did she have to get so scared when he offered that coveted attention to her?

The crack of a bat brought her thoughts back to the game. A high fly ball fell in right field near the fence, and the crowd went wild while the players scrambled on the field to tag the runner before he scored.

Lance returned with a tray of hot dogs, nachos, two cans of soda, and a piece of fry bread. Sadie laughed with joy as they balanced the feast on their laps and tried not to spill anything when, a short time later, the home team scored the winning run.

"What happened to the ice cream?" she asked.

"Sorry, the young lady at the concession stand said it was too hard to keep it frozen in this heat." Lance wiped his mouth with the back of his hand and gathered the paper trash from the food. "Want to stay for the next game?" he asked. "It's a doubleheader."

Sadie looked at her watch. "When did you become so interested in baseball, anyway?" she asked. "I really need to get by my office before the end of the day and check my messages."

Lance nodded. "How about we stay until the next game gets started and then we'll go. I just had a hunch about a baseball glove we found, and I thought I might pick up on something to help me identify the owner."

"Oh, okay." Sadie said, uninterested. "Next game is fine."

From their seats on the top row of the bleachers, they had an excellent view of the entire area. The crowd was constantly changing, people coming and going. It was almost impossible to sit still for very long in the oppressive summer heat, and a lot of folks would wander back and forth to the shade offered by a tent near the concession stand. Sadie couldn't help but notice Lance scrutinizing every individual who walked through the gate. It was something that came with being a police officer, she surmised. You have to know what's going on around you all the time, he'd told her before.

As the teams warmed up on the field, Sadie noticed two women arguing near the batting cage. The younger woman wore the colors of one of the teams, and Sadie thought maybe she was the coach. The other woman had come out of the crowd and appeared to be a little drunk. It looked like the situation could turn physical at any moment. She glanced at Lance and saw that the women had already caught his attention as well.

Lance stood. "I'll be right back," he said, and immediately descended the steps and made his way toward the two women.

Sadie watched as he approached in a friendly manner. The younger woman ignored Lance and yelled again at the other woman. The baseball bat hit the ground as she stomped off. Lance offered to shake hands with the other woman, but she seemed too intoxicated to respond. She waved him away and staggered to the gate. Lance turned toward the stands and then stopped, waiting while the younger woman walked over to pick up the bat she'd dropped a minute earlier. Lance approached her and seemed to be introducing himself. They spoke for a moment until the team began to filter in from the baseball field, surrounding the woman. Lance backed out of the group of young players and headed back to his seat.

"Who was that?" Sadie asked after Lance settled in next to her.

"Do you recognize either one of those women, by any chance?" he asked.

Sadie studied the young coach and then scanned the area. "No, but I couldn't see their faces very well from here."

Lance looked around at the close proximity of the crowd around them. "Let's go," he said.

They left the bleachers and walked briskly to Lance's truck. Not far away, Sadie could see the intoxicated woman unsuccessfully trying to unlock a vehicle.

"Do you think she has the wrong car?" she asked, nodding in that direction.

"Stay here," he said, after punching the remote to unlock his truck.

Sadie stood beside Lance's truck and watched from a distance as he approached the woman. Her car looked well worn. Several scrapes and dents adorned the front fender, and the backseat appeared to be full of boxes and clutter. She could see Lance talking to the woman in his trademark firm-but-gentle manner, and in a few short minutes the woman teetered on her feet and voluntarily surrendered her keys to him with great animation. Sadie smiled. She loved his ways.

Lance pulled his cell phone from his pocket and dialed, talked for a moment, and popped it back into his pocket. He continued to talk to her, finally steadying her against the car to keep her from losing her balance and falling to the ground. Before long a police car pulled up. Lance helped the woman into the backseat, closed the door, and pitched the keys to the officer. The police car drove off and Lance returned to his truck.

"Okay, let's go," he said. They jumped into his truck, traveled a short distance to the main gate, and stopped. He rolled down his window and leaned out to speak to a short Indian woman wearing an orange vest directing cars to available parking slots. He pulled his badge out of the console and showed it to her. "There's a blue Ford sedan about midway down the row by the fence. The driver won't be back until sometime tomorrow. Will it be okay where it is?"

The woman looked past Lance in the direction he'd indicated. "I'll tell security," she said. "Can't be responsible if it gets ripped off, though."

"I understand," he said. "Just wanted to let you know."

The woman nodded and motioned to an incoming vehicle to turn right into an open parking space. Lance pulled out onto the highway and headed back toward the hospital where they'd left Sadie's car earlier.

"Did you have to send her to jail?" Sadie felt concern for the unknown woman.

"She's not going to jail. She's on her way to 'detox.' They'll give her a ham-and-cheese sandwich and a cup of coffee, and let her sleep it off. Then when she's good and sober, they'll let her out."

"Oh." Sadie turned an air vent toward her face and lifted her long hair off her neck. "So she's okay, just had a little too much to drink?"

"Too much to be behind the wheel of a vehicle. I certainly don't want her driving on the same road I'm on."

"Do you really think her car will be okay there?"

"Probably. And she's already got enough problems without trying to come up with enough money to get a car out of impound."

Sadie thought for a moment. "Why didn't you just offer to take her home? I could have followed you in your truck."

Lance looked at Sadie. "From all indications, it appears that her car is her home."

"Oh, you mean she's homeless."

"I'm not sure."

"What's with all the mystery? Who exactly is she, anyway? You act like you know her."

"I don't exactly know her. She's part of an investigation."

"What investigation?" she said. "Don't you think it's time for you to tell me what all happened while I was gone?"

Lance sighed. "We found Buck's identity thief."

"Yeah, I know. Charlie told me." She brushed her hair out of her eyes and looked at Lance. "He thinks Buck killed him . . . which is absolutely absurd."

"The woman I just sent to 'detox' lived in the trailer where we found the dead identity thief. Turns out he was a friend of hers and he'd been murdered while she was gone, before she got home from work."

"Oh, Cynthia Tanner? The woman Charlie was asking about?"

Lance nodded.

Sadie raised her eyebrow. "I might be having a drink or two myself with that being the case."

"She said she'd moved out of the trailer," Lance continued, "and it looks to me like she's living in her car."

"That's sad. Who was the woman she was arguing with?"

"Her little sister."

"Then why didn't you just go tell her sister not to let her drive?"

"The last words her sister shouted at her went something like 'I don't ever want to see your drunk ass again,' so I don't think she'd be very helpful with that attitude." Lance lowered his chin and looked toward Sadie. "Do you?"

"I guess not," she said.

Lance turned his truck into the hospital parking lot and stopped behind Sadie's vehicle. "At least she's smart enough to know it isn't too productive to argue with a drunk."

"You're a nice guy." Sadie leaned over and kissed him. "I'm going to check on Buck again. Don't you think they'll let him go home soon?"

"The way the health system works today, I'm surprised they haven't already kicked him out. Let me know and I'll help you get him home. I'm going to the gourd dance at the community center in a little while. I know several veterans who are dancing. Want to go?"

"No, I'd better not. I've got a lot to catch up on."

"I don't plan to stay for the powwow, but we can grab a bite to eat at the gourd dance."

Sadie laughed. "I swear, Smith, all you think about is what you're going to eat next."

She climbed out of his truck and closed the door. Lance winked at her and backed his truck away. Sadie smiled and waved.

Bounding up the hospital steps, she saw Jelly hurrying through the sliding doors. "Jelly? Are you okay?"

Jelly slowed but continued walking toward the parking lot. "Yes, ma'am."

Sadie watched as he climbed into his old farm truck and sped toward the street. She dismissed Jelly and made her way to Buck's room. She was surprised to see that the redheaded niece had returned. Only this time, she'd brought backup.

Dee Dee stood on one side of Buck's bed, and a man Sadie had never seen before stood on the other side with pen and paper in hand.

Sadie walked to the end of Buck's bed. "You doing okay, Buck?"

Buck seemed relieved to see Sadie. "Other than being bothered by these two vultures, I'd say I'm getting better all the time."

Dee Dee turned to Sadie. "Why do you keep hanging around my uncle, anyway? We really don't need your help anymore."

Sadie felt her face burn with anger while she bit her tongue.

Buck spewed forth a string of Cherokee words that not even Sadie could catch. Everyone in the room froze. Buck began to laugh quietly, and then he looked at his niece. "Go on. Get out of here. You're not too old for me take a switch after you, and that's what I'm going to do as soon as I get out of here."

Dee Dee frowned and threw her nose in the air. "You back-country Indians are all the same." She stomped out of the room, and her companion quickly followed.

Once Buck and Sadie were alone, they both broke out in laughter.

Chapter 29

Sadie parked her vehicle beside Jan's Chevy truck and entered through the rear door of the travel office. One large room housed Jan's desk, a display full of travel brochures, a small kitchenette, and a bathroom. The office was empty except for Jan, who turned in her chair and winked at Sadie before returning her attention to a computer screen while expertly balancing the phone receiver between her shoulder and ear. After a few moments, she cut her conversation short and hung up.

"That was Bob Johnson over at the IGA," Jan said. "He's thinking about taking his wife to Maui for their fortieth wedding anniversary. I told him when he made up his mind you'd be here to take care of everything."

Sadie smiled. "That's great, Jan."

"I can't wait until you take over next week," she said. "I think I've got a bad case of short-timer's attitude, and it's getting stronger every day. Think you'll be ready?"

Sadie plopped down in the empty chair in front of Jan's desk. "Are you kidding me? With everything you showed me before I went to Maui and all the things I learned from Pua, I could start today. I think it's going to be exciting."

"Good." Jan shoved back from her desk. "Everything is still the same. You've got three trips here in the pending file, not counting the prescheduled trips for the bank, and that's it. Pua will be very helpful; she has walked me through more than one mess." Jan laughed and took a drink from a lipstick-stained coffee mug and then held it in her hand for a moment before replacing it on her desk. "You've got to remember the time difference, though, when you're trying to call her."

Sadie nodded. Jan spent the next hour reminding Sadie of things she already knew, but Sadie let her talk. She knew before long the conversation would divert to Jan's son and grandkids just like it always did. Sadie was relieved when it was time to lock up.

The two ladies parted company, and Sadie headed back to the hospital to check on Buck. She pulled into the hospital parking lot and chose a parking space in the row nearest the street. As she walked toward the building, she stopped and watched Buck's redheaded niece, standing next to a car and speaking with great animation. Sadie had disliked Buck's niece from the first time she'd ever laid eyes on her, and so far the woman had done nothing to regain any favor with Sadie. The woman suddenly threw up her hands and wheeled around, climbed into another vehicle, and drove off.

Sadie got out and made her way into the hospital. Walking past an empty information desk, she rode the elevator to Buck's floor and, once there, walked into a room full of commotion.

Two nurses and a nurse's aide talked excitedly at each other while one of them, the youngest of the three, stretched her upper body out the open window as if looking for something. One nurse held onto the young girl as if serving as an anchor so she wouldn't fall out. The other began to wring her hands. Sadie glanced into the restroom and saw that it was empty and then realized Buck was nowhere to be seen.

"Excuse me." Sadie's words startled the nurses. "Where is Mr. Skinner?"

The nurse who had been wringing her hands looked at Sadie with wide eyes. "He flew out the window," she said.

"What?" Sadie rushed to the window, her heart racing, and pushed the nurses aside.

Please don't tell me you jumped out the window, old man.

She pulled the young nurse's aide inside, leaned out, and looked down, expecting to see Buck's twisted body sprawled like a rag doll on the grass below. Instead, the only thing she saw appeared to be life as usual—people walking back and forth on the sidewalk to the parking lot and cars moving about on the nearby street. No Buck.

Sadie leaned back inside. "What in the world are you talking about? Where's Buck?"

The nurse's aide spoke first. "The window isn't supposed to be open," she said. "But every time I tried to close it he told me I had to leave it open in case he needed to change into a bird and fly away."

One of the other nurses spoke next. "He told me the same darned thing, but I swear I thought he was joking."

The nurse who had been quiet finally spoke. "Indians do that, you know. That old man is a full-blood Cherokee. He very easily could have changed into a bird and flew off."

"Right." Sadie rolled her eyes. "Have you checked to see if maybe he just walked down the hall? He could be visiting another patient."

The nurse's aide closed the window and walked past Sadie to the door. "That's what I said. He's around here somewhere."

"Don't close the window." The quiet nurse looked scared. "He won't be able to get back in."

Sadie began to laugh. "Well, if the window is closed and he can't get back in, I guess he'll have to use the front door."

The other nurse spoke. "He can't leave without the doctor's permission. That's AMA."

Sadie wrinkled her forehead.

"Against medical advice," the nurse clarified, "and he'll be sorry. The insurance won't pay if you leave before the doctor gives the okay. "

Sadie chuckled to herself, wondering if the nurse really thought a man like Buck had to answer to anyone, including the advice of a doctor in a hospital or an insurance company. For the next hour, she helped the others unsuccessfully search the hospital for her friend. Finally she decided the most logical answer, since Buck's clothes were also missing, was that Buck had talked someone into taking him home. She was certain he hadn't escaped through the fourth floor window like the nurses seemed to think. Instead, he had probably walked straight out the front door with not one person noticing.

She gave the head nurse her phone number and asked to be notified if Buck showed up. As she walked out the door, she ran headlong into Charlie.

"Charlie, what are you doing here?"

Charlie looked around the room. "I understand your friend has escaped," he said.

"Escaped?" Sadie asked, confused. "What are you talking about?"

"The bank got another threatening phone call today," he said. "We were able to trace it back to the hospital. The switchboard operator says there's no way to identify which extension it came from, but if I was a betting man I'd bet it came straight from this room."

"Why in the world would you think that?" Sadie said, disgusted. "First you try to connect him to a murder and now you accuse him of making threatening phone calls to the bank. You don't know Buck. This is all ludicrous."

"Do you know where he is?"

Sadie raised her chin and spoke sarcastically. "Why don't you ask the nurse? She told me he changed into a bird and flew out the window."

Charlie ignored her comment. "Don't you think it's kind of convenient that he turns up missing every time someone wants to talk to him?"

An officer walked up to Charlie and Sadie. "I'm sorry to interrupt, Sir, but we've searched all the rooms on this floor and he's not here. Do you want us to continue to the other floors?"

"Yes," Charlie snapped, "and the outside grounds, too." The officer disappeared and Charlie turned his attention back to Sadie. "Sadie, you can't always tell a book by its cover. You of all people should know that by now."

Anger flared throughout her body. She swallowed the razor-sharp words she wanted so desperately to scream, then wheeled around and marched to the elevator, leaving Charlie standing alone in the middle of the hall.

✛

As she drove toward Eucha, Sadie's mind raced. She mentally ran down a list of places where she thought she might find Buck. She scanned the sidewalk in front of the courthouse and county buildings, checked out the bank, and then drove slowly past Walmart, searching the parking lot for any sign of him. Realizing he must have caught a ride home with someone, she continued to Eucha. She felt in her heart he was just trying to get home, and it was certainly too far to walk. A smile crossed her face. She could see him in her mind's eye sitting on his back porch watching his horses.

When she turned off the main highway onto the Eucha road, a thought flashed into her mind. Could Buck really be trying to hide from the law? Could he have had anything to do with the death of the identity thief? Her thoughts disintegrated when she rounded the last curve before Buck's house and saw the redheaded niece's Cadillac parked in the front yard.

Relief spread through Sadie's body and she grinned. He must have been hiding in Dee Dee's car at the hospital. It was a simple and obvious explanation, and she couldn't believe she'd missed it. Buck had simply talked his niece into bringing him home.

She parked behind Dee Dee's car and walked onto the porch. She could hear Dee Dee talking on the phone, but decided to knock anyway. She wanted to let Buck know to call her if he needed anything—a thought she was sure would irritate his niece.

Dee Dee appeared at the door holding her cell phone in her hand. She didn't seem to be in a very happy mood.

"What do you want?" she said through the screen door.

"Is Buck here?" Sadie asked.

"No, he's not here. And before you ask, the answer is: I don't know where the hell he is, either. Anything else?"

"Oh." Sadie tried to hide her shock. "I must have just missed him at the hospital, then. He wasn't in his room."

"Must have."

"Do you know when he's going to be released?"

"Not a clue." She looked at the cell phone in her hand. "I can't believe how bad the cell service is around here. You can't even have a decent conversation without the call dropping into oblivion." She looked back at Sadie. "Now if that's it, I'm busy here." Before Sadie could answer, Dee Dee turned her back and began to peck at the cell phone with her long fingernails.

Sadie thought it better to retreat before she said something she might regret. As she backed her car out of Buck's yard, the man she'd seen with Dee Dee at the hospital drove his rental car into the yard and parked. He eyed Sadie when he got out, but then moved to the front porch and entered the house.

Sadie continued on toward her house, thinking about Dee Dee and the man Sadie surmised was Dee Dee's boyfriend. They seemed like an unlikely pair. He always dressed in a cheap suit, and Sadie was pretty sure if Dee Dee opened her mouth very far, she'd be able to see fangs.

She stopped at her mailbox, gathered her mail, and then sat in her car for a moment and thought. If Buck wasn't home, then where in the world was he? She thought about Charlie's words and her anger returned. How dare he be insolent with her?

She dialed Lance's number. He'd know what to do. He always did.

Chapter 30

"Sadie, calm down." Lance spoke sternly into his cell phone. "Charlie's just trying to do his job. . . . If Buck's innocent, the truth will eventually come out. . . . No, I'm not taking Charlie's side . . ." He listened for a few moments before speaking in a more conciliatory tone. "Look, I'm getting ready to go into the community building. Why don't you come on over. You'll enjoy it. . . . Okay, okay. Then how about I give you a call later. . . . Sadie, get some rest. I promise we'll find him. I'm sure he's fine. I'll call you in a little while."

Lance sighed, flipped his phone shut, and dropped it in his shirt pocket. He guided his truck into a space alongside the road that promised an easy escape should he need to leave early and walked toward the steady beat of drums and the aroma of fry bread.

Once inside, he was glad the organizers had opted to use the building instead of holding the gourd dance outside in the oppressive heat. The open windows and multiple electric fans provided a surprisingly pleasant airflow inside the building.

He found a place to stand against the wall, blend in anonymously, and observe the activities. The drum, drummers, and singers were situated in the center of a huge circle. Lance couldn't see the emcee, but he could hear his deep voice as he announced the next song. It would be an honor song for all veterans. Lance smiled inside. He was proud to be a veteran, but more than that, he was proud to be an Indian veteran, knowing that Native people had served their country in the military with great distinction in a higher percentage than any other ethnic group in the United States. He moved closer, momentarily, and nodded to one of the veterans he knew.

The drums echoed loudly in the building and the headman dancers entered the circle, which signaled the other dancers to join in. Each man wore a bandolier and a blanket made of red and blue cloth. They held a fan of feathers in one hand and a gourd rattle in the other. The singers' strong voices carried high above the crowd as Lance began to work his way along the wall away from the dancers, weaving his way among the tables of beadwork, baskets, and other artwork, watching the dancers and spectators with equal scrutiny. It was a habit that wore on him at times, a habit of law enforcement he could never shake, not even for one night. Just when he decided to relax and enjoy the dance, someone caught his eye.

Among the drummers and singers in the center of the circle, an old man stood leaning on a walking stick. He wore a long-sleeved, colorful shirt, new-looking jeans, cowboy boots, and a straw cowboy hat, a feather slid under a beaded hatband. It was Buck.

Lance laughed out loud as he reached for his cell phone and headed for a nearby exit. "The eagle has landed," he said when Sadie answered, and then laughed at her confusion. "I found Buck at the gourd dance," he continued. "I'll make sure he gets home okay. Go home and get some rest." He chuckled again as he closed his phone, reentered the building, and headed straight toward the concession stand.

As he waited his turn to order, he watched Buck sing. His respect for the old man had grown day by day, especially after he'd found the treasure box full of Buck's World War II medals. To everyone around him, Buck looked like an ordinary old man, but Lance knew he was a warrior, a warrior who kept his memories of battle hidden from the rest of the world, just as he himself did. Buck had experienced things in war that many of the people around him today, in this very circle of dancers, would never be able to fathom. Lance realized he was going to have to admit to the old warrior he'd taken his letters, apologize for the intrusion, and return them to him. He didn't look forward to that conversation.

Lance turned back to the counter just as a woman next to him reached for a can of soda. Above her thumb and forefinger, a tattoo of pink roses adorned the top of her hand, reaching all the way to her wrist. Something clicked in his brain, and he looked at the woman's face. It was Cynthia Tanner's little sister. She glanced at Lance, grabbed her drink, and quickly retreated into the crowd.

"Wait," he called after her.

She turned and with a look of panic threw her soda at him, hitting him in the chest, and ran out the nearest door.

"Stop," he yelled and ran after her.

By the time he worked his way through the crowd and followed her out the door, she'd already made it across the street and ducked between two parked cars. Anticipating her route of escape, he cut her off at the end of the street and grabbed her arm.

"Stop! You're hurting me," she screamed.

"Stand still and I'll let go."

Breathing hard, she pulled her arm free. "Who are you and why are you chasing me?"

Lance flashed his badge at her. "I'm chasing you because you're running. People who run tend to be guilty as hell. What's your name?"

"Becky Tanner," she said.

"Cynthia Tanner's sister, right?"

"She's a drunk," she retorted as tears welled up in her eyes.

"Why did you toss your drink at me and run, Becky?"

"I thought you were someone else."

"Like who? Who do you think you need to run from?"

The girl pushed her hair out of her eyes with her tattooed hand and remained silent.

"That's a unique tattoo," he said.

The girl looked at her hand and then shoved it in her pocket.

"Tell me, Becky," he said. "You wouldn't happen to own a baseball glove, or come to think of it, maybe it's a softball glove, one with a drawing on it, would you? One that matches exactly the tattoo on your hand there? Pink roses?"

She wiped her nose on the back of her other hand. "I coach high school ball. I've got a lot of softball gloves. That's how I'm going to college, you know. I've got a full scholarship for softball."

"We found a glove with pink roses on it near the highway, not far from a vehicle someone drove away from a crime scene." Lance tried to read her face. "I think you know what crime scene I'm talking about, don't you?"

"I have no idea."

Lance stared at her for a moment and noticed a cut on her forehead, hidden mostly by her bangs. "Want to come clean here, or do I need to call the Sycamore Springs Police Department?"

"Go ahead," she said in a defiant tone. "I didn't do anything wrong." She looked nervous. "And I don't have to tell you anything. That badge isn't from around here. It could be a fake. I learned a long time ago, you can't trust men."

"I'm sorry you feel that way, but that doesn't give you a license to kill."

"What are you talking about?"

"Did you kill your sister's boyfriend?"

Becky's eyes grew wide. "You can't pin that on me. The only thing I've got to say about that jerk is that I'm glad he's dead—and Cynthia should be glad, too. He was eventually going to kill her, you know. He beat her all the time." She lifted her chin in the air. "Good riddance is all I've got to say. Now, if you'll excuse me, I've got to go." She turned on her heel and walked back toward the community building.

Lance let her go. She was right. He was out of his jurisdiction, and he hadn't witnessed her commit any crime other than soaking his shirt with a soda. He looked at his chest and wiped at it with his hand. It was already almost dry in the summer heat.

He pulled out his cell phone and dialed Charlie McCord. "Hey, Charlie, can you meet me at the community building? I've got two birds in a bush, and I think you might be interested in them. . . . Well, it's a woman with a tattoo and an old man leaning on a walking stick." Lance chuckled, dropped his cell phone in his shirt pocket, and walked back to the building.

The drums had gone silent. The gourd dance had stopped for a while so the dancers and the crowd could take a dinner break. He noticed Becky standing in the long line for food, but he didn't see Buck anywhere. Buck's hat should make it easy to pick him out in a crowd, he thought. He scanned the whole arena. Nothing. He recognized one of the drummers and approached him. "Can you tell me where the singer, Buck Skinner, might be?" he asked.

The young man shook his head. "No. He disappeared right after we finished the last song."

Lance shook his hand. "Thanks," he said. "He does that a lot."

The drummer walked away, and Lance felt a presence behind him. He turned to find Charlie McCord, still dressed in his uniform, standing not far away scanning the crowd.

Charlie approached Lance. "Where are these birds you're referring to?"

"I had my sights on the one that flew out of the hospital window a while ago, but he seems to have flown the coop again." Lance laughed. "The other one is in the food line over there." He pointed with his chin. "Cynthia Tanner's little sister. Her name's Becky and surprisingly enough, she's got a tattoo on her hand that matches the drawing on the softball glove we found near the getaway truck. Seems to me she might be a likely candidate for killing her sister's boyfriend. There's certainly no love lost between them."

"Hmph." Charlie smirked. "Did you question her?"

"Nah, not much." Lance continued to keep his eyes on the Tanner girl as he spoke to Charlie. "She doesn't appreciate my out-of-town badge, and I don't blame her. That's why I called you."

"Well, let's go see what she's got to say, then." Charlie walked straight to Becky Tanner and then escorted her to an exit. Lance went out another door and met them both at Charlie's cruiser.

"Am I under arrest?" Becky sounded scared.

"No, of course not." Charlie opened the back door of the police car. "We just need some information, and we thought you might be able to help us out."

Becky reluctantly slid into the backseat. Lance got in on the other side of the car, but left the door ajar with his foot on the ground in case he needed to make a quick exit.

Charlie took his place in the front seat behind the wheel, started the car, and adjusted the air-conditioning vent toward him. "You getting enough air back there?" he asked. Without waiting for an answer, he retrieved a pen and small notepad from behind the car visor and began to recite her Miranda rights.

"Do you understand your rights?" he asked.

She nodded.

"Can you tell us where you were last Sunday morning?"

"I was at a friend's house," she said, firmly.

"Got a name we can confirm that with?"

"No."

Lance spoke up. "I noticed you have a cut or a bump on your forehead. Did you get that playing softball, by any chance?"

Her hand shot up to her head. "No, uh, I accidentally ran into a door."

"Do you mean a door, or someone?" Lance waited a few seconds before continuing. "Did your sister's boyfriend ever hit you?"

She nodded. Tears filled her eyes, and she began to quietly sob.

"Would you be willing to give us a blood sample so we can eliminate you as a suspect?" Charlie asked.

"Blood sample?" Alarm filled her voice and fear crossed her face.

"The driver of the getaway vehicle smacked their head on the windshield and left behind a little bit of blood," Charlie continued. "Wouldn't take but a few minutes, and then you'd be cleared of any suspicions."

Becky began to cry openly. "I am so sorry," she sobbed. "I am so sorry."

Lance placed his hand on her shoulder. "What are you sorry about?"

"I hated him and I wanted to kill him. I killed him in my mind every time I saw him. He was a monster."

Lance handed her his handkerchief.

She wiped her nose. "He raped me," she said.

"Did you kill him in self-defense?" Charlie didn't sound surprised.

"No. I swear." Becky shook her head. "He was already dead when I got there. A friend dropped me off and I found Cynthia's door open. I went inside and didn't see anyone so I got Cynthia's gun. She keeps it in the hall closet." She blew her nose into the handkerchief. "But when I got back to the bedroom, there he was, lying on the bed. He looked like he was dead, I didn't think he was breathing, so I ran away as fast as I could. When I saw the police car at the manager's place, I hid in the bushes behind the neighbor's trailer until I thought I could get away. Benny always leaves his keys in his truck, so I jumped in and took off."

"You mean you're the one that caused that chicken disaster?" Charlie sounded amused.

"I didn't mean to," she said. "I could hardly keep that truck on the road."

"And you crashed the truck, hit your head, and ran," Lance said, "and in the process you lost your softball glove. Is that right?"

Becky nodded. "Yeah," she said, and then with urgency continued, "but I didn't kill him. I wish I did, but I didn't."

"What'd you do with Cynthia's gun?" Lance asked.

"I don't know what happened to it." Dread crossed her face. "I just freaked out. I had to get away."

"Becky, do you know anyone else who might have wanted to kill Benny?" Charlie asked.

"No," she said. "But I'm glad he's dead."

"Yeah, you already said that." Charlie let out a long sigh. "Are you willing to sign an affidavit stating what you just told us?"

Becky slung her hair behind her shoulders. "I guess so."

"We'll need fingerprints and a blood sample," he added.

Becky nodded. "Okay."

Charlie and Lance both got out of the vehicle and left Becky locked inside.

"I think she's telling the truth," Lance said. "I think she just happened to be in the wrong place at the wrong time."

"You never know. You heard her say she wanted to kill him."

"What about the gun?" Lance asked. "Was it the murder weapon?"

"Don't know, yet. Should have the report back anytime. But, from early indications, it's the wrong caliber. Cynthia's gun was a .32 revolver, a little Saturday night special. The shell casing the detectives found at the scene came from a .45. The print on the casing didn't match any in the database. We'll see what the ME says."

"Like I said," Lance interjected. "I think she's just an innocent bystander in all this."

Charlie leaned against the cruiser. "I do have the victim's real name, though. His fingerprints came up with a match in the state of Hawai'i. He spent a couple of days in the Maui County jail for DUI."

"That's interesting. What's his name?"

"I'd tell you, but I couldn't pronounce it even if I wanted to. I'll get it for you. Turns out he's a Samoan and was living in Hawai'i before he moved to Texas a while back, and then on to Oklahoma. We've traced his fake Hawai'i driver's license back to an identity theft ring on Maui."

"How'd they get the old man's name and social security number?"

"Well, Sport, I'd ask the victim, but he's dead."

Lance rolled his eyes and turned to reenter the building.

"You realize," Charlie said, "if she's telling the truth, this means Buck Skinner is still the only one we have with a motive for murder."

Lance waved as Charlie got back into his cruiser and pulled onto the street. The drums had begun to echo in the building again. He hoped the fry bread wasn't all gone.

Chapter 31

The next morning, Sadie awoke to the smell of smoke. She opened her eyes and sat straight up. She'd overslept, as evidenced by the streaks of blinding sunlight streaming through her bedroom window. Her exhaustion had overtaken her the night before and she'd slept deep and hard, and now her mind felt foggy and her body ached. Where was the smoke coming from? She jumped out of bed and ran to the window. In the east, she could see a plume of smoke snaking toward the sky and, although she couldn't pinpoint it, she knew it must be near the road.

She mumbled under her breath as she quickly dressed, blaming some idiot who had probably pitched a cigarette out his car window. Left unchecked, a fire could spread unmercifully across the parched countryside and swallow up everything in its path.

She dialed Lance's cell phone number as she walked outside, and when his voice mail clicked on she left him a short message, promising to update him as soon as she found the source of the fire. Quickly, she grabbed a shovel from the barn and threw it in the back of her truck. On second thought she went back inside and picked up a fire extinguisher that she knew in her heart would be useless if the fire had gained as much momentum as the smoke indicated. She placed it next to the shovel while Sonny jumped with excitement.

"No!" she commanded. "Stay here."

Sonny looked dejected, but obeyed. Sadie jumped in the truck and raced to the road, where she turned east and drove toward the smoke.

She glanced at Buck's house as she sped past. It looked quiet. The black Caddie was nowhere to be seen. She continued on the road until she topped a hill and could see the source of the smoke. It was perilously close to Jelly Hart's house. She ground to a halt in front of his house and jumped out of her truck, amazed at what she saw.

A huge pile of brush had been placed in the yard next to Jelly's house. Jelly carried a branch and piled it on top. The fire was small considering the great amount of smoke it generated, and it crept around the edges of the grass and lapped at the dry limbs in the brush pile.

Buck sat in a folding chair under a tree in the front yard holding a water hose in one hand so mud wouldn't splash on his clean jeans, grasping a walking stick in his other hand for balance. Jelly's confused dogs stood behind Buck staring at the fire until they saw Sadie and let out a chorus of howls. Buck sprayed them with water to shush them, and then smiled and waved at Sadie.

Sadie ignored Buck and the dogs, grabbed the shovel and fire extinguisher from the back of her truck, and ran toward the fire. "Jelly, what in the world are you doing?" she screamed. "You're going to burn down your house!" She began to spray the edges nearest the house, and as soon as the extinguisher was empty, she picked up her shovel and began to throw dirt on the fire.

Jelly stopped piling tree branches on the fire and stood motionless, watching her, his pink face and bare chest obviously inflamed from his close proximity to the heat.

"Jelly," she shouted. "Why are you just standing there? We've got to put out this fire!" She ran over to Buck, and to his amusement she confiscated the water hose and began to douse the fire with water.

It took almost an hour for Sadie to extinguish the blaze by herself. She splashed her face with water from the hose and then climbed onto the front porch and collapsed on a chair. Jelly and Buck stood in the front yard and stared at her like two pouting youngsters who'd just had their party crashed.

"What in the world are you two doing? This could have been disastrous," she finally said, and then turned her attention to Buck. "And, by the way, I've got a bone to pick with you, Mr. Skinner. Do you realize you left the hospital without permission?"

"Ah, I don't need to be in any hospital. I'm just fine as long as I've got my trusty walking stick handy."

Sadie turned her attention to Jelly. "Jelly, what were you thinking? Your whole house could have gone up in flames."

Jelly nodded. "I'd rather it burn than let someone else have it," he said, quietly.

"What are you talking about?" Sadie asked, perplexed.

Jelly joined Sadie on the porch and sat down. Buck reclaimed his seat in the shade of the tree and began to converse with Jelly's hounds.

Jelly wiped his sweaty face with the back of his hand and pulled a crumpled letter out of his pants pocket and handed it to Sadie. It was from the bank where she used to work—now called First Merc State Bank. Consumed with curiosity, she flattened the envelope on her knee, and then pulled the letter out and studied it. As she read, she became greatly concerned. She refolded the letter and handed it and the envelope back to him.

"Jelly, this letter says you're behind on your house payments. They've already started foreclosure procedures."

"I can read." Jelly sounded angry. "I know what it says. But it's all lies."

"What do you mean it's all lies?"

"They take my money every month. My disability check goes straight to their bank. I never get a penny of it. They've got all my money and now they're going to take my place. You know, when my wife died, a little bit of me died, too. Now that they're going to take my place, I don't see any reason to go on."

"There has to be a mistake." Sadie said, alarmed. "Did you talk to the bank?"

"Oh, I talked to them all right. They don't care. None of them care about anything except themselves. You know, the good Lord tells us in the Bible to treat everyone the way you want to be treated. You're supposed to love your neighbor as yourself. He tells us what to do. He even tells us how to do it. It's just that nobody does it." His lip began to quiver. "The only thing left for me to do is destroy this place."

"Oh, no." Sadie's mind began to spin. "Please tell me you didn't write a threatening letter to the bank."

Jelly stared blankly at her. "Yes, I wrote them a letter," he said in a calm and matter-of-fact tone. "I told them what I just told you. It wasn't a threatening letter. It was just plain old fact. What they are doing is wrong. I told them if they couldn't figure out what they were supposed to do, I would destroy this place. Today is the deadline they gave me, so today is the day I destroy my house."

Sadie exhaled a long, slow breath.

Buck interrupted their conversation. "I'm going to go ahead and walk home."

"Hold on, Buck," Sadie said. "Jelly and I are going to town. I'll drop you off." She turned her attention back to Jelly. "Get cleaned up, Jelly. We're going to the bank."

While Sadie waited for Jelly, she pulled out her cell phone and placed a call to Charlie McCord. "Charlie, I've solved the mystery behind your bomb-threat letter. . . . Well, it's kind of complicated. Can you meet me at the First Merc State Bank branch in Sycamore Springs? . . . Yes, the branch where I used to work—in about an hour. Thanks." She hung up and then called Lance. When she got his voice mail, she left him the same message.

She dropped her cell phone in her purse and approached Buck. She loved his independent charm and dry humor. He reminded her of her late father. Buck had been there supporting his neighbor, not judging his actions, just offering his encouragement for the decision Jelly had already made. If Jelly wanted to burn down his house, then Buck was there to cheer him on, and if the truth be known, Buck would have been the one to take Jelly in when he had nowhere else to go. She wondered if either man had bothered to think that far in advance.

"Buck, are you all right?" she asked. "The nurses at the hospital aren't very happy with you. They think you changed into a bird and flew out the window." She grinned.

A twinkle flashed in his eyes. "I did," he said. "Flew the coop." Then he winked at Sadie.

"Where'd you go, anyway? I looked everywhere for you."

"Went to see my medicine man. He put some herbs on my knee and gave me this walking stick. I feel better already." He placed his hand on his knee and flexed the lower part of his leg up and down. "Then I went to the gourd dance." One of Jelly's dogs got up, made a circle, and reclaimed his place next to Buck's chair. Buck reached down and patted him on the head. "Saw your man at the gourd dance," he said, before moving his attention from the dog to Sadie. "I figured he was looking for me, but when we broke for dinner he was gone. So I caught a ride with someone else and asked them to drop me off at Jelly's. I wasn't in any mood to put up with that niece of mine just yet. Guess it's time to go home and lay down the law. It's time for her and her friend to go back to California." He stood up. "She's family, but she's a pain in the ass."

Jelly came out of the house wearing jeans and a white tee shirt, his pink face clean-shaven, his wet hair slick against his head.

"Come on, you two," Sadie said. "Get in."

As they climbed into Sadie's vehicle, Jelly spoke up. "What about you? You've got ashes in your hair."

Sadie laughed and looked in the rearview mirror to assess her appearance. "That's okay. You're the important customer. Not me."

When they dropped Buck off at his house, Sadie noticed the black Cadillac and the rental car had both returned to Buck's yard. "Looks like you've got company, Buck."

Buck grimaced as he crawled out of the car, using his walking stick to help him gain his balance. "Not for long," he said, as he limped toward the house.

Sadie smiled as she backed out onto the road and continued to Sycamore Springs. Secretly, she wished she could witness the fireworks that were about to go off inside Buck's house. Even though she knew Buck as a gentle spirit, she imagined he could be a tough old leatherneck, if and when he wanted.

When they arrived at the bank, Sadie parked beside Charlie's cruiser, and she and Jelly got out and entered. She could see Charlie inside the manager's office and proceeded to invite herself and Jelly in.

It took only a few minutes for Sadie to explain in no uncertain terms that her friend had an agreement with the bank to transfer his mortgage payment from his checking account. The amount of his monthly direct deposit was more than enough to cover his house payments, and the bank's negligence in transferring the funds had caused enough emotional distress for Jelly that he had almost destroyed his own home.

"The bank could be held liable for any damages," she said, "mental and physical."

The branch manager, Melanie Thompson, sat stoically listening to Sadie. Eventually, she leaned forward, handed the foreclosure letter back to Jelly, and looked at Sadie. "Not my problem. It's already been transferred to the foreclosure department."

"Then get them on the phone." Sadie deliberately raised her voice. "Now," she added.

Melanie looked at Sadie, then at Charlie, who raised his eyebrow in a you'd-better-do-it-now look, before she reluctantly picked up her phone, dialed, and hit the speaker button. Sadie dismissed the clerk who answered and asked for the department manager. Melanie rolled her eyes when Sadie struck up a conversation with a former colleague, a woman Sadie obviously knew well from working together in the past. Jelly sat wide-eyed, mouth gaping, watching the events unfold.

"Miss Thompson says nothing can be done," Sadie was saying, "but you and I both know when the bank is at fault you can take immediate steps to override her decision, transfer the funds that are still in his account, and close out the foreclosure file. Right?"

The woman on the other end of the line spoke with authority. "Absolutely, Sadie. Give me the information and I'll take care of it."

"I'll turn the phone over to Miss Thompson and she can give you the particulars. It was great talking to you. Give me a call sometime and we'll have coffee."

"Will do," the voice on the other end of the line said.

Irritation flooded Melanie Thompson's face as she relayed the information about Jelly's accounts into the phone. Sadie motioned with her head for Charlie to step outside the manager's office.

"I don't know what you needed me for," Charlie chuckled. "Sounds like you still know your way around a bank fairly well."

"I needed you to realize that letter was not a bomb threat, Charlie. It was a man reaching out for some kind of help, and no one would listen."

Charlie picked at the side of Sadie's hair. "Do you know you have ashes in your hair?"

Sadie flipped her hair behind her shoulders. "Don't change the subject. You owe Buck Skinner an apology for even considering he might have called in a threat to the bank from his hospital room. Jelly told me he made the call himself from Buck's room and all he asked was whether or not they got his letter. That's not criminal, Charlie, it's a huge misunderstanding by an incompetent bank manager who doesn't have a lick of common sense."

Charlie looked past Sadie through the glass wall of Melanie Thompson's office and nodded. "I think you're right, Sadie."

"Buck is at home recuperating. I think you need to give him some slack. Lance told me on the phone last night that you picked up Cynthia Tanner's sister for questioning. Doesn't it seem plausible that she simply killed the other Ben Skinner because he was abusing her older sister? That certainly makes more sense to me."

Charlie placed his hand on his hip. "Okay, I might have been wrong about your friend Buck and the phone call, but he is not out of the woods yet on the demise of one identity thief. Buck had a motive for that murder, too. We're still waiting on the lab to match the blood and fingerprints on the getaway vehicle and the gun to someone. It could still be your friend Buck. We're going to need to get his fingerprints."

Disgust filled Sadie. "You never give up, do you, Charlie?"

Charlie put his hand on Sadie's shoulder. "It's my job, Sadie. It's my job."

Jelly emerged from the branch manager's office looking as if he wanted to cry. "I don't know how to thank you, Sadie. You know, my wife took care of all the bank business. She kept everything all neat and orderly." Jelly paused for a moment, pulled a handkerchief from his back pocket, and wiped his nose. "Now everything's a mess. I don't know what I'm going to do without her. It's like part of me is just gone."

Sadie patted him on the shoulder. "You'll be okay, Jelly, but it's going to take some time. Keep reading your Bible and you'll be okay."

"You worked a full-fledged miracle in there," he said. "They would never listen to me. You really do love your neighbor."

Sadie smiled. "Call me next month when your mortgage is due and we'll come in and make sure Melanie fixed the automatic payment." Then she laughed. "Come on, Jelly. Let's go home." She turned and looked at Charlie. "Are you coming?"

Charlie nodded. "I'll meet you at the Skinner place in a bit."

Chapter 32

Sadie dropped Jelly off at his house and made him promise to call her if he needed help with anything. When she got to Buck's house, she noticed the two vehicles she'd seen earlier were still there, so she decided to go on home and call Lance. They could make arrangements to meet at Buck's, and Lance could return the letters he'd told her about.

Sonny met her with his regular enthusiasm—lots of wolf-talk and wagging of tail. Joe stood near the gate under his favorite shade tree, swishing away flies with his tail. As she unlocked the back door, she could hear her phone ringing. She dropped her things and answered. It was Lance.

He was on his way from Liberty to her place now. He'd brought Buck's things with him and wanted to get them back to Buck as soon as possible. She would ride Joe and meet Lance at Buck's in about half an hour. They agreed and hung up.

Her call to Buck to let him know they were coming went unanswered. She left a message on his recorder and dismissed it from her mind.

She grabbed a carrot and walked to the barn to retrieve Joe's bridle. Before she could turn around, the horse had his broad nose in the middle of her back, snuffling. She giggled and turned to the horse, slipped him the carrot, and let him finish eating it before she placed the bit in his mouth and pulled the bridle over his small, attentive ears. She pulled his blanket and saddle from the railing, placed them on his back, and tightened the cinch.

As she worked with Joe, she began to think about Buck and all he'd been through. She hoped she could be as resilient as he was when she reached his age. A wave of uneasiness swept over her. Why hadn't Buck answered the phone when she called? Then she reminded herself that he didn't like to talk on the phone. He'd probably just been ignoring her call.

She patted Joe on the neck and whispered sweet words in his ear, then led him through the gate. Sonny quickly left his resting place next to the back porch and joined Sadie as she climbed onto Joe's back.

"Come on, boys," she said. "Let's go see Buck."

They took a leisurely walk through the pasture and then through a gate near Buck's house. As Sadie got closer, she could see the two cars were still there, and the uneasiness she'd felt earlier quickly returned. With that many people around, surely someone could have answered the phone.

She rode Joe into the yard and found a place for him under a shade tree. She dismounted and dropped his reins to the ground, a signal for him to stand still. "Sonny, stay," she commanded. The wolf-dog found a spot not far from Joe and lay down.

Sadie approached the house and knocked on the screen door. She couldn't hear anyone talking or any movement inside, so she knocked again. Still no answer. Obviously, that's why no one answered the phone; they must be out back somewhere.

She looked toward the empty road. Surely Lance will be here any minute, she thought.

She left the front porch and walked around the side of the house. As she neared the back porch, she could hear Buck's niece carrying on a one-sided conversation, and Sadie wondered who she was talking to.

Sadie stopped just out of Dee Dee's sight. Quietly, she leaned against the house, inching as close as possible for better hearing.

"Just get it over with," Dee Dee was saying. "I don't know. . . . Well, we wouldn't have this problem if you hadn't killed the wrong Benjamin Skinner in the first place."

Dee Dee's words sent a chill down Sadie's spine and pumped adrenaline through her veins. The puzzle began to piece itself together in her mind's eye. Buck's own niece had arranged to have him killed, but the killer had found the identity thief instead of her uncle. Questions swirled in her head. Where was Buck? Where was the killer on the other end of Dee Dee's cell phone call? And where was the driver of the rental car?

Sadie quickly retreated to the front yard, looking for Lance. Where was he? Buck's life was in danger. She couldn't wait. She looked at Sonny and he immediately stood. She held a finger to her lips indicating silence and pointed at the ground beside her. The wolf-dog flew to her side and watched for her silent instructions. Together, Sadie and Sonny walked close to the house to the back porch and crouched.

Dee Dee continued to talk on her phone in an irritated voice. "I don't know, think of something. Just make it look like an accident so they can't tie it back to us. And hurry up so we can get out of here. I've had all of this place I can stand for a while. . . . Yeah, yeah, I know, but it'll be different once he's out of the way and this place is mine." She paused for a moment, then suddenly stopped talking, put the phone down, and walked to the edge of the porch and looked straight at Sadie. "You again? Now what do you want? I didn't hear you drive up."

"Where's Buck?" Sadie asked, trying to muster a relaxed tone.

"I don't know. He's probably disappeared again. That's what he's good at, isn't it?"

Sadie's heart pounded inside her chest. "Where's your friend? The one driving the rental car parked out front?"

Dee Dee looked nervously into the pasture toward the springhouse. "He's getting some water samples to take back with us. We're leaving in a few minutes."

Sadie walked closer to the back porch where Dee Dee was standing. "I thought Buck said he didn't want to sell his water."

"Yeah, well, he'll eventually come around. Besides, he's an old man and he isn't going to live forever." Dee Dee poked at her hair with her long fingernails. "I'm his only living relative. In time, the place will be mine and I can do whatever I want with the water. It doesn't matter to me whether it's now or later."

Sadie moved to the bottom of the back porch steps, her hand holding tightly to the scruff of Sonny's neck, keeping his body close to her leg.

"You know, you're kind of scary, you and your wild dog. I'm going to have to ask you to leave. I'll tell my uncle you stopped by."

"Will that be before or after your friend kills him?"

Dee Dee took a step backward, fear crossing her face. "I don't know what you're talking about."

"I heard your entire conversation, Dee Dee. Two lawmen will be arriving here any minute. Maybe you can explain it to them."

Dee Dee's mouth trembled and terror danced in her widened eyes as she dropped her cell phone. She jumped off the porch and ran toward the creek, picking her feet high in the air as if she was afraid the tall weeds would touch her shoes.

"Stop her, Sonny."

In less than a minute, Sonny stood facing the redheaded woman, teeth bared, daring her to move. Dee Dee screamed. "Call him off! Call him off!"

Sadie heard a truck door slam and ran to the front yard to find Lance walking toward the house. "Hurry," she shrieked, and Lance quickly followed to find Dee Dee cowering on the ground, covering her head with her arms. Sonny stood his ground, barking at her.

"Keep her from leaving and keep her from using her cell phone," Sadie commanded as she ran for her horse. "She's hired someone to kill Buck. I think they're at the springhouse."

"Stop, Sadie!" Lance yelled.

By then she was on Joe's back and had pointed the horse into Buck's property toward the springhouse. Sonny left his prize for Lance to take care of and ran ahead. Sadie and Joe slammed to a halt in front of the springhouse while Sonny raced forward. The springhouse door stood open, with no one in sight. Sadie turned Joe around the springhouse and chased Sonny toward the place where they'd found Buck once before—in the sinkhole.

✢

Buck waited in the coolness of the springhouse while his niece's friend stood outside in the sun talking on his phone. Buck had agreed to let the beady-eyed, skinny city fellow take a water sample home to California with him if he and Dee Dee would leave and go home. Buck was tired of putting up with his niece and her disrespectful attitude, and he didn't trust her friend. The Californian's pale skin resembled a piece of white bread, and Buck had immediately disliked the guy. He'd been around enough people to know a creep when he saw one, and this guy was a creep.

Finally, the man hung up and pushed the cell phone in his pants pocket. Buck watched him turn in a circle as if trying to decide what to do. Buck emerged from the springhouse. "Come on," Buck said. "Let's go. I'm tired of this."

The man quickly turned toward Buck. "Say, can you show me where that sinkhole is you fell in? I've never seen a sinkhole before."

Buck took in a long breath and exhaled. "Will you go home after that?"

The man smiled. "Yeah, we'll go back to California after that."

Buck led his niece's friend around the springhouse, using his walking stick to steady himself as they walked to the sinkhole where Buck had been held captive in the ground for several days. When they got close, Buck heard a click, a sound he'd heard many times before—the sound of the safety being switched off on a semiautomatic weapon. He stopped abruptly, turned, and found the man pointing a Colt .45 at him. Anger swelled inside Buck as he slowly shook his head. "You know, young man," he said, "I've killed better men than you with my bare hands. And the only reason I killed them was because they were wearing a different color uniform than me. They didn't really want to kill me and I didn't really want to kill them. It was just the nature of the beast. Kill or be killed. Don't think I can't do it again if I have to."

"Stop babbling." The Californian motioned with his gun for Buck to move forward. "I have to do this, old man. There's too much money at stake. The water from this spring is the purest I've ever seen." He bent down and picked up a sizeable stone and balanced it in his other hand. "Sorry about this, but you're not going to survive your fall into this sinkhole again, because I'm going to give you a little help by smashing in the top of your head with this rock."

Buck looked past the man's shoulder and grinned. "I'm afraid you're not fast enough. We've got company."

Sonny barked and the man turned. Just as he did, Buck whacked him in the side of his head as hard as he could with his walking stick. The gun launched from his hand into the air as the rock fell to the ground and the man crumpled on top of it. Buck raised the walking stick high and hit him again, this time on his knees. The Californian screamed in pain as Sonny arrived and began to bark loudly just inches from the man's ear.

Joe slid to a halt and Sadie jumped off. "Buck, are you all right?" She ran to the gun, picked it up, and pointed it at the squirming man on the ground.

"Help me! That old man is trying to kill me," the man screamed as he held his knees and twisted in pain. "Call off this crazy dog! Please, call off the dog!"

Sonny continued to bark in the man's face.

"Stay on the ground and be quiet or I'll shoot you," she said.

"What?!" the man cried. "You can't shoot me!"

"Oh, yeah? There's no one here to stop me, and Buck will back up any story I want to tell."

Buck pursed his lips and nodded, and then held his walking stick in the air and looked at it. "This creep cracked my walking stick," he said.

"That's okay," she said. "You can ride Joe back to the house." Suddenly, she could hear Lance's truck. She waved Lance in their direction. "Or, better yet, it looks like you can ride in an air-conditioned truck."

"What were you thinking when you took off like that?" Lance yelled as he flew out of his truck. "Are you all right? You could have been hurt."

"I didn't have time to stop and explain," Sadie said. "I was afraid I'd be too late, and as you can see, I'm just fine."

"Call off your dog," Lance sounded perturbed as he turned his attention to the man who'd started squirming again on the ground.

"You didn't leave Dee Dee by herself, did you?" Sadie said, alarmed. "She's just as guilty as this guy."

Buck looked at the ground and shook his head.

"She's in fine hands," Lance said, "having a conversation with Charlie McCord."

"Good." Sadie called to Sonny. "*Eluwei!* Quiet!" The dog ran to her side.

Lance leaned over and snapped handcuffs on the man. "Your girlfriend rolled all over you. Get up." He grabbed the man's arm and pulled him to his feet.

"My head," the man screamed. "My knee. I want to press charges. That man tried to kill me."

"With what? A walking stick? Give me a break." Lance shoved the man toward his truck.

"Oh, no, you don't," Sadie said. "Buck's riding with you. This guy can walk."

Lance took the gun from Sadie and pushed it into his jeans at the small of his back, and then helped Buck with his cracked walking stick into the truck. Sadie took the soft rope she always kept attached to Joe's saddle and knotted it to the man's handcuffs just as the man tried to limp away.

"Looks like your knee's not quite as bad as you let on," she said. "Start walking."

Chapter 33

Buck sat in a worn, overstuffed chair in his living room, lost in his thoughts, trying to make sense of all that had gone on the day before. Sadie and Lance sat across from him on a matching sofa. Finally, Lance placed a small box and a pile of letters on the cluttered coffee table between them.

"I want to apologize to you for taking your things from the old house," Lance said.

Buck stared with no emotion at the things on the table.

After a few moments, Lance continued. "To be honest, I wasn't sure we'd ever be able to find you alive. The trunk was the only thing I found in the abandoned house by the springhouse and, frankly, I thought the structure might fall in on me while I was there." Lance laughed as if trying to lighten the mood in the room. "I thought whoever left them there must not want them anymore. When I saw they belonged to you—well, I'm sorry. These are your personal items and I apologize."

They all sat in silence for a few minutes before Buck finally spoke. "It's good," he said, as he looked directly at Lance. Then he flattened his right hand and pushed it forward in a downward motion in front of his chest, indicating he had no ill feeling toward Lance for taking the letters.

Buck resituated himself in his chair using an old, wooden cane for balance. His eyes traveled to a blank space on the wall. "I don't know how that girl could have any Skinner blood running through her veins," he said about his niece. "She thought she could just throw me away like old trash, all for a dollar." Buck looked at Sadie and Lance. "That dollar isn't going to help her much now that she's in jail.

"There's something wrong with this world," Buck continued. "Nobody cares about anybody anymore. The government wanted to take my place because someone stole my social security number. They wouldn't listen to me." He reached into the top pocket of his overalls and pulled out a piece of venison jerky and offered it to Lance and Sadie. Respectfully, they each tore off a small portion and handed it back to him. He bit off a piece and ate it before continuing. "The bank was going to take Jelly's place, and they had his money all the time." He sounded angry. "They wouldn't listen to him, either. That's not right. I'm real glad you could straighten that mess out for him, Sadie."

Sadie smiled and nodded. Then she and Lance continued to sit quietly, listening to the old man.

"Everything's all messed up," Buck said. "I spent four years fighting in a war so I wouldn't have to take this kind of crap off anyone." He leaned forward and cursed under his breath. "Sons of bitches."

"Buck, have you ever lost your social security card or any other type of identification?" Lance asked. "We haven't been able to figure out how the identity thief came up with both your name *and* your social security number. Sometimes these folks pick numbers randomly out of the air, but this guy had your name, too."

Buck shook his head. "The only time I can remember doing anything like that was during the war."

"Was it in Hawai'i?" Lance asked.

"Matter of fact, it was." He leaned back in his chair. "I was stationed on the island of Maui," he said, "with the 4th Marines. That's where we lived between battles. I don't know what happened to my personal belongings after I got wounded and shipped back to the States. I guess someone could have taken them." He thought for a moment, and then used his cane to help himself stand. "Come here," he said.

Sadie and Lance followed him into a bedroom and Buck pointed to the map of the Pacific Rim that Lance had seen earlier. Buck used his forefinger to trace hand-drawn lines on the map and began to speak with enthusiasm, as if he'd never shared this story with anyone before. "Here's the Marshall Islands," he said. He turned and looked at Sadie and Lance. "We sailed straight into battle from San Diego. I hope I never see another ship as long as I live." He turned back to the map and pointed. "Here's Roi-Namur. We took Roi within six hours of landing, and twenty-four hours later we'd secured Namur Island. That was February 1, 1944."

"Wow, you remember the exact day?" Sadie asked in amazement.

"Unfortunately," he said, and then continued his story. "They took us back to Maui, where we set up camp and learned how to jungle fight." He returned to the map and slowly followed another line with his finger. "The next battle was on the island of Saipan." He pointed to a small island on the map. "See? It's the most northern island in the Marianas." He looked at Sadie. "That was on June 15, the same year."

Sadie nodded, as if embarrassed that she'd commented about his memory earlier.

He turned his attention back to the map. "Here's where we landed. The Navy had been bombing them for two days before we got there. We had troops invading all along here," he said as he outlined the west coast of the island. "The Army Infantry followed us in the next day and secured the airfield right here. Without the airfield, and the whipping our Navy put on their aircraft carriers in the Philippine Sea, the Japanese didn't have any way to resupply their forces." He let his hand fall to his side as he leaned on his cane. "We beat them, but it sure cost us a lot of men. I thought I'd died and gone to hell, it was so bad." He tilted his head as if trying to remember exact details. "The battle lasted for twenty-five days and they said some sixty-six hundred men from the 4th died. They said the Battle of Saipan was the turning point in the war in the Pacific. Too bad I only lasted about half that long." He absentmindedly rubbed his upper left arm and then pointed at the map again. "These other lines show where my division went on to Tinian and Iwo Jima." He headed back to his armchair and sat down again. "You've heard the saying 'war is hell'? Well, take it from me, it is."

"What happened at Saipan, Buck?" Sadie asked after they had all sat down. "What did you mean when you said you only lasted half that long?"

"I was one of the lucky ones," he said. "I took a round through my arm. Bullet went clean through." He held up his arm and pointed at a place above his elbow. "And I took a lot of shrapnel in my legs. I got knocked out from a bomb blast and lost a lot of blood, but my buddies carried me back to the beach where the field doc patched up the bleeding and put me on a transport back to a ship. I don't remember any of it, though. I was unconscious for days, or weeks, I don't know. Woke up days later in a military hospital in Honolulu. They said I had a real bad concussion. I couldn't hear anything for a long time. From there they shipped me back to the States and my stint as a Marine was over."

"So you never went back to Maui?" Sadie asked.

"No. Never did. I don't know what happened to all my stuff. Didn't think it was all that important."

"Would you ever like to go back?" she asked.

A faraway look came into Buck's eyes. "They have the most beautiful flowers there. They even grow flowers on trees," he said. "There's a tree there that has round red flowers on it, a little less than the size of a baseball." He indicated the size with his hand. "It looks like a pin cushion. The tree grows up high where the air is cool and the mists swirl around the mountains." Buck could see the mountains rising above the ocean and the crooked blooming tree, all so vivid in his mind. "It's the prettiest thing you've ever laid eyes on. They said the flowers were sacred to the goddesses of the hula dance."

Buck tried to lighten the mood, afraid he'd shared too much when he saw tears well in Sadie's eyes.

"Have you ever seen a woman dancing hula?" Buck continued. "It's nothing like people make it out to be back here. It's real pretty. It's real nice, the way the real hula dancers do it, that is."

Sadie looked at Buck and then to Lance. "I know where we can get some discount tickets to Maui," she offered, and then smiled.

Buck turned back to the letters on the table. "Thank you, young man, for bringing these to me. It's time for me to put the war behind me. The man at the Veterans Office down at the Cherokee Nation says I have to open the wound and let the pus out if I'm ever going to get over it. I have a feeling these letters are going to cut it wide open." He looked at Lance with watery eyes. "I'd forgotten these things were still in the attic down there. *Wado.* Thank you."

Sadie and Lance rose to go. "I'll let you know what happens with your niece," Lance said. "Right now she will have to be held for arraignment and that won't be until Monday, at the earliest."

Buck used his cane to help him stand. "It don't matter. I would like some help getting these vehicles out of my yard, though. Can you do that?"

"You bet," Lance said. "I'll get the keys and take care of it right away." Lance shook hands with Buck, and Buck watched as he and Sadie walked out of his house holding hands.

✛

When Sadie and Lance walked into her kitchen, the red light was blinking on her phone. She checked the caller ID and saw that Pua had called. Sadie picked up the phone, dialed Pua's number, and then grew silent as she listened to Pua for a few minutes.

"No, no, no." Sadie's heart began to break. "Oh, Pua, I am so sorry. . . . I know." Sadie turned away from Lance and grabbed a tissue while she continued to listen to Pua. "Pua, if there is anything we can do, please let me know. She was such a delightful person. I know you are going to miss her greatly. Please, keep in touch. Aloha."

Sadie put the phone down and burst into tears, no longer able to hold in her pain. Lance took her in his arms.

"What's wrong, Sadie?"

"Tutu Lehua died in her sleep last night, Lance. Pua's mother."

Lance looked confused. "But, Sadie, you barely know her."

"I know, but she was so sweet. I just loved her. She was able to talk about Pua's father for the first time ever while I was there. Pua said it was like a heavy burden had been lifted from Tutu's shoulders. She kept talking about me and how she'd been able to talk about him because I am Cherokee, and he was Cherokee, and she felt like I was a kindred spirit. Oh, Lance, this is just awful. I feel terrible."

"Pua's father is Cherokee?"

Sadie smiled. "You know how everyone thinks they have Cherokee ancestors, well, that's what they think. But they couldn't even tell me his name." Sadie wiped her nose with the tissue. "He was killed in the war."

Lance took Sadie's face in his hands and wiped tears from her face with his fingers. "I'm sorry, honey."

"Pua wants me to come back to Maui when they scatter her ashes." She looked at him pleadingly. "Lance, will you *please* go with me this time?"

Lance nodded. "Okay."

Chapter 34

Charlie shuffled through the stack of papers on the corner of his desk and retrieved a brown envelope from the medical examiner's office. He used his pocketknife to unseal the flap and then pulled out the report. He leaned back in his chair, took a sip of coffee, and almost choked on it when he started reading aloud, "Causes of death are asphyxia and anaphylactic shock due to the severe allergic reaction to the ingestion of mushrooms."

"Damn, crooks are so stupid," he said, and started laughing aloud. The victim was already dead when the Californian shot him in the head.

Charlie picked up the phone and dialed. When Lance's voice mail clicked on, he left a message. "Hey, Smith, you're not going to believe this. Give me a call when you get a chance." He hung up, put his feet up on his desk, and began to laugh again.

✣

It had taken Sadie a full week to convince Buck to accompany her and Lance to Maui. He had come up with every imaginable excuse. It was too far. He'd been there before, and didn't need to go back. He was too old to make the trip. He didn't know anyone there. Who would look after his place?

Sadie had an answer for every objection. It was most likely the only time she'd get Lance to go, and they could keep each other company. It would be good for him to get away after the ordeal he'd been through; help him forget about his niece and her sleazy boyfriend. Her uncle and aunt had promised they would look after both her place and Buck's. And, as a final argument, Sadie offered to pay his way. He would never agree to her paying for his part of the trip, but he finally agreed to go. A week later, they were on their way.

✛

The plane began its descent. Sadie pointed out Haleakalā and the West Maui Mountains to Buck and Lance. When the plane reached the south side of Maui, the pilot banked hard to the right and circled back north toward the airport.

"Look," she said, pointing out the window with excitement. "That's Ma'alaea. That's where our vacation rental is."

Lance craned his neck to see. "Where?"

Buck shifted in his seat. "I don't know which is worse," he said, "airplanes or ships. I may not ever be able to walk again." He looked out the window. "It sure looks a lot different," he said.

"Do you recognize anything?" Lance asked.

"No. I've never seen it from this high up before. We only rode in and out of here on ships. Looks a lot different."

Lance had returned a call from Charlie shortly before they boarded the plane in Tulsa and then relayed the information to Sadie. She began to rerun the events in her head.

The ballistic tests, he'd said, revealed that the shell casing found at the crime scene in Cynthia Tanner's trailer, where the Samoan identity thief had died, matched the gun Dee Dee's boyfriend had in his hand when he attempted to kill Buck. But the medical examiner's report held the most shocking revelation: The identity thief was already dead when the killer pumped a round into the back of his head. He'd died of anaphylactic shock. Evidently, the big man had an allergic reaction to some mushrooms he'd eaten. His throat had simply swelled, closed off his airways, and caused him to suffocate. A search of the crime scene had indeed uncovered a bag of dried morel mushrooms.

Sadie could hardly believe her ears when Lance had told her the story. That is simply bizarre, she'd remarked, shaking her head.

They released Becky Tanner, Lance had explained, but Dee Dee and her boyfriend were still in jail, charged with conspiracy to murder Buck. Sounds like they're going to have free room and board for a while, he'd added.

At Buck's request, Sadie had taken him to visit Dee Dee in jail before they left on their trip to Maui. When he saw her, he told her he never wanted to see her again. Dee Dee tried to blame it all on her boyfriend. When she said she was innocent, Buck simply turned his back to her and walked away. Sadie's heart broke with sadness for Buck, knowing his niece was his only living relative.

Sadie's thoughts came to an abrupt halt as the plane's brakes screeched on the tarmac, just as they had on her first trip, and then the plane slowly taxied back to the airport terminal and parked at the gate. The passengers disembarked and made their way through the open-air airport and down the escalator to the baggage claim. Buck's knee had healed so well he didn't even need his cane, but Sadie found a place for him to sit anyway where he could guard the carry-on bags while she and Lance gathered their luggage.

After all the bags had been collected and rolled out onto the sidewalk, Sadie guided them to the rental car window. The process moved more quickly this time. Lance drove and Sadie directed him as they rode through Kahului and Wailuku on their way to the condos, a different route than she had taken on her first visit. She watched Buck as he gazed out the windows of the car.

"It looks a lot different," he said in a childish voice.

"This is Kahului," Sadie said, repeating many of things Pua had told her. "It's hard to tell when you drive out of Kahului and into Wailuku, but Wailuku is the seat of Maui County, where all the county buildings are."

Lance drove slowly down the street, past Queen Ka'ahumanu Shopping Center and Maui Community College, the Maui County Fairgrounds and Baldwin High School. They passed under a small bridge that appeared to be very old, and Sadie announced they had just entered Wailuku. After a few blocks, she directed Lance to turn left at an intersection onto a highway that would take them directly to Ma'alaea. They passed a rock church with magnificent stained-glass windows and a circular driveway. The structure appeared to be at least a hundred and fifty years old.

"I've been there," Buck erupted from the backseat.

Lance slowed the vehicle. "Do you want to stop?"

"Maybe before we go home, we could come by and go inside." Buck's voice wavered. "It's a real nice church. They used to feed the men meals there on Sunday afternoon," he added. "It was the best food I had while I was here."

"I'll find out from Pua how we can make arrangements to get in, Buck," Sadie said. "Okay?"

Buck nodded.

They continued toward the south side of the island, driving past dozens of mature monkeypod trees that flanked the highway, their high limbs arching gracefully over the road. The trees eventually gave way to sugarcane fields, and before Sadie knew it, she was back at Ma'alaea Banyans renewing her acquaintance with the front desk clerk. She had arranged for Buck's room to be next to the one she'd rented for Lance and her in case he needed anything.

After leaving their things in their respective rooms, they walked a short distance down the street to a restaurant near the Maui Ocean Center, where they watched boats, large and small, sailing in and out of Ma'alaea Harbor. They ate fish and rice and indulged in lilikoi cheesecake while an animated Buck told war stories, nonstop. Sadie watched him with admiration. She had never seen him display such excitement. She and Lance leaned back in the booth and watched Buck point through the huge glass windows at the ocean and describe where the ships would wait in the harbor to take the men into battle.

Lance put his arm around Sadie's shoulders and pulled her close. "I'm glad you came up with this idea to bring Buck and me here," he said.

Sadie fell into his chest and kissed him on the cheek. "Me, too," she said. "I'm so glad you came with me this time. Isn't it wonderful?"

When they could eat and drink no more, they walked slowly back to the condo building.

"Let's get some rest," Sadie said. "Pua's coming early in the morning to take us on a tour of part of the island. The ceremony to scatter her mother's ashes will be the following day. After that, we're on our own to do whatever we want."

Buck nodded and closed his door behind him; Sadie and Lance did the same.

The next morning, Sadie made an early morning run to the grocery store and returned with eggs, bacon, and everything she needed to make a hearty breakfast in the small kitchen of the condo. As soon as the coffee was ready, Lance invited Buck to join them on their lanai to enjoy the view of the ocean while they ate.

Buck sopped his runny fried eggs with toast and spoke with a full mouth. "I've been up and ready to go for hours," he said. "I'm ready to see this island again."

Joy filled Sadie's heart, tempered with sorrow. She felt more certain than ever that convincing Buck to come back to Maui had been the right thing to do, but she hated that the main reason for the trip was to say her final good-bye to Tutu Lehua. Life was so full of unexpected twists and turns.

She looked at Lance while he and Buck continued to talk, and she realized how much she truly loved him. Maybe it was time for her to reconcile that fact with herself.

A knock at the door snapped Sadie out of her thoughts. It was Pua.

"Welcome to our island," Pua said, as Sadie opened the door and invited her in.

After introductions, Pua hugged Sadie and kissed her on the cheek, then did the same to both Lance and Buck. Turning her attention to Buck, she said, "I understand you've been here before, Mr. Skinner, during the war."

"Please, Miss, call me Buck," he blurted, and everyone laughed.

"As you wish," she said, and nodded her head.

In a few short minutes they had climbed into a van and Pua was driving toward Kahului. "I thought I would take you by Giggle Hill," she said, turning to look at Buck. "That's where the Marines' camp was, right?"

"Yes, ma'am." Buck nodded, his face glued to the backseat passenger window.

They passed through the edge of Kahului, past the big-box stores, and before they reached the airport road, turned right at an intersection onto Hana Highway. Emerald-green sugarcane fields dominated the nearby landscape against the backdrop of the majestic dormant volcano—Haleakalā. They passed the Kaunoa senior center and a small area of luxury homes in Spreckelsville before rolling into a small tourist-looking town.

"This is Pa'ia," Pua said. "We can stop here on the way home and look around if you'd like." She drove past the Pa'ia Town Center and Charley's Restaurant and Saloon. "If you're lucky, you might run into Willie Nelson in Charley's," Pua said, and laughed as she continued to drive along a curved road flanked with more hearty fields of sugarcane and pineapple. "Here's Mama's Fish House," she said, pointing to her left. "They have fabulous island food."

Continuing around the island, the road rose high above steep cliffs. "This is Ho'okipa. The surfers and the windsurfers love this area." Then she pointed back inland. "You can see Giggle Hill from here."

Sadie turned and caught a glimpse of Buck's face. His earlier jovial attitude had turned somber. He looked as if he'd seen a ghost.

"Do you remember any of this, Buck?" Sadie asked, concerned.

"Yes," he said quietly.

"Some people refer to this area as the Ha'iku, or Kokomo, area," Pua said, as she continued along the highway and turned right onto Kokomo Road toward Giggle Hill. The conversation inside the van waned as Buck struggled to see out all sides of the van at once. Finally, Pua pulled off the road at the bottom of a hill and turned off the van in front of a 4th Marine Division Memorial sign, next to a park and children's playground.

They got out of the van and Lance helped Buck crawl out of the backseat. When Buck had gained his balance, he stood and stared. A light mist fell on their shoulders and a huge rainbow formed directly in front of them. Sadie marveled at the beauty of a place where men like Buck had joined together to offer their lives for their country. Pua and Sadie migrated to the memorial; Buck and Lance pointed at their surroundings and talked about the 4th Marines, roads, tents, and airfields.

"Look at this," Sadie remarked, and started reading aloud. "Battle of Marshall Islands, Battle of Saipan, Battle of Tinian, Battle of Iwo Jima. December '43 to November '45. That's a lot of war."

They stood silently staring at the memorial for several seconds before Sadie spoke again. "I'm so sorry about Tutu Lehua," she said. "She seemed to be in such good health and so vibrant."

"I know," Pua said, "But I am glad that she passed so peacefully, even if the pain in my heart may never go away." Pua looked at Sadie. "And, I'm so happy she got to meet you. I asked her after you left why she could tell you things she'd never shared with our family." She smiled. "She said because you were the first one to ask her." A tear streaked her left cheek. "I'm thankful you came into our lives."

"I loved meeting her," Sadie said. "I will never forget her." They hugged and cried together.

Lance approached and put his arm around Sadie. "Are you two all right?" he asked.

The two women smiled and wiped their faces. "Yes," Pua said. "Are you ready to go?"

"Buck wants to drive up this road," Lance said, pointing toward the mountain. "He says there's a waterfall he wants us to see."

They all climbed back in the van, and Pua drove while Buck spoke freely about where he'd camped as a Marine and where he'd walked to different places on the island. He'd point and say, "This used to be the field hospital," and, "We used to have a baseball diamond right where that house is now."

The lush vegetation grew dense, the air felt damp, and the houses became scarce as the van climbed higher up the mountain. Finally, Buck pointed to a small trail and asked Pua to stop. She found a safe place to pull off the road and parked.

"We'll have to walk from here," Buck said. He exited the van with vigor this time.

Sadie could hear rushing water in the distance as they followed Buck on an unmarked, well-worn path into thick, jungle-like vegetation. Cooler temperatures brought a chill to Sadie as they continued to slowly climb. Then, out of nowhere, the four walked into a clearing and stopped directly in front of a stream of crystal clear water cascading down a thirty-foot rock wall into a pool. They all stood, motionless, staring at the grandeur of it all.

Suddenly, Buck took off around the right side of the pool toward a tree covered in red blooms. When he reached the tree, he stretched for a bloom, but it was too high. He looked around as if trying to figure out how to climb on the wet foliage behind the tree to get a better angle.

"Lance, please don't let him climb up there," cried Sadie. "He's going to fall."

At that moment, Buck slid to the ground onto his hands and knees. Lance ran to Buck and helped him stand.

Buck looked up at the gnarled and twisted tree. "That's *ohia*," he said. "I want one of those flowers," he continued, in a matter-of-fact tone.

"Okay, hold on," said Lance. "I'll get you one."

Lance circled to the right, testing his footing and slowly working his way up and back around to the tree. He pulled out his pocketknife and cut off three blooms, pitched them to Sadie, and climbed back down.

Sadie gave a flower to Buck, another to Pua, and kept one. "These are beautiful flowers, Buck," she said. "It appears that you have picked these flowers before."

"I will tell you the legend of this tree," Pua said, and she began to speak.

"One day Pele, the goddess of the volcano, met a handsome young man named Ohia. She desired to have him as her sweetheart. He confessed that he already was in love with another young girl, Lehua. This enraged Pele and she used her magical powers to transform the young man into the ugly Ohia tree. Lehua was terribly sad and pleaded with Pele to return the young man back to his human form. Pele refused, so Lehua begged the gods to help her to be reunited with Ohia. Instead of changing Ohia back to a human, the gods transformed Lehua into a lovely blossom to adorn the Ohia tree. Now when anyone picks a Lehua blossom, it will rain because the lovers have been separated."

Pua stopped speaking and, as if on command, light rain began to fall. Buck fell to his knees. Sadie and Lance ran to his side to help him up. "Are you okay?" they said in unison.

Buck stared at Pua and his lip began to quiver. "Please tell me where you learned that," he said.

"My mother taught it to me," she said. "Her name was Lehua. She was named for this bloom."

Lehua's words echoed in Sadie's head. *I called him my Ohia . . . he was Cherokee . . . he died in the war.* Sadie's heart drummed inside her chest.

"Buck, did you know a woman named Lehua when you were here on Maui?" Sadie asked.

"Yes," he said and nodded as Lance pulled the old man to his feet. "And I have never stopped thinking about her."

"Oh!" A guttural cry escaped from Pua's throat. "What is your name?" she cried.

"Benjamin," he said.

"Which is 'Peniamina' in the Hawaiian language," she said, and then in a quiet tone she added, "You are supposed to be dead."

Sadie's knees felt like rubber. "Oh, no. I can't believe this," Sadie said. "Could it be—?"

" —that he is my father?" Pua finished Sadie's sentence and walked closer to Buck. "Tell me what you called my mother—her pet name—the name no one called her but you."

"Baby," he said. "I called her the Cherokee word for baby—*Usdi.*"

Pua and Sadie gasped at the same time, as bewilderment crossed Lance's face.

"Usi," Pua said. "You mean Usi. Right? My name is Pua Usi. My daughter's name is Usi. We were given the name my father gave my mother before he was killed in the war."

"Lehua must have dropped the 'd,'" Sadie whispered, trying to digest the events happening before her.

Buck looked at the ground. "Now, I wish I *had* died. I never dreamed . . . I don't know what to say."

Pua fell against Buck and sobbed. The rain began to pour from the sky.

"I think we need to find someplace dry to finish this conversation," Lance said. He took Buck by the arm and guided everyone back down the path. When they reached the van, he turned to Pua. "I'll be glad to drive. I think you two have a lot of catching up to do."

Pua hugged Lance and gave Sadie a kiss on the cheek. "Yes, we do." She sounded dazed.

✢

When they arrived back at the condos, Sadie and Lance gave Buck and Pua some private time and retreated to the lanai to sip tea and stare at the palm trees and the ocean. In the distance, Sadie could see the island of Kaho'olawe. Pua had finally taught her to pronounce it: "Ka-ho-oh-lah-vay"—not so hard after all.

Below, they could see Buck and Pua walking slowly along the water's edge. Pua stopped, picked up something from the beach, and then tossed it into the ocean.

"They've got a lot to work through," Lance said, "and it's not going to be easy. If Buck really is her father, and it sounds like he is, then this is going to take some adjustment."

Sadie nodded, took a drink of tea, and leaned into Lance. After a moment, she sat straight up.

"Oh, my gosh, Lance, I just realized something. Usdi must have been Dee Dee's Cherokee name. The name she hated so much she had it legally changed—from Usdi to Dee Dee." Tears welled in her eyes. "He lost Dee Dee and got a daughter and a granddaughter in return." She wiped at her eyes and leaned back against Lance. "I just wish this could have happened before Lehua passed."

"You know," he said, "life turns on a dime. You should never put off for tomorrow what you think you should do today. Tomorrow may never come." He scooped Sadie into his arms. "And based on that philosophy, I need to tell you something." He kissed her gently and then said, "I love you, Sadie, and don't you ever forget it."

Sadie melted into his chest. "I love you, too, baby."

About the Author

Sara Sue Hoklotubbe is a Cherokee tribal citizen and the author of the award-winning Sadie Walela Mystery Series. She grew up on the banks of Lake Eucha in northeastern Oklahoma and uses that location as the setting for her mystery novels to transport readers into modern-day Cherokee life.

The American Café (University of Arizona Press, 2011) was awarded the 2012 WILLA Literary Award for Original Softcover Fiction by Women Writing the West, won the 2012 New Mexico–Arizona Book Award for Best Mystery, and was named 2012 Mystery of the Year by Wordcraft Circle of Native Writers and Storytellers.

Deception on All Accounts (University of Arizona Press, 2003) won Sara the 2003–2004 Writer of the Year Award from Wordcraft Circle of Native Writers and Storytellers.

Sara and her husband live in Colorado.